Ancient Matriarchs

We Stood
Beside Them:

Other Wives of the Ancient Patriarchs

Angelique Conger

SOUTHWEST OF ZION PUBLISHING / LAS VEGAS

Angelique Conger/Southwest of Zion Publishing
7401 West Washington Ave
Las Vegas, NV 89128
www.AngeliqueCongerAuthor.com

Publisher's Note: This is a work of fiction. Names, characters, places, and incidents are a product of the author's imagination. Locales and public names are sometimes used for atmospheric purposes. Any resemblance to actual people, living or dead, or to businesses, companies, events, institutions, or locales is completely coincidental.

Book Layout © 2014 BookDesignTemplates.com

We Stood Beside Them/ Angelique Conger. -- 1st ed.
ISBN 978-1-946550-41-5

Remembering the lost women
Who stand beside their men in righteousness.

"We cannot force anyone to do anything, or we become like the Destroyer, and fight on his side, rather than Jehovah's. That is the hardest thing to learn." - Eve

CONTENTS

PART ONE

Elia

Chapter 1

Friends

Best Friends.

Always together, it seemed.

Cainan and I became known as 'Best Friends.' Cainan lived in the house next to mine as we grew up. His sister, Grace, often chased us out of mischief, and sometimes even danger. She often growled about the trouble we caused her.

Cainan's Papa, Enos, stood tall in my eyes. Though he had great responsibilities in the community as leader in both religious and community matters, he always stooped to my level to visit with me and Cainan. On those rare occasions he found me without Cainan, he bent to look into my eyes and spoke kindly to me.

Cainan's Mama, Rebecca, could be counted on to give us sweet treats through the day. Later, as I grew, I trusted the advice she gave. She never led me wrong and seldom offered advice unless I asked. I loved Cainan's Mama and Papa almost as much as I loved my own.

Mama insisted I learn to cook and clean, create pots, weave baskets and cloth, spin thread, and other womanly tasks. All the time I worked with her, I longed to be out in the sunshine, running and riding with Cainan.

While I helped Mama, he joined his papa and the other men, learning to herd the animals, build homes, plant and weed the fields and harvest. They kept him as busy during the day as Mama and my sisters kept me.

In the evenings, we ran into the last of the sunshine to spend the end of the day together. We would sometimes grab our horses from their stalls, ride through the village, then race across the meadow. Sometimes we dropped into the grass to search for berries in the bushes, or other sweet treats. We would gather all we could carry in either a bag or basket and bring them to our mamas.

It is no wonder we grew to love each other over time.

There was a time I did not believe he could love me. He could be my good friend but not love me as anything more.

We shared everything, including secrets. When Cainan spoke of his interest in Abiyah, in the days we were both about fifteen summers old, dark jealousy crept into my heart and I soaked my pillow with sad tears. Still, I hid my sorrow and encouraged him.

I told him of the little things girls like, and I offered to carry messages and little gifts to Abiyah, all the while wishing I could scratch her brown eyes out. Cainan was my friend. How could I share him?

After many days of listening to him speak of her soft white hands, I found lemons to lighten mine from the sun. When he praised her golden hair swept back in beautiful curls, I brushed my burnished copper hair back and tried to coax curls from its straightness. When he admired her tiny feet and tinkling laugh, I stared at my long toes and listened to my loud laugh. Nothing like Abiyah, I feared I would lose his friendship.

Then one day, he found me sitting under a cherry tree in the orchard. He picked a double handful of the huge, dark globules and plopped next to me in the grass. As though he had never been interested in another girl, he offered me one.

I raised my eyebrows.

"Ah, El. Take one. They are ripe and taste good. You will like them." Cainan said, holding his hands filled with cherries toward me with a grin.

How could I resist his smile? I took three from him and popped one into my mouth, chewing the sweet fruit from the seed. "You are right, Cainan, these are good."

He handed me more.

"I have missed you, Elia. Where have you been?"

I kept my eyes on my hands. "You were with Abiyah. Her hands are white, her feet small, and her golden hair sweeps back in curls. All these I will never have." I dared to glance up into his eyes. "Why are you not with her now?"

"She hangs on me, like she fears I will disappear. Not like you."

I raised an eyebrow. "I thought you liked her attention."

Cainan popped a cherry into his mouth and chewed it, then spit out the seed. "No. I thought I did, but I find it tiresome to always have to entertain her. We are not comfortable together, Abiyah and I. Not like me and you. I can tell you anything. I cannot tell her of my friendship with you. Her brown eyes flash and she expresses ugly thoughts." He glanced up at me. "I never expected such ugliness from a pretty girl. You never say such things."

I popped another cherry into my mouth and smiled.

"I mean it, Elia." He took my empty hand in his. "I never looked at you that way before. You are my friend, my best friend. I had not thought of you as anything else. But, El, I am looking at you now. You are beautiful."

"But I have big feet and brown hands."

"They keep up when we run and hold the reins on your horse confidently." He stroked my hand. "I like the brown. It shows you have spent time outside exploring with me."

"My hair will never form lovely curls. It will hang straight down my back."

Cainan tucked a strand of hair behind my ear. "I love your copper-red hair, straight or wavy, it matters not to me. El?"

I dashed a tear from my eye. "What, Cainan?"

"I am sorry if I hurt you."

"Oh?" I kept my face averted from his.

He dropped the uneaten cherries in his lap and touched my chin, gently turning it toward him. "I am a stupid man. I forgot how much I love being with you. Abiyah has nothing I want that would take me away from you."

"Thank you." I sniffed away the crud in my nose and wiped the falling tears. "I thought I had lost you to her. I was afraid we would not be friends any longer. I missed you."

His hands dropped to my shoulders and he tugged me into an awkward embrace. "I missed you, too. I will never forget you, El. You are my best friend."

Five years later, his embrace had become less awkward.

"Elia, you are my best friend. I want you to be with me forever."

I squeezed him a bit tighter. "I want the same thing, Cainan. I cannot imagine a life without you as my friend. Are you suggesting it will not happen?"

Cainan pushed me back from him so he could look into my eyes. "No, dear Elia. I am asking you to be my wife, so we can be together always."

"Your wife? You love me?"

"How can you ask that? You know I do."

I giggled at his crestfallen look. "Yes, I do." I became serious. "And yes, I would like to marry you. Will our parents allow it?"

His eyebrow lifted and his smile twisted into a half-frown, one side tilting down. "Hmm. I would hope so. They have allowed us to be friends since we were big enough to walk. We should go ask them. Whose parents should we ask first?"

I thought only a moment about that question. "Yours. Your papa is leader of this village and is Jehovah's leader. We should ask them first."

Hand-in-hand, we walked from the nut orchard to his papa's home where we met with Enos and Rebecca.

"Mama, we need to talk with you and Papa," Cainan said as we entered through the kitchen.

"Oh? Papa is in his study. I will get him."

She offered us a piece of cake and asked us to sit while she found Enos. We sat together at the table, munching on the treat as we had since we were little. A small shiver raced through my stomach and I looked at Cainan. He smiled and reached out to squeeze my hand.

Enos and Rebecca entered the room and he sat at the table while she cut each of them a piece of the cake. She set the cakes on the table and joined us. I smiled as Enos caught her hand in his and gave her a gentle squeeze.

"Mama, Papa," Cainan jumped right in. "We want to be married."

Enos stopped the bite of cake on its way to his mouth and set it down. "You do?"

"Of course, they do." Rebecca laughed and playfully swatted at Enos. "They have been friends since they were tiny."

I looked at Cainan and he shook his head a bit.

"We have been waiting for you to come to us about this," Enos said. "What took you so long?"

"I just asked Elia today! What makes you think I should have come to you about this sooner?" Cainan glared at his papa.

"He means that we have expected this for years," Rebecca said, defusing Cainan's frustration. "You and Elia have been close. We knew you would come to us with this request. We have been waiting."

"You have?" I choked on my cake.

"Of course, we have." Enos and Cainan both pounded on my back. "Who else would our Cainan marry, if not you?"

"Oh. I had not thought about it like that."

"So, you give us your permission?" Cainan glanced from his papa to his mama and back, staring into their eyes while he waited for the reply.

Enos let us wait a long breath before answering. "Yes. You have our permission. When?"

I stared at Cainan and he gazed into my eyes. "Soon. We need to ask Elia's mama and papa. Soon, though."

Rebecca laughed. "Then you two had better go ask her parents."

My mama and papa did not laugh with us. Papa took Cainan out to his shed for a man-to-man conversation. Cainan told me later that Papa wanted to be certain he would take care of me. He understood Cainan's status as son of the village leader and wanted to be certain of Cainan's love for me.

Three weeks later, Enos married us. With gifts from friends and family, plus the items both Cainan and I created, we moved into a home left empty for months by a family who no longer believed in Jehovah and left to live elsewhere. We were soon settled and comfortable there.

Papa Enos suggested we go visit Grandpapa Adam when we could.

~ ~ ~

A short time after our marriage, we left for Home Valley, planning to visit with Grandpapa Adam and Grandmama Eve. We rode our horses and traveled alone, seeking to be alone together away from the eyes of our families and friends.

The trail had been traveled enough we had no trouble following it. The weather was beautiful, and we stopped often to gaze at opening flowers wafting lovely fragrances in our direction, tall waterfalls, gurgling brooks, and listen to baby birds cheeping in their nests. We saw a part of the world new and exciting to us, away from Cainan. We arrived after three weeks of slow riding.

Little boys ran with us through the village and directed us to Adam and Eve's home. Grandmama Eve welcomed us with the warmth and open arms Mama Rebecca had warned us to expect. We had to wait to visit with Grandpapa Adam, for he left only days before on a teaching journey. We had nothing pressing us to return home, so we settled into one of the many guest houses.

We spent time with both Rebecca's parents and with Grandmama Eve. They never turned away help, and soon Cainan spent much of the day in the fields and shops with the men while I worked beside the women. I offered silent thanks that Mama had insisted that I learn these skills and was not embarrassed in front of all these new friends.

Eventually, Grandpapa Adam returned and welcomed us as warmly as Grandmama Eve had. We settled in comfortable chairs in their home to visit.

Grandpapa Adam turned to Cainan. "We did not expect your visit, or I would not have left when I did."

"No, Grandpapa, we did not send word ahead." Cainan grasped my hand and squeezed it tightly for a moment, then relaxed and kept his hand around mine. "We have come for a blessing on our marriage. Papa suggested we needed your blessing."

Grandpapa Adam nodded and smiled. "Your Papa is correct. It is best to receive the blessings of Jehovah in the beginning of a marriage. When would you like this to happen?"

"What is required? Do I need to do anything in advance?"

Grandpapa scratched his chin beneath his beard and glanced at Grandmama Eve. "You are right, Eve, this beard needs to be shaved." He gazed at us, sitting close together in front of him.

"Sometimes, a sacrificial offering is required, but I think not this time. Do you have people you would like to witness this?"

Cainan turned his eyes toward me. "Is there anyone here you would invite?"

"Just your Grandpapa Joram and Grandmama Doren. You?"

"They are the only ones close to invite. Everyone else is in Cainan." He turned his gaze back to Grandpapa Adam. "Only Grandpapa Joram and Grandmama Doren. Is that enough?"

"Perhaps. But if you wait a day or two, you may have someone else to invite. Let us set the day for the afternoon three days from now after our Sabbath services. Will that work for you?"

Cainan glanced at me, raising his eyebrows in silent question. I nodded.

"Of course, Grandpapa."

In the afternoon two days later, little boys shouted the joyful news that more visitors were entering Home Valley. I followed Grandmama Doren outside, curious to see who would cause such a great commotion. Two pair of bullocks pulled a tall wagon with a white fabric cover. Cainan stepped close to me and put his arms around my waist.

"My Grandpapa Seth and Grandmama Ganet," he breathed into my ear. I could hear the strain in his voice and turned to see him wipe away tears.

"How long since you have seen them?"

"Many years. They were not always here when we returned to visit and Papa never knew for sure where to find them in their travels to teach of Jehovah. Papa always hoped they would return the same time we did. And, now they have." Cainan pulled me forward to join the throng waiting to greet them.

Seth and Ganet sat on the high seat, gazing across the crowd. I thought Ganet searched for her mama and papa, her brothers and sisters, but her gaze focused on Cainan and me and her smile broadened.

"You were right, as usual, Seth. Cainan is here," Ganet said with a laugh. She gazed past us, searching for someone else. "But, not Enos and Rebecca." Her voice fell a bit.

Seth climbed down from the high seat and turned to help Ganet. He allowed the young men and boys to take care of the wagon and bullocks, reminding them they would need the baskets in the back, then took Ganet's arm and walked purposefully toward us.

I stepped closer into Cainan's embrace. Seth and Ganet stopped in front of us, and engulfed Cainan in an embrace. Ganet turned to me.

"You must be Cainan's wife?"

I nodded unable to push words past my teeth. It did not matter, for her arms surrounded me, loving and welcoming me.

"Grandmama Ganet, Grandpapa Seth, this is my wife Elia. You have heard me speak of her before." Cainan pulled me close once more.

"We have, and we have waited to meet this lovely friend of yours." Ganet smiled at me. "We are glad you decided to make her your wife. Friends make the best wives and husbands."

I reached my hand out to shake Seth's, but he grasped it and pulled me into a bear hug. "Hugs are expected in our family. Welcome, welcome."

Grandpapa Seth kept his arms around me as he walked toward Grandpapa Adam's home. "Come along. We have things to discuss."

I swiveled my head back to see Cainan similarly led by Grandmama Ganet. He shrugged.

Grandpapa Seth's warm arms guided me to Grandmama Eve's kitchen, and we entered without knocking. She turned to welcome us. She hastily brushed the flour from her hands and the front of her robe.

"Adam warned me we would have more company, so I thought I'd make a strawberry pie. I am glad it is you, Seth." Grandmama stepped into Grandpapa Seth's embrace.

"Who else?" Seth questioned. "Yum. Strawberry pie. My favorite."

"I remembered you like it and the strawberries are red and sweet." Grandmama Eve turned to welcome Grandmama Ganet with a kiss on the cheek. "So good to see you again, dear. I have missed you."

"And I missed you. I did not argue when Seth told me we were to return to Home Valley."

"Just in time," Cainan said.

Grandmama Ganet's eyes opened wide. "In time? In time for what?"

"Grandpapa Adam told us someone would be here to witness his blessing on our marriage. He suggested we wait until after the Sabbath services tomorrow," Cainan said.

"Papa always knows we are coming, even when we do not send a message ahead." Grandpapa Seth laughed.

The next afternoon, we crowded into Grandpapa Adam's little study. Eight of us were about all that would fit. There, with Grandpapa Joram and Grandpapa Seth as witnesses, we knelt on a small altar in front of Grandpapa Adam as he blessed our marriage, using sacred words and offering sacred blessings. Tears fell from our eyes as we kissed at the end of it. Papa Enos had been correct — as always. We would not have wanted to miss this blessing.

After the rite, Grandpapa Adam spoke to Cainan about sharing the words of Jehovah with our brothers and sisters in the near future.

Chapter 2

Storm

The early years of our marriage were spent happily in Cainan. We worked among the men and women of the community, sharing in their efforts and enjoying the bounty of our work. In time, sons and daughters were born into our family.

Cainan often traveled with Enos teaching others the words of Jehovah for the first few years. Sometimes, he traveled with one of the other young men. Later, we traveled together with our little family. I learned to appreciate the words of Jehovah and the love they carried for the sons and daughters of Adam and Eve. As we traveled, we learned to listen to His warnings.

One afternoon, when we had traveled for many days between villages, one came into view. A tall wall surrounded tall buildings. Tall green trees brushed the clouds. The village enticed us. Little Henya had new teeth coming in, bringing with it the usual unhappiness along with the whining and runny nose that go with it. We were all tired of traveling and ready for it to end, at least for a few days.

Cainan had learned to pray before entering a new village. The practice drew us to our knees at the sight of this village. I wanted to sleep in a bed and be warm for one night.

When Cainan told me this village was a bad place to stop, tears slipped down my cheeks. I hid them in Henya's curls as she, too, cried.

"Elia, I am sorry, dear. Jehovah would not have us enter this village. I do not understand why. There is a reason. You have heard the stories from Mama and Papa and from Grandmama Ganet and Grandpapa Seth. They insisted on entering a village even though warned against it. Each time, they paid dearly for it. Remember the stories of Grandmama Ganet? She was nearly sacrificed to the huge serpent god Zil."

I shuddered at the memory of the story. Serpents had increased in numbers over the past few years. We had lost bullocks and milk cows to them, recently. I wanted nothing to do with false gods and their sacrifices.

"Are you certain this village is unsafe?" I hated giving up on the opportunity for a warm bed.

Cainan touched my shoulder. "Yes. I am certain. We want our children to be safe, do we not?"

I sighed and watched the warmth of my breath rise as I allowed my shoulders to slump. "I do. I was looking forward to a warm bed."

"One awaits us, yet. Be patient."

The sun would soon set and Cainan set up our temporary home of huge mammoth skins around a skeleton of long poles, tied together at the top. With it set up, I moved our packs inside and started a small fire, willing it to heat up quickly. Our tent kept us warm most of the time, after the fire chased away the cold air. I had no real reason to complain.

As I began our dinner, the children ran in and out of the small door, each time flipping the flap open, allowing cold air to chill the inside of our tent. Already grumpy, I growled at them to stay out or come in.

"We will, Mama," Zerach said, "but we wanted to tell you about our visitors."

"Visitors?" I lost some of my grumpiness.

"Yes, Mama. Papa says they come from the east."

"Not from the village?"

"No, Mama. Papa says to be sure we have enough food for extras."

I glanced into the pot of stew on the fire. Enough for us, but not enough for extras. *How many extras?* I dipped into the bag of mixed grains for another double handful and allowed it to trickle through my fingers. The earthy fragrance brought a smile to my face as I remembered the last harvest we participated in.

Cainan had drizzled warm wheat across my face to wake me during the night. We had slept on the threshing floor, out of the wind and away from our children. There had been few nights alone since Zerach's birth ten years before. Now, I felt a stirring within me, a tiny movement signaling a new life growing there. I touched the spot, welcoming the movement.

Adira chattered to her brother at the door flap, reminding me to add extra vegetables. I dipped into different bags of dried peppers, mushrooms, and onions, dropped them into the pot, and stirred them in. I retrieved two potatoes, washed away the dirt, and cut them into the stew. Now it looked like enough for extras.

I sat back on my heels and watched the stew bubble. Visitors were coming. Perhaps I should consider something sweet for the end of the meal. I considered what to mix up for a moment, then started to mix a berry tart using some dried berries picked earlier in the year by our children.

"Elia? Could you come out?" Cainan called.

I pushed the tart into the fire, brushed the flour from my hands, and stepped out of the tent.

"There you are." Cainan draped his arm across my shoulders. "Elia, I would like to introduce you to our visitors. This is my older sister, Sara and her husband, Ophel. I have not seen them in many years. They moved to Home Valley when I was little."

"Sara?" I stared into the green eyes of the older woman. Her bright red hair, much like Cainan's, had faded, becoming a light brown. When I looked closely, I saw the shape of my beloved Cainan in her face. "It is you! How did you get here?"

"We travel to visit with Rebecca and Enos," Ophel said. He coughed to break up the roughness of his gravely voice. "How far are we from Cainan now?"

Cainan glanced at me and shook his head slightly. "We are a distance from there. We left two months ago." He reached into a barrel and dipped up some water.

"Two months? Constant traveling? That is almost as far as we have traveled." Ophel scratched the back of his head.

"No, not constant traveling. We stopped at a few villages. I would guess you are about two weeks from Cainan and Mama and Papa's home." Cainan poured the dipper of water into a cup and handed it to Ophel.

"Spend the night with us," I said. "We would love your company. I have more than enough stew for all of us."

"Is that what I smell?" Sara asked, sniffing the air in appreciation.

"Yes. And I must go check on the dessert." I glanced at a nearby tree, whose branches and leaves danced as the wind increased. "Come in out of the wind."

Gedalya and Henya crawled over their uncle and aunt that evening, while Zerach and Adira listened to them share stories of their mama and papa when they were little.

Cainan stepped outside before we crawled into bed, taking Ophel with him.

"What did you do?" I asked as he crawled back into the warmth of our tent.

"I gathered the animals together, securely surrounding them with our heavy wagons."

"Why?"

"I am not certain why. I only know I had a feeling that the animals need protection."

~ ~ ~

During the night, the wind increased. It whistled down the smoke opening and rattled the heavy skins surrounding our protective enclosure. Children cried out, wind caused dreams disturbing their sleep. Even Sara cried out in her sleep. The night brought me little rest. Cainan wrapped his arms around me, protecting me from the wind. I snuggled close to him, trying to block out the sound. Patches, the family dog, lay by the children's feet whining at the noise.

At last, an eerie half-light filtered through the smoke hole, bringing with it a silence. The children awoke and wanted to climb through the door and run outside. Cainan stood in front of it.

"Not now. The storm is only resting."

Ophel laughed at the idea and began to push past Cainan.

"Wait a while, Ophel. Listen. Do you hear it?"

The children sat still, silently listening. In the distance, we heard the sigh of a breeze. Ophel stood, hand raised to push open the flap, listening as the slight ruffle of a breeze against the tent increased. Within a few short moments, the light darkened and raging wind buffeted the walls and screamed down the smoke hole, scattering the coals and blowing smoke into our faces.

I bent to add fuel to the fire.

Cainan touched my upper arm. "No, Elia. Better not. Wait until this is over."

He knew something I did not. I silently shook my head and banked the remaining hot coals to prevent them blowing into our possessions and causing a fire problem. Instead, I searched through our bundles and found bread and jam, which I cut and handed to the others.

We sat on our beds and listened to the rising wind rage at the mammoth skins. We knelt on the soft rugs that covered the earth as Cainan led us in prayers for protection. Then, once again, we sat on our beds and listened. I wanted to sleep but could not in the noise of the storm.

I gathered Henya into my arms, while the other children crowded as close as they could on either side near my feet.

"Jehovah blesses us," Cainan said. "The strength of this storm would have blown away the skins that surround us by now if he did not."

"What about my pony, Spot, Papa?" Zerach asked. "Will she survive this? Can I bring her inside?"

Cainan gathered him into his arms and ruffled his hair gently. "She is as safe as I can make her, Zerach. Jehovah protects her."

Adira snuggled close to Patches, laying her head on him. Great tears slid quietly down her cheeks.

When at last the force of the wind blew on past our little camp, the silence caused me to shiver. How had we lived through this, except through the grace of Jehovah? I gazed at

Cainan. We sat in the silence a long moment, gazing at each other, waiting.

"Is it safe to leave, yet?" I whispered.

The silence spread out, uninterrupted by the sound of even a slight breeze. Sara turned toward her brother with a silent question. The children turned slightly and stared at their papa. Patches pushed her cold wet nose into his lap, eyes focused on him.

Cainan pushed himself up to stand, wobbling to and fro a bit until he found his balance. "I think it is safe. Wait here while I check."

Ophel pushed away from Sara's arms. "I will go with you."

Cainan nodded and untied the flap to the outside and stepped into sunshine, followed by Ophel and Patches. Sara scooted toward me and held my hand. The children scooted closer, drawing comfort from us.

"Elia! Sara!" Cainan called. "Come out and see the blessings of Jehovah. Bring the children."

I unfolded my legs and stood, shaking out the cramps. Sara pushed herself up and stretched, following me to the door flap. I bent enough to push through into bright sunlight. I stared all around us.

The trees that only the day before had been covered in golden leaves or dark green needles now stood strangely naked. Nothing hung from the few that stood upright. Most had broken near the ground. Some lay in piles of broken branches and trunks in crazy angles. One huge beech stripped of leaves and branches quivered from the storm, a tall maple impaled through it near the top.

I stood with my mouth hanging open, staring at the damage around us. How had our tent survived? And, what about our animals and wagons? I walked toward the animals with my mouth gaping open wide. Our two wagons and Sara and Ophel's wagon stood in a triangle, untouched by the winds. Inside, the animals lay calmly. I counted the bullocks. All ten sat in the middle, chewing their cuds. Zerach's pony, Spot lay with fresh grass hanging from her mouth. The other horses lay beside her, munching on green grass. The milk cow pushed off her back feet and stood to allow her calf to nurse. Sheep and goats lay together, contended.

I stood on my toes to look inside the wagon. It looked as it had when I left it the night before. Nothing seemed to have even been touched by the winds. Cainan dipped into a barrel and filled the trough with water I had been certain would be blown dry. Ophel dipped a bucket into another barrel and poured oats into the feeding troughs beside one of the wagons. The animals stood and shook the dust from their pelts and wandered toward the water and food.

I managed to find my voice. "How did they survive when the trees all around us did not? For that matter, how did we sit safely within our tent?"

"The hand of Jehovah protected us."

The children trooped into the enclosure, shouting and jumping toward the animals with Patches jumping and barking joyfully at their heels. I glanced upward to see a clear, blue sky. The sun shone on us, warming away the chills we felt the day before. It stood only a hand above the morning horizon. I believed the storm lasted longer, it certainly felt like it lasted forever.

"Elia, look at the village," Cainan said pointing toward the village we had been warned to avoid.

I stared, then turned in a circle, searching for the village, thinking he had pointed in the wrong direction. There was no village. No buildings. No tall trees. No walls. Nothing. It was completely gone.

Chapter 3

Promises

We traveled together as a family for many years, before Cainan determined it would be safer for the children and I to stay in Cainan where his brothers and others protected the community with walls and guards. Men were known to raid travelers, robbing and killing the weak. Cainan feared for our safety along the trails and left us home.

He, however, continued to travel, sometimes with others; more often alone. I feared for his safety, but he reminded me that Jehovah protected those who trust Him. How could I argue with him? On the trips when he returned later than expected, I fell to my knees in prayer for his protection more often.

I worked in my garden, harvesting late vegetables when he arrived on one return much later than I expected from his travels to Shedolamak. My arms had burned brown from working in the sun. I glanced up to see a glow surrounding him.

"Are you well, my husband?" I cried upon seeing him. I held my arms beside my body, fearing to touch him.

"Yes, my Elia. I am well. Why?"

"There is a … a glow about you. What caused that?"

Cainan glanced into a bowl of water, seeking to see what I saw. "Oh. It must be from my visit."

"Your visit? To Shedolamak?"

"No, my dear. With Jehovah. He met me on the road. Oh, Elia, I have never felt such love in all my life. His words filled me with great joy."

His eyes glazed as he gazed past me. He shook his head. "I stopped along the way and knelt to pray, concerned that I had failed to be perfectly obedient."

"You? Less than perfectly obedient? I struggle to understand that." I stared at him.

Cainan took me by the hand and led me inside. I twitched, afraid I would be shocked by his touch, but it did not shock me.

"What?" he asked.

"I feared your touch would hurt. It did not."

"Why would it hurt?"

"You have been with Jehovah."

He smiled and took my hand, leading me to our comfortable chairs.

We sat facing each other. He held on to my hand. "Yes, me. I have been less than perfect. I bowed in repentance, praying for forgiveness. After much prayer, I received my answer. I am forgiven."

"Is that not what you teach the people every day? That when you humbly repent, Jehovah will forgive?"

"It is. And I have received that forgiveness." He traced my hand absently with a fingertip.

"What happened next?"

"I prayed for my brethren, those here in Cainan, and in Gog, and Selah, and Shedolamak, and all the other communities I have visited. I begged for forgiveness for them." He focused on his finger on the back of my hand.

"And?" I did not want to disturb his thinking.

"He spoke to me. Me! His gentle voice filled me with love. His strength, His love. How can I describe them? It is not possible to describe, only to know it here." He drew my hand with his to touch the center of his chest. "He forgave me of my sins and promised that those I teach can receive forgiveness, as they request it. He promised that men and women will be saved. My heart continues to swell as if to burst."

"What took you so long to return home? I expected you weeks ago."

Cainan traced my face with his finger. "And you feared for me, Elia? For that, I am truly sorry. Jehovah commanded me to meet with Grandpapa Adam. I journeyed toward Home Valley, but Grandpapa met me along the way. He traveled without knowing why or where he should go."

"What did he tell you?" I fought back tears of joy.

Cainan stood and began to pace. "He agreed that I should have prayed for forgiveness. He reminded me that my assignment for now was to continue to teach Jehovah's plan for the happiness of our people. And, one day he will share the High Priesthood with me. I am overwhelmed."

I stared at him for several long breaths. "It does not surprise me. Cainan, son of Enos, you are a good man who cares."

He sat and put his arms around me. "I love you, my friend." He kissed me.

"Even with my big feet and brown arms?" I asked.

"Because you have big feet and brown arms. You are willing to do what must be done. Jehovah loves you and your willingness to be obedient."

It took many days before the glow about him faded, but I will always remember the glow and his joy that day.

We visited Cainan's parents, Rebecca and Enos, to share the news.

While there, he shared something new to me. "Grandpapa Adam interviewed me, searching my soul. He then lay his hands on my head and blessed me. He charged me with a responsibility to share the commandments of Jehovah with my brothers and sisters, not just those who left Cainan in search of something different, but those men and women on this earth who lost their way, or those who never knew where to find the truth." He reached for my hand.

"It is a big responsibility, son." Papa Enos said, clapping his hand on Cainan's shoulder.

"I am overwhelmed and humbled by such a commission. Mine, to teach my brothers and sisters of Jehovah's great love." He turned his eyes toward mine. "I have learned of love with Elia and our children. Can Jehovah's love be greater than the love of a mother, who willingly draws near to death every time she gives birth to a child?"

"Yes, son. Much greater, for he created this world and all things on it," Mama Rebecca said, touching him gently on the cheek.

"And in time," Cainan added, "through His great love, He will come to this earth and offer Himself as a sacrifice to atone for each of us who have lived or ever will live."

My heart nearly burst with his loving words. "Such great love," I whispered, "to offer Himself for unworthy children."

Once more, we traveled together, taking long journeys with our children, returning when possible to visit in Cainan. When travels became too dangerous for a time, we left our children with my mama and papa.

Traveling with our children had always been dangerous. Now, however, we did not fear as much, for we knew Jehovah watched over our family while Cainan served him.

~ ~ ~

Four years later, we returned to Cainan. Mama Rebecca and Papa Enos had been to Home Valley. I noticed Papa Enos more thoughtful. He spoke more carefully.

"What has happened," Cainan asked them when we met with them for an evening meal. "You are changed."

"Am I?" Papa Enos asked.

"You are," I said. "What happened on your visit to Home Valley?"

"My parents joined us there. We did not expect them to be there. We left here suddenly, not knowing why we traveled to Home Valley. How would Mama and Papa know to come?" Awe filled Papa Enos' voice.

"Why were you all there?" I asked.

"Good question, Elia," Mama Rebecca said. "Jehovah needed Enos to visit with Grandpapa Adam."

"Why?" Cainan and I asked together.

"Jehovah commanded Grandpapa to ordain me to the office of High Priest and as a special witness to Jehovah," Papa Enos said almost in a whisper.

Cainan leapt from his seat to embrace his papa. "This is wonderful news."

"How do you feel about that, Mama Rebecca?" I asked.

Her genuine smile filled me with warmth. "We are blessed to have this opportunity to serve Jehovah. Grandpapa Adam blessed me with peace. I know Nat and Ziva, our children who were taken from us, are safe. They are in Nod for a reason. I have a peace I have not had in many years."

I took her hand and squeezed it. "A blessing of peace is more important at this time than any other. You are blessed."

"I am. We are."

In the next days, Papa Enos gave up leadership of the village. Cainan's older brothers, Jon and Yavid received the shared responsibility of leading the community.

When we were alone, after all the decisions had been made, Cainan breathed a sigh of relief. "I am happy for Jon and Yavid. They are well trained in the protection and leadership of this community. I am happy no one turned to me. I could not have accepted such a responsibility."

"Oh?" I asked. "Why?"

"We are to leave to teach others again. There are brothers and sisters who yearn to be reminded of Jehovah's commands. It is my responsibility and blessing to travel to teach them."

I bit my lip. Would he leave me behind with the children, as Jon had suggested?

"How long will it take you to be ready to travel?" Cainan asked.

"I am to go with you?" Surprise leaked into my voice.

Cainan caught me around the waist and spun me around. "You are my eternal companion. Remember the promise given by Grandpapa Adam? Yes. You are to travel with me."

"What will Jon say?"

"Jon has no say in this. We are to travel with our children once more."

"Even Zerach and Adira?" I asked. "Zerach has met a young woman here in Cainan. He would be sad if he were expected to leave her behind."

"A woman? Who?"

"Nyssa. They were friends as children."

"And he cares for her?"

"He sees her every time we come back. I think he will be talking with you soon about marrying her."

"It should be soon. We leave in two weeks."

"I suppose that is enough time for a young couple," I mused.

"You asked about Adira. Does she have one she loves?"

"She has seen much of Meir. He is often here with her."

"Two of them. Papa is leaving to teach soon, as well." Cainan closed his eyes in thought. "We will see what Zerach and Adira have to say about this tonight when we gather for our evening meal."

"What?" Adira and Zerach cried in unison when Cainan told the family of our coming travel plans.

"I cannot leave," Zerach said. "I asked Nyssa to marry me today. We were going to speak with you tonight after dinner."

"No, son. You cannot —"

"Papa! I love her. I will marry —"

"Yes, you will marry Nyssa, not travel with your mama and me." Cainan interrupted.

"— Nyssa." Zerach spluttered. "You said I could marry her?"

"Yes, son. What does her papa say?"

"We have not been over to ask him. We planned to ask him after we spoke to you tonight."

"When?" I asked.

"After we eat," Zerach said. He began to bolt his food.

Adira slapped her hand on the table. "Mama, Papa," Adira said. "I cannot go away again now. Meir will forget me."

Cainan turned to her. "Forget you? If he loves you, he will not forget you. Are you certain he loves you?"

"I am, Papa. Meir loves me."

"He will not forget you if he loves you."

"Must I go with you?" she asked. Tears welled up in her eyes.

"We will see what happens in the next day or so."

Adira dropped her spoon and pushed herself away from the table. "No," she cried as she ran from the table toward her room.

I stood to follow, but Cainan waved me to sit back down.

"Give her time to accept it," he suggested.

After dinner, I went to find Adira. She had left.

Later that night, Adira returned with Meir. "Papa, Meir would like to talk with you."

I glanced up from my mending to see Meir walk into Cainan's office with him. Adira sat next to me.

"Are you certain of this?" I asked.

"Yes, Mama. Meir did not want me to leave. Marriage is his idea."

"Do you love him?" I asked.

"I do, Mama, or I would not have talked to him."

"Be certain. Marriage lasts for a long time."

We sat together. She held my hand while we waited.

The door finally opened. Meir came out of the office and glanced around the room.

"Adira?" he said when he saw her sitting by me.

Cainan followed him out of the office and smiled.

Adira jumped from her seat and hurried into his arms. The two of them rushed out the door.

"You gave them your permission?" I asked.

"How could I not, Elia? He loves Adira. She loves him. Like we loved each other so many years ago."

I batted my eyelashes at him. "And do you not still love me in the same way?"

He strode through the room and sat next to me. "You know I do, though more now. We have always been best friends. Our love continues to grow."

When we left Cainan two weeks later, we left both Adira and Zerach, newly married by Papa Enos.

Chapter 4

New Home

Years later another son was born. I often teased Cainan that he ran out of names, for he named this son Mahalaleel, I called him Maha. To prove he had not, he named our next child, a daughter, Shir.

Soon after Maha's birth, our family began to travel once more. Before we left, Cainan's brother, Jon, who had been responsible for the safety of the community of Cainan for longer than I can remember, came to our home begging us to take along brothers or other men as guards.

"The land is no longer safe to wander alone as it was in Grandpapa's days, or even in Papa's. I fear for him and Mama. Wicked men would take them captive if they could. They will take you, or Elia, or your children." Jon stood in front of his much younger brother, barely able to contain himself.

"No, Jon. I have been given a command to travel in search of those who are ready to hear of Jehovah's great love. We are commanded by Jehovah and will be protected by Him." Cainan spoke in a quiet, contained voice.

"But Jehovah requires us to use our good sense to stay safe. You cannot keep your family safe and travel alone." Red crept into Jon's face.

Cainan stood and embraced Jon. "I have been commanded to travel alone with my family, trusting in Jehovah. I will do this. I know you love us and want only the best for us. Believe me, if I could, I would take a guard. I cannot. I will not."

Jon stood, spluttering. He had lost this same argument with Papa Enos too many times. He gave me a quick embrace, shook his head, and turned to leave. "If you change your mind …"

"You know I cannot."

"I know. But I wish you could. It is dangerous." He swirled his cape around his shoulders and left.

"Is it dangerous?" I asked. "Jon would not worry needlessly."

Cainan drew me close. "Jon is right to fear for us. It is dangerous out there. But we have been commanded to leave the safety of Cainan and travel once more. Jehovah will protect us."

I gazed into his face and found peace in his bright green eyes. "I trust you. Jehovah will protect us."

Cainan held me close for a long time before breaking the silence. "Are you ready to leave in the morning?"

"All but the last basket of clothing and Maha's cradle."

"Good. We leave at first light."

We left our married children and grandchildren in their homes in Cainan, taking with us only Maha, Liba, our five-year-old daughter; Matan, our ten year-old son, Karni, our thirteen year-old son; and Yaffa, our fifteen-year-old daughter. We traveled in a large wagon pulled by six bullocks, trailing horses, sheep, goats, and two cows.

Along the road west, we passed other wagons. Some of those within rode past us staring forward as though they did not see our wagon nor hear the snorting of our bullocks and the noise of our children. Occasionally, a child would stare and wave toward us, tugging on his mama's skirts or his papa's robe, begging them to look. The parents never did. I knew these people were not among those we were commanded to teach and stayed quiet.

Sometimes, riders would join us, riding beside our wagon and visiting with Cainan. Some of these stayed less than a hand's span of the sun's movement across the sky. Others rode with us for several days, joining our fire at night, sharing their food with ours, and listening to Cainan speak of Jehovah. A few of these begged for baptism. Cainan complied, baptizing them in a river or deeper hole in a stream. Always, they would fall on our necks with tears of gratitude before turning down another path or road along the way.

We missed our companions when they left us. Still, we knew they had other places to travel, different than ours. Within days, another group of riders, on horseback or in wagons, would join us, eager to visit, willing to hear of Jehovah's love.

Our family traveled slowly along the road west for many weeks, in no real hurry to get anywhere. We followed the direction of the Spirit, stopping for a night only once in a small village. The rest of the time, we camped far away from other people. Tall mountains grew ever larger ahead of us. Low, green hills rose from flat plains, rising ever taller to sharp, rugged mountains topped with ice and snow. Greens, browns, and violets colored its slopes, enticing our eyes upward toward Jehovah.

At last, we entered a small village at the base of those mountains, set in a beautiful green meadow. We watched laughing children chase each other through the streets as our heavy wagon trudged behind them toward the village green. Two of the older boys detached themselves from the game and ran ahead.

Cainan pulled the bullocks to a halt on the edge of the green and helped me climb down from the tall wagon seat. Yaffa handed a wiggly Maha into my arms and followed. She helped Liba down. Karni and Matan scrambled off the back and came to stand beside us, eyes following the noisy village boys running across the green from us. They stopped and spoke to two adults who strolled in our direction, the boys following behind in a noisy mob.

"Welcome to Persyn. I am Rixon and this is my wife, Zonara," the man waved toward the woman. "We are the leaders of this poor village."

"Thank you." Cainan nodded to Rixon. "I am Cainan, son of Enos, son of Seth, son of Adam. My family and I would like to become a part of your village, if we may."

I felt my eyebrows draw together. Until that moment, I had no idea this was our destination.

"Son of Enos, you say?" Rixon lifted an eyebrow.

"I am. This is Elia, my wife, and our five youngest children."

Zonara touched Rixon on the elbow. He winked at her, then turned back to us. "As I said to you before, Cainan, son of Enos, son of Seth, son of Adam, you are welcome in our humble village. We work hard for the little we have." He pointed up at the mountain. "We live on the wrong side of the mountain. It keeps the rain and snow away, sharing but little with us."

"Oh?" Cainan's eyes followed Rixon's moving finger as it pointed higher.

"We get enough water from it to grow a few crops to feed our families, but not much more. Ours is a difficult life. If you would like to join us for that, you are welcome."

Cainan glanced at the weary crops, drooping in the heat of the day and up at the mountain. "Yes. This is the place for us. We will join you here."

The children behind Rixon and Zonara shouted and danced in excitement, swooping past them and gathering in Karni, Matan and Liba. They shouted and danced among us a moment then raced away.

"Karni, watch for your brother and sister," I called.

He turned, running backward. "I will, Mama."

~ ~ ~

Zonara and Rixon led us to a guest house. Cainan stopped the wagon beside it and unhitched the bullocks. About then, the children returned. They helped take our animals to a fenced field previously used by a family who deserted Persyn the year before.

That evening, the community welcomed us and invited Cainan to teach them. The children and I sat along the side of the village hall, listening to him speak of Jehovah's love for his children. The reminders of Jehovah's love for all the children of Eve and Adam filled the villagers with hope.

In the weeks and months that followed, the people of Persyn responded to Cainan's message, and became strong in their love for Jehovah. We settled in the village, becoming a part of their community.

I enjoyed being part of a village community once more. I did not realize how much I missed sharing with other women. Zonara became a good friend, like one of my sisters — or Cainan's.

Cainan traveled to nearby villages to teach those people, as well. Sometimes, he traveled with other men; other times, he traveled alone. I feared for him on those journeys when he traveled alone. There were more bandits now who traveled the roads, taking from the innocent and unprotected. However, Cainan reminded me that as Jehovah's follower, he would be protected. I trusted Jehovah, I trusted Cainan, and I faithfully waited for him each time he left us.

During those days, I was kept busy with Mahalaleel. A rambunctious child, he kept us busy. Even as a toddler, he climbed to the top of the tallest cottonwood trees where the branches were thin. I often stood at the bottom of the tree with my heart pounding in fear that the branch would splinter and Maha would plummet to the earth. Somehow, he never did.

Maha loved high places. As he grew old enough to leave my watchful care, he climbed high into the surrounding hills with the other herding boys. He climbed higher than other herders of sheep, goats, or other animals. He would return after days, full of stories of great flying birds and animals that lived in the highest reaches of the hills.

As Maha became older and big enough, he trailed the sheep and goats into the hills with the other boys. He often returned with wild stories of finding the bones of some huge animal. I laughed with him.

One day when he returned, he lugged a bone with him.

"I brought you something, Mama," he said.

"What is it?"

"A jawbone from some creature that lived here long ago."

"That is a big jawbone."

"I told you I found the bones of some huge animals. Did you not believe me?"

"I guess I did not. I do now. This is large enough to use as a table."

"That is what I thought," he said.

He turned it into a table we used in our sitting room.

41

After that, he scaled the mountains, reaching almost the very top, and shared stories of leopards, foxes, and antelope scrambling across the rocky slopes.

Maha loved Jehovah and His teachings almost as much as he loved high places. Perhaps, he felt His presence in those high places. Sometimes he whispered to me of the nearness of Jehovah's spirit there. I hoped he would draw close to Him and be a son to continue the patriarchal order of the Priesthood.

We were soon blessed as a family. When we took Maha and our other younger children on one of our family trips to Home Valley, Grandpapa Adam took Cainan into his office, as he often did. I sat in the kitchen with Grandmama Eve while the children ran outside. As matriarch to our family, she welcomed everyone who visited with a warm meal and freshly baked treats. I loved helping her grind the grains and mix sweet breads together to share with the other guests. The fragrance of baking breads and other treats reminded me of our visit early in our marriage.

"Tell me of your life in Persyn, Elia." Grandmama Eve brushed the flour from her hands and sat beside me.

"It is a lovely place, nestled against the tall mountains. The people there are good and humble. They love Jehovah and seek to do what is right. Our lives are not easy. Barely enough water trickles from the high mountain lakes to provide us with sufficient water for growing. There is enough to eat, but little extra. We rarely have extra for coming years of drought."

"It sounds like a lovely place. Cainan is busy teaching?"

I leaned back in my chair. "Yes. He often travels to villages on the plain and to other villages in the mountains. He leaves us home more, especially now that Maha is growing older, although he often takes Maha with him. But, Nadav is growing and stays with us when they are gone."

Grandmama Eve glanced out the window to where Maha played with a ball of strings with the other young men. "He loves his play."

"That he does. His greatest joy has always been to find the highest place around. It surprises me that he is not in the tallest tree," I said with a small laugh.

"He told me he feels closer to Jehovah in the mountains."

I smiled. "He has told me the same. His connection to the animals is unusual. I watched him one day, when we were foraging in the hills. He wrestled with a great brown bear as though it were a friend. I dared not shout out, fearing the animal would forget its friendship with Maha."

Grandmama gasped. "A bear?"

"Yes, a huge brown bear. No one else I know wrestles with bears, nor plays with the lions and tigers of the mountains, yet I have seen my Maha race with the great cats and wrestle with bears."

"Interesting. He is a big boy."

"He is."

We heard Grandpapa Adam's study door open and leaned forward, expecting to see him and Cainan walk toward us. Instead, Grandpapa Adam called my name.

"Elia? Would you join us, please?"

I glanced at Grandmama Eve. *Why would they want to speak with me?* She shrugged and smiled as I slowly stood and marched down the long hall to Grandpapa's office. I suddenly had a sense of how Cainan must feel when he joins Grandpapa Adam in his office each visit.

The door closed behind me and I stared around. Cainan sat in a chair near a low fire. He glanced up at me. He looked like a lost little boy.

"Please have a seat, Elia," Grandpapa Adam invited.

I breathed deeply and found my way into the seat next to Cainan, who glanced my way, raising his eyebrows slightly. I reached out to him and he grasped my hand, squeezing tighter than usual, increasing my concern.

"Relax, you two," Grandpapa Adam laughed. "This is a wonderful time."

Cainan relaxed the strength of his grasp and I smiled my thanks.

"We are here to honor your husband," Grandpapa Adam said.

My eyes opened wider and I glanced at Cainan. He stared intently at me.

"Elia, it is Jehovah's wish that your husband be ordained as a prophet, given the special responsibility to testify of His love and to call others to repentance."

I turned from Grandpapa Adam toward Cainan and stared. "He already testifies of Jehovah's love and calls others to repentance. Is this different?"

"It is. He will receive the High Priesthood as he fulfills the responsibility of a prophet."

"But he is so young, not yet one hundred years." I argued.

"That is what I said," Cainan whispered.

"Age is no indicator of ability to call others to repentance. You, Cainan, have followed the commands of Jehovah, including those you received on that day He met you in your travels to Shedolamak."

I watched Cainan breathe in deeply, then let the air escape from his lungs. With it, I watched his fears and questions fly away. His shoulders lifted, his back straightened, and he held his head up. I smiled with his transformation and set my now free hand on his arm.

"When will it happen?" Cainan asked.

"Soon," Grandpapa answered. "Your parents and grandparents will be here within the week."

"I did not know Mama Rebecca and Papa Enos were coming to Home Valley. Did you?" I looked at my good husband, who shook his head.

"They do not know why they come, but they will arrive soon."

Grandmama Eve laughed when I asked her about it. "Your grandpapa knows these things. Jehovah shares with him. You will see."

They arrived within the week, Grandpapa Seth and Grandmama Ganet arrived from the far north, while Papa Enos and Mama Rebecca rode into Home Valley from a village south of the community of Cainan. They arrived on the same day.

While we sat together, sharing a meal in Grandpapa Adam's and Grandmama Eve's home, Grandpapa Adam shared the news with them. Grandpapa Seth, who sat beside Cainan, pounded him on the back. Papa Enos looked at him across the table with pride and joy. Both Grandmama Ganet and Mama Rebecca gazed at him with love.

"I knew it would come," Mama Rebecca said.

Grandmama Ganet nodded. "It could not have happened to a nicer grandson—or granddaughter." She glanced toward me.

I cleared my throat. "Will our lives change much? I know Cainan will have greater responsibilities, but ..."

"And you, as his wife, will have greater responsibilities. People will look to you, as his wife. Can you support him in your actions as well as your words?" Grandmama Ganet asked.

"Oh. I did not think of that." I thought of my behavior, not bad, but my thoughts of others were not always the best. "I guess I have some repentance ahead of me."

Grandmama Eve laughed. "We all do. We will help you."

"And will you help me, too?" Cainan asked.

"Of course, that is why we are here." Papa Enos said.

We spent hours together, the women in Grandmama Eve's home and the men at the altar, both Cainan and I learning of our new duties. On the next Sabbath, Grandpapa Adam introduced Cainan as the newest prophet to the people of Home Valley. After the Sabbath service, we adjourned to Grandpapa

Adam's study, where the three prophets lay their hands on my good husband's head and ordained him to be a Prophet, seer, and revelator. Then, the four men lay their hands on my head and gave me a sweet, wonderful blessing that has helped me to support Cainan all the years he has been a Prophet.

Chapter 5

No Sword

Life changed after that day in many ways, and in others, it stayed the same. I continued to be Mama and Grandmama to my children and grandchildren and responsible for our home and garden. I continued to visit with the other women in Persyn and assist them when I could.

Some people looked at me differently, however. They heard about Cainan's new responsibilities and thought I would behave in a more prideful manner than I had before. I did not understand, for I had not received new responsibilities, Cainan had.

In time, most of those stopped looking at me as someone different and accepted me as one of the women of the village once more.

We stayed in Persyn long enough to watch Mahalaleel grow into an honorable and obedient young man. He still loved high places, and often hiked into the mountains.

One day he came to us. "I need to leave Persyn. It is time."

"Where will you go?" I asked him.

"Laish."

"Are you going to visit your grandparents there?"

"Yes. I prayed. I received word that I am sent to go to teach there."

Cainan smiled. "I received the same word. When do you plan to leave?"

Maha sat on a seat across from us. "I plan to leave in the morning, if I can get supplies ready by then."

"You may want to wait until the next day," Cainan suggested. "I will have time to help you get your travel supplies together. Besides, you should not leave tomorrow. It is the Sabbath."

"I can wait one more day," Maha said, nodding. "Then I must leave."

I stood and went to my storage closet and gathered together food for him. The trip would be long. He would not have time nor place to cook every day. I included travel bars for those days.

I set the supplies on the table. Maha came in with his pack. "Thank you, Mama." I walked with him down the hall and helped him gather together bedding and other supplies to keep him warm as he rode the distance from Persyn to Laish.

We celebrated the Sabbath together the next day, remembering the good things Jehovah had provided to our family and to the people of Persyn.

Maha bore strong testimony of his love for Jehovah, His goodness, and His blessings. He could be an excellent servant for Jehovah.

We rose early the next morning to embrace Maha as he left. He mounted his horse and took the lead line for his pack animal. "I will see you again, Mama, Papa."

Our son, Mahalaleel tapped his heels into the horse's ribs to urge him forward. We watched him ride out of sight.

"Will we see him again?" I asked.

"We will. Jehovah will watch over him," Cainan replied.

We turned and returned to our daily activities. I wondered how far Maha had traveled, where he spent the night, and why he needed to visit Grandpapa Seth and Grandmama Ganet.

Even as I wondered and worried about Maha, I stayed busy. I had a garden next to the house that needed weeding and watering often. The garden kept us in fresh vegetables and were vital to our having food to eat during the raining time.

I also helped in the fields, weeding and harvesting during the hot times of the year. My skin turned brown in the sun as it did every year. Getting water to the garden and the fields continued to be a struggle. The mountain beside us shielded the rains and kept us from receiving all the water we needed during the year.

We heard from Grandpapa Adam that Maha passed through Home Valley on his way to Laish. His trip had been commanded by Jehovah. He would be safe.

While we knew Maha traveled with Grandpapa Seth, Cainan received a message from Jehovah. We were to go visit Grandpapa Adam and Grandmama Eve in Home Valley. Beyond that, we were leaving Persyn for a time. I did not know if we would ever return.

Our family bade our goodbyes to Rixon and Zonara, and all the others we had grown to love in a community celebration the night before we left. Our children ran through the village center, chasing after the others of the village until I called to them to come home to bed.

We brought with us Nadav, and our two youngest daughters. Liba stayed in Persyn with her husband and new child. We knew we would return often to visit.

We climbed into our wagons early the next morning and rode down the mountain trail toward our beloved family

We taught children of Adam to remember the commands of Jehovah as we traveled. Some listened, though many more refused to hear our message. We often found ourselves bowing before Jehovah, begging him to soften the hearts of the people we met. Why would they not listen?

We did all we could. It was never enough.

Men and women preferred to live lives of debauchery and grief. They had the opportunity to repent and find true joy. Instead they preferred to experience fraudulent days, filled with laughter, wine, and wickedness.

When we entered Home Valley, we discovered Mahalaleel and a young woman.

"Mahalaleel!" I cried as I threw my arms around my son. "I did not know you were here."

"I came with Vida. Grandpapa Seth suggested we come to Grandpapa Adam to receive his special blessing on our marriage."

"Marriage?" I asked. I peered closer at the woman who stood near my son.

"Yes. Mama, Papa. This is Vida. She is the reason I traveled to Laish. I helped Grandpapa Seth teach of Jehovah to others, but my true purpose was to find and marry Vida."

I gazed at this beautiful girl. She had tied her long brown hair into a bun at her neck. Tiny curls, unlike any I would ever have, escaped and fluffed around her face. Her dark brown eyes pierced into mine. Intelligence shone through.

I opened my arms and embraced her. "Welcome to our family."

"I am happy to be part of it," Vida said.

Her musical voice entranced me. "I can see why you love her," I said to Maha as I hugged him once more. "Vida is lovely."

"I knew you would love her."

That Sabbath, while the younger children played outside in the protecting care of our daughter, Shir, we went into Grandpapa Adam's study with Grandmama Eve and listened to those simple and marvelous words given when Father married

Adam to Eve. Those words filled me with a joy I cannot express except through the tears that leak from my eyes.

Maha insisted on riding with us to Cainan. He wanted to introduce Vida to our family, maybe even stay there. We rode together, visiting and learning more about each other.

Cainan lifted a hand one day, stopping Vida and me mid-laugh. Our children had been trained well in our travels. At Cainan's signal, they raced to the side of the wagon and stood silently waiting for directions.

Cainan directed us off the trail into tall bushes. We sat on our horses and the children stood beside the wagon while a crowd of noisy, belligerent men rode past.

"We heard they rode this way. It will not be difficult for all of us to overwhelm them. They are two men, two women, and lots of children, after all. Women are weak."

I glanced at Vida. 'Weak?' I mouthed, pointing to her and to myself.

She shook her head. 'Not me, nor you,' she mouthed. 'If they attack us, we will show them.'

What will we show them with? I do not even have a stick with which to beat them. We need training.

The men shouted and cursed as they passed us, threatening our lives.

When we moved out along the trail a span later, I brought my concern up to Cainan and Maha. "What are we supposed to do if we are caught by men like those who just passed us? How do we protect ourselves? I carry no sword. I carry no stick. What do Vida and I do?"

"I carry no sword, either," Cainan said. "My brother Jon believes I will end up dead one day, killed by one of these men who seek to take my life."

"You do not carry a sword?" Vida gasped.

"What will I do with one sword? I cannot fight off twenty men with one sword. I have been promised that if I trust Jehovah, He will protect me."

"You depend on Jehovah completely? You do not even carry a knife?"

"I have my belt knife. You have yours. I use mine for eating, however. I do not plan to fight, nor do I practice to fight with it. I travel alone, or with my family." He waved at the children giggling as they danced along beside the wagon, now the danger had passed.

He continued. "We travel alone. We do not bring a guard with us. How can those we seek to teach trust us when we bring with us a guard of men with knives and swords?"

Maha took Vida's hand. "We trust Jehovah, totally and implicitly."

Vida glanced to Maha. "Do you carry a weapon?"

Maha laughed. "Why? I travel like my papa, alone many more times than not. A sword would give me false bravado, make me think I could win against a group of men. No," he shook his head. "I trust in Jehovah.

~ ~ ~

We traveled back to our home in Cainan with Maha and Vida. He planned to build a new home for her there in the home village of his grandparents.

As so often happened when we traveled, we passed groups of travelers who did not recognize our presence. Sometimes, they turned toward the sound of our bullocks as they passed with a stare of wonder in their eyes. When these unseeing travelers were strong, heavily armed men with foul curses sliding from their tongues, I bowed in gratitude to Jehovah that He protected us from them.

One afternoon we came upon a fight between men on horses. We rode into a thick stand of bushes to hide and wait for it to end. We put our hands around the muzzles of our horses and bullocks, keeping them quiet.

As we waited, we listened to the sounds of the fight. Swords clanked together with grunts and shouts of anger and pain. Thuds echoed as men pounded one another with their fists. The terrible noise frightened me, causing me to fear the men would come into our bushes. I pressed my head into my horse's neck trying to block the violence from my ears.

The shouting ended and I wanted to move on, but Cainan held me back. "Wait a bit, dear, until we are certain they are all gone."

We stood within the bushes until the sound of the men faded into the distance. We stood with our hands over the mouths of the animals another long moment until Maha peeked out and looked around. It seemed forever before he stepped back into the thicket.

"They are gone. It is safe. We can continue our travels." He helped Vida onto her horse and mounted his own while the rest of us mounted our horses or climbed into the wagon, then pushed through the brush and back out onto the road.

I closed my eyes as we passed the blood soaking into the ground. I hoped none had died, but Nadav said they had carried away the bodies. I bit my lower lip to hold back the tears, thinking of the men who lost their lives to a ridiculous fight.

Cainan saw my eyes sparkle and nudged his horse between me and the battle site. "It is as Grandpapa told us it would be, my love. Men sell their souls for a bit of metal. They take the lives of others because of an argument or a disagreement. They have lost the love for others given to them by Jehovah."

"We see it everywhere we go. I wish it was not so." We trotted on past the battle site trying to avoid the evil we had seen.

Other such battles forced us from the road more often than we wanted. Eventually, we safely made our way into the land of Cainan.

The day before we arrived, Vida admitted to nausea caused by her being with child.

"How can it be?" she asked. "We have only been married a short time."

I helped make her comfortable. "When did you last have your moon time?"

She counted back. "Perhaps seven weeks?"

"Ah. Enough to be sick."

Although I anticipated a quiet life in Cainan, it did not happen. Within months, Adira sent word with her oldest son that her newest babe would be born soon.

She didn't need me to help bring the child into the world. Cainan's sister had trained to be a healer. She had been called.

But I had missed the births of many of my grandchildren. I hurried to be at her side.

The delivery did not go well. The baby had not been as active in those last days. I feared problems.

I did not want to add to Adira's fears, but I grabbed her hand. She gripped my hand hard.

"I am frightened, Mama," she said. "It is not the birthing of the baby. I fear he will not live."

"No!" I cried and squeezed her hand even harder. "Jehovah will bless your baby."

"If he still lives. I do not know how. He has not moved all day."

"Babies get quiet before their birth —"

"No, Mama," Adira said, tears filled her voice. "I have birthed other babies before. This is different."

She clung to my hand as she went through the squeezing pains of childbirth. Grace finally urged Adira to push the child from within her after more than two spans.

"You have a daughter," Grace said.

She handed the babe to her daughter, Raya, and worked to remove the last of the afterbirth from within Adira. Adira focused on the cramping pains and Grace's voice.

I watched Raya's face as she worked to get the tiny child to breathe. She worked hard, even blowing gentle breaths into the babe's mouth.

The little girl's chest rose and fell. I held my breath, watching for her chest to fill with air again. It did not happen.

By the time Grace held the remains of the afterbirth in her hands, her daughter looked at me and frowned and shook her head.

"No!" Adira cried out.

I wrapped my arms around her and held her close. She tried to push me away.

"Give me my baby!" she cried. "Let me hold her."

Raya wrapped the tiny girl in a blanket and handed her to Adira.

"Mamas need to hold their babies," she said.

I fell to my knees next to the bed and prayed for a blessing on the child and on my daughter.

Adira unwrapped her daughter and held her bare little body next to her bare chest, with the blanket covering them both. She held the babe's heart near her own.

She cooed and spoke softly to the baby, singing little songs.

Tears rolled down my face. I touched the babe's face, and then turned away to help Grace.

Grace glanced at Adira, and looked at me, and shrugged.

I helped change the bedding beneath Adira. She hardly noticed as we moved her. Grace took the bloody bedding out.

I knew Meir sat outside the room, waiting to welcome his new child to the world. I could not bring myself to go out and tell him.

I sat on the chair next to Adira's bed and set my head in my hands, praying softly for Jehovah's help. How would I get the baby away from her mama?

I do not know how long we sat there like that. The light changed in the room, growing darker as the sun moved toward setting.

I became aware of a small sneeze and a snuffling sound in the bed next to me. I turned, expecting to see Adira sniffing her tears up.

Instead, the babe sniffed, searching for her mama's breast and food. Adira had wrapped her in the blanket and held her close to her breast.

"What —?" I asked.

"Her heart felt mine and began to match it's rhythm. She woke with a sneeze."

"A sneeze?"

"Um hum. A little sneeze. She thinks she is hungry," Adira said.

"She would be, after that."

~ ~ ~

We stayed less than a year in Cainan before we were called to leave and teach of Jehovah once more. Vida had delivered another son in that time.

Before we left, we met with all of our children in a big family gathering. We gave and received love from our children and grandchildren. Cainan took each child and grandchild into his study and offered personal guidance.

While the older ones received Cainan's blessing, the littlest children and I went into the kitchen to make small cakes for everyone. We laughed and told stories leaving flour scattered in the kitchen. I planned to clean it after the children left.

The children shared the treats with the other children and adults.

"These are lovely," Nyssa, Zerach's wife, said. "I did not think young children could cook such nice treats."

"They need some direction from an adult, but they do a good job," I told her. "Try it some time. You may be surprised."

Cainan called Zerach and Nyssa and their children into his office.

I visited with the others while Cainan offered counsel and blessings to Zerach's family.

Early the next morning, Cainan and I and our two youngest climbed into the wagon. Our horses were tied to the back to follow behind. We waved to Jon, who stood guard at the gate that day.

"You are leaving again with only your wife and little children?" Jon asked.

"I must. You know I must depend on Jehovah to protect us. He has done so before. He will do so now."

Jon shook his head and opened the gate for us to ride through.

We rode across the land, traveling in whichever direction Cainan was led. He talked with travelers about Jehovah. Some believed him. Many did not.

Occasionally, Cainan led us into a village, where we stayed a few days to teach the people. We never went into larger cities. Many times, however, we rode around the walls of a village without attempting to enter.

After many months of traveling, we arrived at the mountains far south of Persyn. We entered a dusty town. They had built wooden walkways far above the ground.

I lifted my eyebrows at Cainan.

He shrugged.

"How long are we here?" I asked.

"A day, a week, a month? I do not know until we are given other directions," Cainan said.

As we rode down the street, no one showed us any attention or offered any assistance.

Once more, I lifted my eyebrows. "Now what?"

"We go a bit farther. Perhaps the leaders will find us by the time we get to the village center."

We rode in silence down the main street. Buildings rose on both sides of the street. The buildings were neither falling apart nor looked like they were owned by people of substance. They were common, simple homes.

"These people should be willing to listen. If their homes are any indication, they are not filled with pride," Cainan said.

By the time we arrived at the village green, children were following us, as they often did in new villages. Two men stood at the edge of the village green, waiting for us.

"We shall discover now if the people of this village are willing to learn of Jehovah," Cainan murmured.

I nodded and tucked a hand beneath his elbow. We had seen this before.

Cainan pulled the bullocks to a halt and stepped down out of the wagon. He turned and took my hand to help me get down, before stepping toward the men.

"I am Cainan, the son of Enos, a son of Adam. This is my wife Elia. We have come to live with you for a time, if you are willing."

"A son of Adam?" One man asked. "We have not seen a son of Adam in many years. Does he still live?"

"He does. We saw him not many months ago," Cainan said.

"That is good. I have heard Adam is a good man."

"He is. I have come to teach you of Jehovah."

"I am Tuval," the first man said. He nodded toward the man beside him. "With Yether, we are the leaders of this village."

"I am happy to meet you." Cainan stepped forward to grasp his elbow. "What do you call this village?"

"This is Pisidia. Are you certain you want to stay here? Our village is poor. Although the rain falls in its time, we rarely get more than we need. Worse, the earth refuses to bear fruit. We struggle to grow enough for all to eat," Yether said.

"For now, we would like to stay," Cainan said.

"If that is so, we will take you to the guest house. After you have been here a few days, you may change your mind."

"We may, but I doubt it," Cainan said. "Some of you are waiting to hear more about Jehovah's love. I am here to teach you of that love."

Tuval and Yether led the way to the guest house. By the time we arrived, others followed us, murmuring in the background.

Our children jumped out of the wagon and joined the other children playing around us. Children always made friends faster than adults.

"This is our guest house," Tuval said when we arrived. "It is furnished with beds, tables, and chairs. You and your family can move in today. If you decide to stay more than a week, we will find a different home for you. This is small for a family."

"Thank you," Cainan said.

"I have a stew cooking," a woman who stood behind me said. "I will be happy to share it with your family. Your children are playing with my children."

I turned to her. "That would be nice. I feared we would be eating cold travel bars again tonight."

"Oh, no. I would not let you do that," she said. "I have enough for my family and yours." She pointed down the street. "My house is five houses down the street that way. Come in a span. That should give you time to get settled in."

"We will. My name is Elia. My husband is Cainan."

"I am Chava. Come in a span." She turned and strode down the street toward her house.

"You will have one friend," Cainan whispered to me as we lifted out our baskets of supplies from the back of the wagon.

"You can put your wagon beside the house," Yether said. "I will show you where to put your animals so they are safe."

Cainan helped me with the baskets we would need, then settled the wagon next to the house before unhitching the bullocks. He and Yether led the animals down the street to a barn while I carried the baskets inside.

I set the basket of food in the kitchen. I appreciated the offer of a meal. Cooking this late in the evening would mean a late meal.

I walked through the small guest house. It held a small sitting room, the kitchen, and two small sleeping rooms. It would be enough for our small family.

Cainan came into the house, followed by the children.

"What is for dinner?" Ebron looked at the cold fire space. "No fire?"

"It is hot outside. Too hot for a fire tonight."

"Hot?" Hadad asked. "It is cool. The rain will come soon."

"I am hungry," Ebron said.

"I know," I said with a little giggle. "Chava invited us to eat with her family. You were playing with her children."

"Oh! Datan and Pili? We get to go to their house to eat?" Ebron cried.

I nodded and the boys cheered.

Chapter 6

Floods

I wondered why the walkways stood so high above the ground. The dry earth struggled to grow enough food to feed the small village. Why would the walkways be so high up?

The rains came and we learned why. High flood water raced beneath the boardwalks. Any who fell off were swept down the mountain.

The first year there, Hadad fell off the boardwalk. His brother, Ebron held to his hand, and I held Ebron's hand.

"Hold on to him!" I screamed, dropping the basket of vegetables I planned to take to Chava.

"I am, Mama!" Ebron shouted. "Hold on to me, Hadad!"

I bent to grab for Hadad's other hand, while still holding onto Ebron.

"Stop!" a voice shouted from behind me.

I heard a splash as someone jumped in the water behind me. I could not turn to see who would risk their life for me and my son. I had to hold both boys' hands. The rain tried to wash their hands from mine. *Oh, Jehovah, help!*

Hadad's body rose from the water and he stood on the boardwalk once more. Tuval clung to the boardwalk's support. I grabbed both boys into my arms, holding them close to me and watched Tuval struggle to pull himself from the rushing flood back to the boardwalk.

A hand reached out for Tuval's and pulled him up onto the walk. I turned to see who would have helped this brave man. Cainan pulled him into the center of the walk.

"Are you well?" Cainan asked.

Tuval nodded. "I will live. Take your family home. Today is no day for a woman and children to be out."

Cainan lifted Hadad into his arms, then put an arm around me. "Come. You should be home."

"I was taking vegetables to Chava —"

"Not on a day like today. Wait until the rains lessen. Do not bring the boys out into rain like this. It is not safe."

"I know that now." I went with him back up the walk.

We turned off at our porch and entered the home we had been given to live in.

"When you need to go out in the rain, be certain I am with you. You cannot keep the boys from falling," Cainan warned me.

I nodded. After that, I did not leave the house in the rain alone until the boys were bigger and stronger and could help me stay on the slippery walkway.

During those years, our boys became great friends with Chava's children. They spent many days through the years together as they grew and matured. The friendship between Ebron and Pili reminded me of my friendship with Cainan. They spent many hours together riding and hunting, working in the fields, and standing side-by-side on the threshing floor.

If I thought working to grow food at Persyn had been difficult, I remembered it fondly while struggling to drag grains and vegetables from the earth surrounding Pisidia. Tuval had been correct that first day when we entered the village. I often remembered his words, 'The earth refuses to bear fruit.'

We dumped manure from the horses and cattle on the land, scratching it into the hard-packed earth. After years of work, feeding our family became easier, no longer an exception. Even then, it continued to be a constant battle to fill the soil enough to keep it from packing hard during the cold rains.

The people of Pisidia willingly listened to Cainan and the teachings of Jehovah. Cainan stayed busy for years, teaching and guiding them in the ways of the Lord. Our time there began to be sweet and joyful.

It did not surprise me when Ebron and Pili came to Cainan, asking permission to be married. All our neighbors joined us in the village green on the day of their marriage.

Cainan spoke the words of the rite that married them, though he did not give them the blessings that only Adam had been given the right to perform. As I welcomed Pili into the family, I whispered to them that they should go to Home Valley as soon as they could. They would need the sacred blessings from Adam.

We continued to work hard in the fields and gardens, building up the earth to help it provide us with food.

Then, not many years later, Ebron's friends, Calum and Huw, climbed the mountain in search of missing goats. In their search, they found a strange, soft, rock—gold. Strangers passing through the village recognized it as something of value. He told them how men in Nod and other parts of the world melted it or pounded it into beautiful objects. He showed them a circle of it around his finger.

"If you find more of this and trade it with others of other lands, this substance will help you to feed your families," he said.

At first, they did not believe the stranger. Huw rode off with the stranger and a bag of the gold, not returning for many months. His wife began to sorrow, fearing he had been overcome and murdered for the rocks in his pack. Finally, Huw returned with three full wagons of food and supplies.

"Where did this come from?" Cainan asked.

"From the men in Nod. They traded me these three wagons and all that is in them for the small pack of gold I took with me," Huw replied.

Men surrounded him, asking questions. Huw shared the bounty of the wagons in a great feast that evening. Cainan feared this would become a problem for the people of Pisidia.

It did.

Too many of the men in the valley tired of the struggle to grow food and raise animals. One by one, they slipped away, into the mountains in search of the gold-rock.

Fewer people dumped manure in the fields, fewer were left to coax the water through them, fewer came to harvest and prepare the grains for storage. Fewer stayed to milk the cows and goats. Fewer men helped shear the sheep and goats. Only women were left to care for the animals. Soon, the fields lay fallow and the animals escaped their pens. The village of Pisidia became a dry and barren place.

The men, and some of the women, climbed the mountain and dug in the earth, plucking the gold from it. Men from other communities found our little village, offering to trade grains, dried fruits and vegetables, and other supplies we could not produce near the mountain, for the gold. Now, instead of struggling to live, they had their needs satisfied by the gold they dug. Among their purchases, they paid for men and boys to plant and harvest their fields and care for the animals. Once more, the village became a pleasant place to live.

Except, along with the gold and trade, the people of Pisidia traded away their humility and love and dependence on Jehovah, becoming a hardened, prideful people. Cainan's duty to teach the people of this part of the land became much more difficult.

When Mama Eve and Papa Adam traveled through the land, they stopped to spend time with us. The men were hardened.

Mama Eve tried to walk down the street on the wooden walkways. Men walked past her and pushed her off. I ran to help her up.

She shook with frustration. "How could they push an old woman like me from the safety of the walkway?"

"They are hardened. It is no longer safe for women to be here. I fear for Grandpapa Adam, as well."

"Why?" Grandmama Eve peered into my eyes and onward into my soul.

"They seek for gold they can trade for food, rather than the life-giving word of Jehovah. Few work the fields, they prefer to dig in the dirt of the mountains for the yellow rock that can never feed their children."

"How can you and Cainan stay here?" she asked.

"I do not know. We wait on word from Jehovah. Cainan will stay as long as he believes there is someone to listen to him. For now, that is only our sons and their wives."

"Time to leave this place," Grandmama Eve said. She took my arm and held it tightly. "Do you not think?"

"I do. Now, for Jehovah to agree."

~ ~ ~

Grandmama Eve and Grandpapa Adam only stayed with us for two weeks. Grandpapa Adam went with Cainan into ours and other surrounding villages, attempting to share the love of Jehovah with them. The men refused to hear. Their women had become too hardened to care.

When Grandmama Eve embraced me, she whispered in my ear. "Jehovah does not expect you to live among such hardened people."

"I know, Grandmama. Cainan said as much last night. We hope the boys will leave with us. We want to leave before the rains. If not, we will leave as soon as we can safely travel when they end."

The rain came early that year. Efron and Hadad loved their wives and their parents. But they, too, could see that Pisidia was no longer a place for men who loved and trusted Jehovah to live. The Destroyer had enticed the hearts of our village friends.

By the end of the rain, even Pili, Efron's wife, and Gila, Hadad's wife, agreed that they must leave. No good woman could feel safe among the hardened men who came to dig for the gold.

We watched Ebron and Pili's children one wet afternoon while they walked along the boardwalk to visit a friend. When Ebron and Pili came to get their children from our care, Pili was wet clear through. Her cloak and hood should have kept her dry.

I raced to a back closet to get towels for them. "What happened?" I asked when I returned to the sitting room.

"Men knocked her off the boardwalk," Ebron growled. "If I had not been there to catch her hand and drag her back onto the walk, she would be down the mountain, with the trash the floods carry with them."

"Your wife is not trash!" Cainan cried.

"No. But the men of Pisidia do not know how to treat a woman. They treated her like trash, as something of little value. We are leaving when the rain ends."

I sighed. "I prayed you would decide to go with us. I did not want you to be hurt. I did not want you to have an experience like this. These men are terrible."

"We thought she would be safe with me along," Ebron growled. "We were wrong."

"I have not been outside since the rain started. I do not dare," I said.

"I will not allow it. Your mama is important to me," Cainan added.

"I do not think Hadad and Gila will stay. Nor do I think Pili's mama and papa will stay."

"They should plan to leave with us," I said. I took the towel from Pili and carried it to the closet and dumped it in the basket with other towels waiting to be cleaned.

"I am going to have a chat with Gila," Pili announced. "She should not have to nearly fall into the raging flood to decide to leave these men. Pisidia is not a good place for women and families."

The rain fell longer than usual.

By the time the earth dried enough we could travel again, we had a group of families who traveled with us. Not only did our sons and their families leave, Chava and her husband came. Tuval and Yether brought their families in wagons pulled by oxen. They rode their horses and joined our little caravan of travelers.

"Where will we go?" Tuval asked.

"Away from these mountains and this gold," Cainan said.

We traveled east toward Home Valley, searching for a place that would accept a band of believers.

At last, we found a beautiful valley, not far from Home Valley. The fertile ground promised food for us. A river flowed across the side of the valley. We would have a place to grow our crops and water to drink. A small forest grew near.

We camped near the river in the valley while Cainan, Tuval, and the other men walked through the forest, searching for wood to build homes.

"What did you find?" I asked when the men returned. "Those trees are beautiful. I would hate to see you cut them all down for homes."

"There is enough wood for a few homes," Cainan reported. "If we are careful, we should not have to cut trees to build our homes."

"I see trees growing along the ridge in those hills," Yether added. We should be able to find enough wood to build warm homes for our families before the rain falls again."

We cheered. The children came running from playing among the flowers to see why we cheered.

"We have a new home," Gila told her young daughter.

"Where?" she asked in her childlike simplicity. "I do not see any houses."

"Not yet, dear," Hadad said. "But before it is cold and wet again, we will have homes built for you and all the other children."

"And," Pili added, "we will have fields of grain harvested to feed us during the rain times. You will like our new home."

"Yippee!" the children cheered together.

The men took time to help us plow enough land to plant grains so we would have food to eat. Then they dragged in many logs and built us new homes and furniture.

We women planted vegetable gardens and searched for other food we could eat until ours had grown. Men hunted and brought us meat to eat, so we did not starve.

Before the rain fell again, our new little village of Oren stood near the river, close enough we could get water but far enough we would still be safe when the rains flooded.

We loved this new little village. When strangers came, seeking refuge, we accepted them, with a warning that we would share the words of Jehovah with them.

Some stayed. Oren grew. Others found no joy in listening to the commands of Jehovah and moved on. We wished them well and safe journeys, knowing they were not people who would be happy with us.

Chapter 7

Gathering

We traveled to Home Valley again. Grandpapa Adam invited all the family to join him in Home Valley for a special family council. Those of us who gathered enjoyed meeting others of our family from around the land. We traded the specialties from our part of the world with others.

I traded some of my pots for those from far away. I enjoyed the sweet taste of jellies and other foods they shared with us.

Then, as the men gathered, I sat with the other daughters of Eve in a beautiful warm field as she told her story. In the next days, I heard Ganet's story and Rebecca's. Their lives were inspiring. They worked so hard to follow the commandments of Jehovah.

Eve suggested that those of us who are wives of the prophets who did not have time to share our stories should write them for others to read. My heart thumped against my chest.

What did I have to teach these women? When we broke up with the promise to write our story, I spent many weeks fussing and fuming over the assignment. My life has not been inspiring.

As I wrote this, however, I have learned that there is more to inspiration than flashes of light and speaking with Jehovah.

I have followed my husband across the land and lived in harsh places under difficult conditions. I have trusted Jehovah in all we did. Life has not been easy. I doubt it will ever be easy for any of Jehovah's children.

I suppose my life may have something for others to learn. I hope you will agree.

May Jehovah bless you,

Elia,

Wife of Cainan

PART TWO

Vida

Chapter 1

Visitor

I am Vida.

I lived in the mountains of Laish as a child. I loved the cold, white snow that fell each year instead of the rain. I plucked icicles from the edge of the roof and sucked on them for water, always careful to stay far away from the edge of the roof overhang.

Grandmama told me stories of when Ganet and Seth came to live with us. "A boy stood under the edge of the overhang and one of the huge carrots of ice fell on him."

"I know better than to do that. It is dangerous!" I cried.

Grandmama nodded her head. "Everyone thought he died. But Seth went into his home with his parents and prayed to Jehovah for many spans. When he left the house, the boy lived."

"How did that happen, Grandmama? I thought when you die, you are gone forever."

"Usually, you are. However, sometimes those who obey the laws of Jehovah can call them back to life. The boy had died. I know because it was my older brother, Mowob.

"Seth brought him back to life. When I ask Seth about it today, he tells me he did not do it. Only Jehovah has the power to restore a life. He had only begged for Mowob's life for his parents and family."

I never forgot that story, especially when I sat in my Uncle Mowob's lap and played with his children who were my age. If Seth had not returned him to this life, I would never have known my uncle.

As I grew, Ganet and Seth were important in my life. They lived in a home next to ours. When they were home, I could run to Ganet for sweets.

She offered me the advice and support that a grandmama offered. She became a third grandmama to me. I love her, and she loves me.

Mahalaleel came to visit one summer when I had lived more years than others thought to be wise and still be unmarried. We became friends. How could I ignore him when he lived with my special grandmama?

He climbed the highest mountains with the herders, often climbing higher than the others dared. He brought back the bones of long dead animals and told stories of what their lives must have been like.

He enthralled me.

I had always been the girl who loved being with the women. I loved cooking, sewing, weaving, and gardening. Maha loved being out of doors, climbing mountains. He raced wolves and fought bears!

Other girls loved to be out in the wild outdoors. Not me. How did Maha ever decide I would be the woman he wanted for a wife?

But he did.

He asked me to walk with him into the hills one afternoon. I packed a meal in a basket for us and waved goodbye to Ganet. She smiled at me in a knowing way. I did not know why she did.

Maha led me to a beautiful meadow, not far from our village. He spread out the blanket he carried. I set out our simple meal and we sat down on the blanket to eat.

"Vida," he said. "You are a quiet woman. You listen when Grandpapa Seth speaks. I like that."

"Seth has much to say that I must learn."

"He does. Perhaps that is why Jehovah sent me here to live with him."

I handed him a piece of poultry I had cooked.

He took it and kissed my hand.

"What is that for?" I asked pulling away from him.

"I find you fascinating. You chat with Grandmama like she is your best friend. You listen intently to Grandpapa. You cook delicious food and sew beautiful clothing."

"I do the things women are taught to do. I also go to the threshing floor during harvest and help with the threshing." I lifted a shoulder. "I am a woman, doing womanly things."

"And you have men ..." He took a bite of the chicken and smiled at me.

"Friends. Nothing more."

"No one you wait for? No one who has stolen your heart?"

"Do I look like men want to drag me away with them to be their wife? I am nineteen. All the women my age already have a child, some have two." I stared at my hands. They were larger than many of the girls I knew, but they did more.

Maha took my hand. "I am happy no one has claimed you to be his."

"Why?" I looked up into his blue eyes. A lock of brown hair drooped into one.

"I like you, Vida. Can you not see that?"

"Why? I do not hike into the mountains or ride horses with the wind."

"Those are things men do to impress women. You are a beautiful woman. Your soul impresses me."

I glared at him. "My soul?"

"Your soul. Your sweet, obedient, willing soul."

"If you think I would be compliant if you expected something different than what Jehovah has taught? You would be wrong." I gathered my skirts and began to stand.

He grabbed my hand. "No! Nothing like that!" He pulled me down and let my hand go. "It is your trust and faith in Jehovah that draws me to you. I do not know how other men do not see your beauty. I do. Perhaps Jehovah has clouded their eyes to save you for me?"

My glare returned.

He winked.

"I jest, but only a little. I do not understand how you have escaped being married to another man."

"I have been busy learning to be a wife and mother with my mama and Ganet. I do not go out onto the green or to the well flaunting myself, as I have seen other girls do."

"For this, I thank you. I would never have come to know you."

"You are serious?"

Maha took my hand in his. "I am very serious. Will you be my wife?"

"Your wife?" I giggled. "You do not even know me."

"I know you well enough."

"I do not know you well enough." I pulled my hand from his.

"If you get to know me well enough, will you marry me?"

"That is a big question. How will that happen? I do not have time to walk into the hills every day. I have work I must do."

"I will spend time with you. I will show you the man I am. I am more than the man who climbs high mountains —"

"You wrestle with the bears."

He grinned. "They are my friends. You never know when it will help to have a bear for your friend."

I lifted an eyebrow.

Maha swallowed and cleared his throat. "I do not tell this story often." He scratched his face beside his eye. "On the way here, I ran into a gang of robbers. They wanted to take away all I had. They were digging through my pack when a big brown bear roared into my camp."

"What did you do?" I squeaked.

"I screamed."

My jaw dropped. "You screamed?"

He giggled. "The men saw the bear and screamed louder." His giggles became laughter. "When the bear raced toward them, roaring as he ran, they dropped everything and ran. They did not remember to mount their horses. They just ran out of my camp, dropping my possessions as they ran. One stumbled over a log."

He howled with laughter.

I pictured the robber stumbling over the log with a big brown bear snapping at his back side. I giggled with him.

"The bear roared one more time, then came to me. He rubbed against my leg like my mama's cat does."

"He rubbed against your leg?"

Maha nodded. "He did. I scratched him behind his ears. Mama's cats always like that. He did, as well. He snuffed up at me. I gave him a bit of dry meat from my pack. He scarfed it down, nodded at me, and lumbered away."

I held my stomach where it hurt from laughing. "Did you see those men again?"

"No," Maha said, laughing still. "I brought their horses with me. I wouldn't want them to starve. That bear did me a favor."

"You would return them if you saw them?" I asked.

His laughter ended suddenly. "Yes. If they admit the horses are theirs, I will return them. I have cared for them well."

~ ~ ~

Maha was true to his word. He came inside to spend time with me while I did the things I must. He held the hank of yarn between his hands while I rolled it into a ball that would easily unroll when I wove it into a blanket. He covered his tunic with a towel and helped me mix and knead bread. And he accepted a needle from me and stitched together a seam, among the other things he helped me do. Through it all, we talked and laughed and learned more about each other.

One day he came to my door and asked me to come outside. "I have a gift for you. I do not think your mama will appreciate it if I bring it inside," he said.

His grimace concerned me. I grabbed my cloak from the peg behind the door and called to mama. "I am going out with Maha. I will return soon."

"Take your cloak," she called back. "It is cool outside."

"I know, Mama. I have my cloak." I hurried out the door, closing it behind me. "What is your surprise?"

"Close your eyes," he said. He put his hands over my eyes. "Do not peek."

I giggled. "You have a surprise for me, and I cannot see it?"

"Yes. Follow me."

He led me down the steps, warning me of each one, then turned. We walked a few steps before turning again.

"Stop," he whispered. "Keep your eyes closed. I will remove my hands. Wait."

His hands fell from my eyes, but I kept them closed, wondering what his surprise would be. I smelled an animal, but we were outside where there were many animals.

"Open your eyes now, Vida," he crooned to me.

I opened them. A black horse with white splotches stood in front of me.

"This is for you," Maha said. "If you are going to be my wife, you will need a horse."

"She is beautiful," I cried and reached my hand up to touch her nose. She whuffed and bounced her head.

"Give her this," Maha said, handing me a carrot.

I held it out and she took it from my hand. She slurped it in, barely touching my palm with her lips, and crunched on it. I quivered from the soft tickling touch of her lips.

"What will you name her?" Maha asked.

I gazed at the splotches on her body. "Someone has painted white on her. I will call her Paint."

"What do you think of that?" Maha asked the mare.

The horse bounced her head in my direction.

"I think she likes the name. Paint, meet Vida. Vida, meet Paint."

"She is beautiful, but … but … Maha —"

"What? I can give my future bride a gift."

"Maha, I do not know how to ride a horse."

"You have never ridden a horse? How can that be?"

"I have never left Laish." I shrugged. "When we go out into the snow, it is in a wagon or a sledge. I have had no reason to know how to ride."

"It is time you learned."

I rolled my lips inward. "Yes, ... I suppose it is."

He turned toward me and took my dress in. "No. You will need a different dress. That one would not allow you to put your leg over Paint's back."

I glanced down. The dress I wore fit me comfortably, but the skirt would slide up high on my hips or tear if I tried to sit on Paint's broad back.

"I suppose I need to go change. What do you recommend?"

"I recommend a wide skirt, if you have one. I wear trousers. If your brothers left trousers, that would be even better."

"Mama would be appalled if I wore Jonathan's trousers," I said. I had never considered wearing them. Women did not wear trousers.

He shrugged. "Do you have a dress with a wider bottom, so your legs do not show?"

I thought about the dresses in my trunk. "Perhaps. Wait here. I will return."

I ran into the house and changed. Maha still stood next to Paint where I left him when I returned. "Better?" I asked.

I wore a blue dress cinched at the waist with a flowing skirt.

His eyes roved from the top of my head to my feet. "Much. Come."

He helped me up into the saddle and gave me instructions on how to sit and how to hold the reins. He led Paint down the street with me on her back.

"She is yours. She is your responsibility," he said as he showed me how to brush and care for her.

Each day, Maha visited with Paint. We soon were riding up the mountains and into the valley with me guiding Paint.

Even when the snow fell, I hurried across the space between our kitchen door to the barn behind Seth's home and slipped in to feed and brush Paint. I loved caring for her.

One day, near the end of the cold snow time, Maha found me in the barn early in the morning. "You love that horse."

I looked over her back toward him. "I do."

"Do you think we know each other well enough now?"

"We know each other. But, well enough? For what?" My eyes caught his, then I dropped them to Paint's back.

"To be my wife? Grandpapa Seth will be leaving when the snow begins to melt. I would like him to perform the marriage rite. Will you marry me?"

I had hoped he would ask me that question many times since he asked that day in the heat of the summer and we shared a meal in the meadow. "Will we be leaving Laish, as well?"

"I wi —" he stopped and stared at me. "Is that a yes?"

I nodded. "Yes. I will marry you, if Papa agrees."

Maha sat on a log. "What do you think? Will he agree?"

"You have been in our home all this time. What do you think?" I brushed Paint's back flank and came around to the other side, patted her back, and put the brush away.

Maha's lips slowly lifted. "He loves me. He will say yes."

"Are you certain. He may not want to lose me to the world. You are taking me away."

His lips fell into a frown. "I would not want to lose my daughter to a son of Adam who will take her who knows where. He may say no."

"Who else will have me? I have been with you so long ..." My voice dropped. "I do not want to be with anyone but you. Papa will have to say yes."

Papa gave us his permission, after spending time with Mahalaleel standing in the field as it snowed.

Seth married us the first warm day. Snow still lay in patches on the ground, but we were warm and joyful in the gathering room.

Chapter 2

Blessing

After our marriage, Seth and Ganet left Laish to follow the commandments of Jehovah and teach others his laws. They gave us permission to stay in their home until we were prepared to leave. I wanted to stay and go at the same time. Maha knew of my mixed feelings and allowed me to take my time.

A month after Ganet and Seth left, Maha came in with a frown. "Vida," he said. "I have heard from Jehovah once again. He brought me here to find you. It is now time for us to leave."

"Where will we go?"

"Grandpapa Seth suggested that we receive a blessing from Grandpapa Adam first. After that, I do not know. I only know that it is time for me to leave Laish."

"I would love to meet Adam and Eve."

"Then it is settled," Maha's face lit up. "We will leave the day after the Sabbath."

I stopped stirring the pot and stared at Maha. "But the Sabbath is the day after tomorrow."

"We have to prepare our possessions today and tomorrow, then."

"We do not have much to take."

"It will fit in our saddlebags and on the backs of the pack horses."

"We are riding horses?" I gazed into Maha's eyes, then dropped the spoon back into the pot and stirred.

"We will arrive there faster on a horse. There is no reason for us to take a wagon," Maha said, reaching for a piece of flat bread.

"Dinner is almost ready. Must you take that now?"

"I am hungry."

"You can wait."

"Yes. I can wait." He dropped the flat bread back to the plate without biting into it. "I traded the wagon your parents gave us."

I turned around. "Why?"

"We need to reach Grandpapa Adam's faster than we could in a wagon. Can you ride that far on Paint?"

"I guess I can. I do not have a choice." I fought the lip that wanted to slide out into a pout. I had agreed to go with my new husband.

"I could return the grain and dry meat, but we will need it in our travels."

I reached for bowls to set on the table. "Will we freeze out in the open on horses?"

"Your cloak will help keep you warm. If it gets too cold, you can wrap one of those wonderfully warm blankets you wove around you."

"I can take them with us?" I asked, as I dished food into our bowls.

"Yes. That is why we will need pack horses. I would not force you to leave those special possessions behind." He bent to kiss me. "I love you, Vida. I wouldn't want you to be sad."

I smiled and returned his kiss. "Thank you, Maha. Your thoughtfulness reminds me why I married you."

"Jehovah saved you for me."

"There is that."

Three mornings later, we loaded the pack horses with the packs and prepared to mount our horses. Mama and Papa came out to wish us well.

"Stay safe," Mama said.

"Are you certain you will be safe traveling with just the two of you? I have heard of robbers out there," Papa asked.

"We will be safe. We will not be alone. I have others guarding me. And, Jehovah will watch over us as long as we obey."

"You will be guarded? By whom?" Papa asked. He looked around. "I do not see anyone."

"No. You will not. My friend watches and protects from a distance. We must go."

He helped me up into the saddle and we rode away. I knew who Maha's guard was, but Papa would never understand. We rode out the gate of Laish, our laughter drifting back to Papa and Mama.

Maha took it slow. I had not ridden Paint often during the cold snow times and would need time to become accustomed to the saddle again.

Paint had been in the barn during the snowy times and wanted to stretch her legs. She pulled on the reins and encouraged me to allow her to run.

"Is it safe to run?" I asked.

"For a short distance, perhaps. Paint is smart enough to avoid the gopher holes."

"Then I will allow her to run a bit. Are you coming?"

"I have the pack horses. Be careful!"

I eased up on the reins and bent low over Paint's neck. "Go, Paint. Time to run."

She stretched out her neck and legs, racing along the trail. The wind blew through my long brown hair, tangling it behind me. I did not care. I leaned my head back and shouted my exhilaration.

After riding a short distance, I sat up and pulled gently on the reins, reminding Paint that Maha and the pack horses still had to catch up with us. She came to a stop and turned to face them. Maha's horse loped along behind me. The pack horses ran behind him, our pots rattling and banging against their sides.

I should not have raced along the trail, but I loved it more than I thought I would. When Maha and the pack horses caught up with us, I giggled and turned back to face along the trail toward Home Valley.

"What are Eve and Adam like?" I asked. "I have heard about them. I fear I will stammer in their presence."

"Grandmama Eve is the humblest woman I know. She bakes wonderful treats and spreads love to all. You will love her."

"Grandmama Eve is humble?" I struggled to believe it.

"Humbler even than Grandmama Ganet. Grandpapa Seth is her son. He is so much like Grandpapa Adam that some people struggle to tell them apart."

"They are kind like Ganet and Seth? I look forward to meeting them."

"You will like them." He grinned at me.

As we rode along the trail toward Home Valley, Maha entertained me with stories of his visits with Adam and Eve.

"We did not live there in Home Valley. Papa traveled often, like Grandpapa Seth. Mama and us children traveled with him often. We ended up visiting Grandpapa Adam and Grandmama Eve every year or so, until Papa settled in Pisidia. Even then, Papa went to report to Grandpapa every year or so."

"It would be nice to have had memories like that with Eve and Adam."

"They are your grandparents, too. They are the first parents on this earth."

"I know, but they seem so far away."

Maha leaned over and touched my arm. "You will not feel that way when you have been with them for a span.

~ ~ ~

Maha knew his grandmama.

In less than a span in her home, Grandmama Eve had me comfortably sitting at her kitchen table while she mixed a cool lime drink and told me stories. I soon felt like her best friend and long-lost granddaughter. Oh. I was.

Papa Adam readily agreed to give us his marriage blessing. "When should we do this?" he asked.

"When you are ready," Maha replied. "I needed to hurry here from Laish to receive the blessing. Now we are here, we can wait."

"On the Sabbath?" Grandpapa Adam's eyes twinkled. "Can you wait that long?"

"Grandpapa Seth married us already. We can wait for the Sabbath," Maha said with a laugh. "It is only three days away."

We enjoyed the privacy of a small guest house. When we left the guest house the next morning, Maha's face lit up.

"Mama and Papa are here!"

I gazed around, searching for someone who looked like Maha. I saw no one with blond hair. Only a couple, each with red-hair, riding horses toward Grandmama Eve and Grandpapa Adam's home. "Where? Who?"

He hurried us along. "There!" He pointed at the couple with the red hair. "That is my mama and papa."

"Oh."

He hurried me along the path toward them, calling out.

I did not expect to meet his parents so soon. I hoped they would be as welcoming and kind as Ganet and Seth. I grew up next door to Ganet and Seth. I did not know these people who were Maha's parents. I slowed my steps.

"Come, Vida. You will love my parents," he said, pulling me forward.

"Will I?"

"Yes. They are good people. Trust me."

"They taught you. They must be."

"Papa received the Priesthood while I was young. He is good like Grandpapa Seth. Mama is brave. You will like her."

We stopped on the path outside Grandmama Eve's home and watched them step off their horses. Two children stepped out of the wagon that followed behind them.

"Maha!" one of the little boys squealed as his feet hit the ground. "Mama! Mama! Maha is here!" The little boy ran into Maha's arms and squealed with joy as Maha spun him around.

"Hello, Nadav." Maha set the boy on the ground. "I did not expect to see you here with Mama and Papa."

"They did not say anything about you coming to meet us, either."

The man with warm red hair hugged Maha. His wife, with burnished copper-red hair and golden eyes, hugged Maha, as well.

95

"Mahalaleel!" she cried and threw her arms around my husband. "I did not know you were here."

Maha put an arm around me and pulled me closer. "I came with Vida. Grandpapa Seth suggested we come to Grandpapa Adam to receive his special blessing on our marriage."

"Marriage?" She bent forward to peer at me as she would a bug or vermin.

"Yes, Mama, Papa. This is Vida. She is the reason I traveled to Laish. Although I helped Grandpapa Seth teach of Jehovah to others, I discovered my true purpose — to find and marry Vida."

The red-haired woman's gaze softened as she stared at me. I wanted to reach up and brush my hair back, but Maha held me close. I gazed back into his mama's eyes.

"Welcome to the family." Her arms opened wide to embrace me."

"I am happy to be a part of it," I said.

I must have said or done something right, for Maha's mama gave him another hug. I heard something like, "… see why you love her. … is lovely." The corners of my mouth lifted. She liked me.

On the afternoon of the Sabbath, Grandpapa Adam led us into his study. Maha's mama, Elia, his papa, Cainan, Grandmama Eve, and Cainan's other grandparents, Joram and Doren followed us in. The big study felt small with all of us in it.

Grandpapa had moved aside his desk and brought out a small altar. He asked Maha to kneel on one side and me to kneel on the other. Our gazes strayed from his face to each other as we listened to the sacred and special blessing.

My body tingled from the top of my head to the end of my toes and back again at the marvelous blessing. I will never forget the way I felt or the wonder and love in Maha's eyes as he gazed at me.

Seth had been right. We did need to have Grandpapa Adam pronounce this special blessing on us.

We received hugs and kisses from all the parents and grandparents. A little sadness swept across me for a small breath as I thought of my parents. I would have liked for them to have been able to attend that special event.

"What was that?" Maha asked.

"That? That what?"

"That sudden shadow across your face."

"Oh. Mama and Papa would have loved to hear that blessing. But it is not to be. Mama and Papa are in Laish and cannot leave, even if they wanted to. The snows have stopped. They have only a short time to grow food to feed themselves for next year." I lifted a shoulder and smiled. "I am here with you. That makes me happy."

He bent and kissed me.

I do so like his kisses.

We stayed only another week in Home Valley. Maha wanted to return to Cainan with his parents and family. He said it was to introduce me to his friends. I wonder about that. Maha does not normally brag, but I heard the pride in his voice when he spoke with his papa about traveling with them back to Cainan.

"Where will we stay in Cainan?" I asked.

"There are guest houses there. The people have learned to draw together to help each other in times of trouble. You will like it in Cainan," Elia, er, Mama Elia said.

It would take time for me to remember to call her Mama Elia. Perhaps not, though, for she is as kind and gentle as Ganet, though her feet are longer and her laugh bigger. She loves Maha. That is enough for me.

Chapter 3

Home

I blessed Maha each day of the ride to Cainan that he had given me Paint and taught me how to ride her. I often rode next to El— Mama Elia on our journey. I learned that she and Papa Cainan had been best of friends since childhood. I often thought I would have liked to have had that gift with Maha.

On the road Papa Cainan lifted a hand one day. Elia stopped mid-laugh. I followed her example. Her children ran to the side of the wagon and stood, watching their papa for more directions.

He pointed and we moved off the trail to stand silently as noisy, belligerent men rode past. They searched for a group who traveled down the trail, a group much like ours.

"How hard is it to find two men, two women and a few children?" one man toward the back of the group called out.

"Where is that Cainan? He should be easy to find. They have a heavy wagon," another man grumbled, looking directly at us, though not seeing us.

"I have heard of that Mahalaleel. We can easily over-whelm them," one bragged and added a filthy curse. "After all, women are weak."

'Weak?' Mama Elia mouthed pointing to herself and me.

I shook my head. 'Not us. Not me, not you,' I mouthed. 'If they attack us, we will show them.'

I glanced down at my pack. I had no sword. How would I fight back?

More curses were shouted as the men passed us. They used our men's names. They threatened us!

A span later, we moved on down the trail toward Cainan. I rode close to Maha. The words of the men left me shaken. I did not know how to protect myself. How could I?

"How do we protect ourselves?" Elia asked, voicing my concerns. "What do we do if we are captured by men like those who were searching for us? I carry no sword."

"I carry no sword, either," Cainan said. "My brother Jon believes I will end up dead one day, killed by one of those men who seek to take my life."

I gasped. "You do not carry a sword?"

"What will I do with one sword? I cannot fight twenty men with one sword and only me. Jehovah promised me that if I trust Him, He will protect me."

"You depend on Jehovah completely? You do not even carry a knife?" Surprise filled me.

"I have my belt knife, as you have. We use them for eating. I do not plan to fight. I do not practice fighting and I do not plan to begin. I travel alone or with my family. One knife, one sword will not make a difference against many." Cainan waved at the giggling and dancing children who walked beside the wagon.

"We do not bring a guard with us. How can I be trusted to teach of peace with a guard of men with swords and arrows?"

Maha took my hand. "We trust Jehovah totally and implicitly."

I glanced to his side, though I knew the answer. "Do you carry a weapon?"

He laughed. "Why? Like my papa, I travel alone more often than I travel with others, until now. A sword would make me believe I could win against a group of men. You know who protects me."

"Jehovah," I breathed.

"And the bears," he whispered.

I snorted softly. If he hadn't shared that bit of information with his parents. I would not.

In the days before we arrived in Cainan, I began to struggle with nausea. I did not understand why. I rarely suffered with sickness. Now, however, every morning I woke with a stomach that wanted to expel its contents.

Elia touched my forehead. "You do not burn."

"No. I am only sick to my stomach. I feel like my stomach wants to empty itself of the little bit of food I ate."

"What are the chances you carry a child?" she asked.

"We have only been married a few months. Is that possible?"

"When was your last moon time?"

I stopped to think about it. We had been riding two weeks. Before that, we were in Home Valley. "About seven weeks ago, before we left Laish."

"There is a good chance you are with child. I will watch for something to help your stomach. There are plants that help."

I sighed. "Anything would help. The rocking of the horse makes it worse."

"I remember those days." Mama Elia gripped my hand before riding close to Cainan and spoke softly to him. He turned and glanced back at me.

"What can I do to help?" Maha asked. "I worry about you."

"Your mama thinks I may carry your child already. If I do, there is not much you can do."

"A child? Already?" He rode close enough he could wrap his arm around my waist. "Would you do better if you rode in the back of the wagon? I can make a space for you with blankets so it will not be as hard or bumpy."

I nodded, unable to speak.

Maha jumped into the wagon and tied his horse to the back. In not many breaths, he stepped to the front and took the reins from his younger brother who directed the bullocks. He pulled them to a stop.

"Wha—" Mikya, his brother yelped.

"I need to help Vida into the wagon. She is ill."

"Oh. Why did you not tell me? I could have stopped them."

"I am sorry. I should have said something. Can you take Paint and tie her to the back beside my horse?"

"Sure, Maha." He jumped off the wagon and stood next to Paint and held her still so I could step off onto the wagon.

Maha led me into the back of the wagon and showed me a pallet of blankets to lie on. I sank down onto the blankets and closed my eyes. Maha pulled a light blanket up over me.

"Close your eyes, Vida. Rest. We will be in Cainan tomorrow."

Mikya jumped back into the wagon and started the bullocks forward. I expected the wagon to rock and increase my sickness. It did not.

I closed my eyes and listened to the creak of the wagon. Tomorrow we would arrive and I could stop traveling for a while.

The wagon rocked me to sleep.

When I woke, the wagon continued to roll forward. I peeked out the back to see the sun had passed its zenith. We should be stopping soon for a meal. Could I manage food?

I would need to eat. The child within me needed food.

~ ~ ~

Elia made me comfortable in her home when we arrived in Cainan.

Mama Elia and Papa Cainan's children welcomed us home with a big family dinner. I did not eat much. All the sisters guessed I carried a child within me.

Maha's older brothers and sisters invited us to dinner over the next few days. I learned to love these happy people.

Maha scouted around the community and found a home for us. It had been left behind when the occupants decided they no longer wanted to obey the commandments of Jehovah. They were not asked to leave, but they no longer were comfortable among believers.

Maha's sisters helped me gather dishes and bedding and other items I needed to set up a home. I carried in the blankets I had woven and the few jars I had brought from Laish.

Maha's brothers helped him build a bed, table, and other furniture. We soon moved into our own little home.

My body soon adjusted to the differences of having a child growing within me. The sick stomach ended and I could return to my normal activities.

I enjoyed having a home to care for as I planned for our child. Maha went into the community and found that he could be useful to others working in the fields and following the sheep and goats into the hills to graze.

The bears of the north had not followed us all the way to Cainan. I worried that Maha would depend on them for protection when he followed the sheep and goats into the hills.

"Vida!" he cried one evening as he returned from the hills. "You will never believe who I met!"

I looked up from the loom where I worked on a blanket for our child. "Who?

"My friend Growl, the big black bear from the north. He missed me and followed the scent of our bullocks and horses. He waited outside the walls of Cainan for a week before he saw me lead animals into the hills."

"Did he not frighten your sheep?"

"He would have, but Mikya was with me. He stayed with the main flock while I searched for a missing ewe and her lamb. Growl found me and showed me where the ewe and her lamb were. They were so tired, they were no longer afraid of him. We had a nice wrestle."

"Do you speak to the bears?"

Maha laughed. "Well, yes. I do speak to them, but he does not speak as we do. Somehow, I understand his meaning."

"You have been friends with the bears for many years. I am not surprised you understand them."

"He introduced me to a brown bear who lives near here. Growl did not want me to be here without the protection of a bear."

"They truly do protect you?" Amazement filled my voice.

"They do."

Maha put his arms around me. "The bears will protect you and our children, as well."

"Me?"

"They have protected you in our journey here to Cainan. Growl told me of men who followed us, intent on hurting us. He roared into their camp and tore it up. He killed none of the men, but they fled and never returned to follow us."

"I did not know."

"Mama and Papa do not know, either. For now, I would prefer to keep it that way. Mama is not happy about my friendship with the bears."

"Mama Elia knows of your friendship with the bears. She has come to terms with it."

"Growl and the others would prefer that you do not share the knowledge of their protection. They like to be seen as dangerous."

"They will be. Do they not fear being hurt because of a man's fear?"

"Not yet. Maybe later they will."

I no longer feared for him when he went with the other herders into the mountains. I knew the bears would be there to protect him. The bears had been given to him by Jehovah. We were blessed.

I learned to enjoy life in a larger community. I did not meet all the members of the community, but as Maha's wife, and daughter and granddaughter of Cainan and Enos, everyone knew me.

They treated me with kindness and courtesy. I learned to love them. Most especially, I loved Maha's brothers and sisters and their families. His uncles were gracious and treated us kindly.

Jon offered Maha the opportunity to be a part of the city guard. He declined.

"I have traveled across the land without a sword. I cannot begin to use one now. I must depend on Jehovah to protect me."

Jon shook his head. "You will want to do something besides herd the sheep. You will be known as a son of Adam and will be hunted by the men of the earth who follow the Destroyer."

"That may be, but I cannot carry a sword."

I trusted Maha and I trusted Jehovah to protect us.

One morning, after the nausea no longer troubled me, Maha and I packed a lunch and rode our horses out of the community. He led me along a path to the east.

The air changed. It tasted of salt. Moisture increased. Soon we crossed over a little hillock. Waves rolled in toward us.

"The sea!" I exclaimed. "You brought me to the sea."

"You showed me the mountains and the snow in Laish. You need to see the sea. But we need to leave the horses here."

He stepped off his horse and came to help me off Paint. He took the basket with our lunch and the blanket and kicked off his heavy riding slippers. I removed mine, as well.

Maha took my hand and walked with me down the slope toward the sea. He set the blanket and basket above the waves.

"We will come back for these later. Come." He took my hand again and pulled me toward the water.

We ran along the waves, jumping over them as they rolled in toward us. I giggled as I splashed in the water.

"I expected it to be cold," I said through my giggles."

"Not this time of year. It is cold and gray during the rains. Now it is warm and blue."

I leapt another wave. We raced down the beach and back up again. I flopped on the sand giggling.

"This place is wonderful. No wonder I have heard good things about the sea. Everyone should have an opportunity to come to the sea at least once."

Maha plopped next to me. "I agree. The sea is a wonderful place."

A small creature crawled toward me in the sand. I watched it crawl until it came close to me. Before it neared me, it turned and scooted off in another direction.

We dug in the sand and covered our feet in it. As the sun rose past its zenith, we returned to our blanket and lunch basket. As we ate, we watched the waves begin to move in toward us again.

"We must go," Maha said. "It is late, and we will want to be home before it gets dark."

I slipped my riding slippers back on my feet and set the used dishes back in the basket. Maha folded the blanket and tucked it into the basket.

We mounted our horses and rode back to Cainan, happy to have been together at the sea.

Chapter 4

Wave

Our first child, Eneas, grew quickly. He loved the sea and begged to visit often. He loved to dig in the sand and jump the waves rolling to the shore. I, too, loved the sea. I loved the cooling water in the hot time of the year. We went as often as we could during the first fifteen years we lived in Cainan.

We had five children. As oldest, Eneas cared for his younger brothers and sisters. He would keep a close eye on them when we went out to the sea.

One day, I stared out to the sea as dark clouds formed and the wind became stronger.

Eneas glanced at me, a worried look in his eyes. "Something is not right," he murmured to me.

"No. We should hurry home to safety," I agreed.

We gathered the little ones onto their ponies. I pulled Lucina, our youngest daughter, in front of me, while the others climbed onto their horses, all the while fighting a dread that filled my soul.

Eneas checked to be certain all the children were seated on their horses and shouted for me to go as he raced to jump up onto his horse.

I rode away, leading the little ones toward the safety of home. I expected Eneas to trail behind on his horse.

The gale raged behind us, spinning and turning. The sea heaved. Great waves rolled inland, splashing cold droplets of water against my back. Fear tickled my spine.

I raced ahead on my black mare, Beauty, hoping to reach the safety of Cainan's walls. The children on their ponies rode close on either side of me.

The storm raged around us, tearing at my clothing, threatening to drag me from my horse. I fought to stay on Beauty, glad to have Lucina clasped between my legs and the horse's neck. The children screamed in the wind. I led them over the low barrier of sand, and on toward Cainan. Fear gripped my throat.

When we arrived at the gates, Maha held them open for us. I raced through, followed by three of our children. I turned and looked for Eneas.

He was not there.

"Where is Eneas?" I shouted into the blast.

"Mama," Gera cried. "I tried to tell you, but you could not hear my scream. The waves caught Eneas and his horse."

"Caught him?" Maha shouted to be heard above the wind. I heard the horror in his voice.

"The water caught up to him, … tripped his horse, …"

I gripped Lucina and stared toward the sea, expecting to see Eneas ride through the gate.

He did not.

"Tripped his horse? How can water trip a horse?" I ran toward the gate Maha slammed before I could pass through.

"Mama, Eneas fell off his horse. He was … was … washed back into the sea." Tears poured from Gera's eyes. "Mama, Eneas is gone!"

A wave crashed into the tall wall surrounding Cainan.

"We have to go find him," I shouted, clawing to open the gate.

Maha grabbed me from behind. "You cannot go out there. It is not safe here. Listen to the water bashing into the wall. Look at the sky!" Maha shouted.

I looked up to see a giant, dark black, almost green, cloud. Rain poured. The wind tore at the walls and gates.

Maha dragged me toward our home. "You cannot go out there. The wind and waves will take you away."

"But … Eneas!" I cried.

"We will look for him when the storm passes. If you go out into that, you will be lost to us, as well."

I fought him all the way to our home.

"He is my son, too, Vida," Maha cried into my ear as we opened our front door. "I will help you find him when this is over."

I sobbed as we hid in the center of the house. Maha gathered the children around us and prayed. Tree limbs and other debris crashed into the walls of our home so loudly I could barely hear the words of his prayer.

We sat listening to the windstorm for more than a span.

When the battering reduced, I jumped up and raced toward the door.

Maha caught me by the elbow. "Where are you going?"

"To find my son."

"I told you I would go with you, but not now. The storm has not passed. It is the quiet in the center. I have seen it before. Wait. It will hit us again soon."

"More wind?" I stared into Maha's eyes.

"Yes, Vida. More wind will batter us. It is still dangerous."

The wind began to bang against the door again. Maha was right. The storm returned.

We huddled in the center of the house once more. I wrapped my arms around my remaining children. Maha's arms wrapped around all of us.

Exhausted from fear and tears, the children sat staring at the walls, until, even as the wind and rain battered our windows and doors, the youngest children closed their eyes and slept.

Eventually, the wind blew away from us. We left the sleeping children and walked out, wondering what we would find.

Maha had to push hard to push away a tree that lay across the doorway. When I could finally step outside, I stood still with my mouth agape. Huge tree limbs were broken and scattered in front of our home.

Tree branches impaled doors in the houses near us. Roofs had been lifted from houses and lay upside down far away. Trees had been stripped of all greenery. The few bushes remaining lay flat against the earth, their leaves and many of the branches blown who knew where.

Yaffa, Maha's sister joined us in the path outside our home. "I heard Eneas is missing."

Where did she learn that Eneas had disappeared? I could only nod. She wrapped her arms around me and held me tight.

"I will stay with you while the men search for him," she breathed into my ear.

I pushed away. "No. I am going with them. I must find him. He was with me. I lost my son." I brushed hair off my face and tied it back into a tail at my neck.

Maha caught me by the arm. "You do not have to go with me. I will find him," Maha begged. "Please stay here with Yaffa. It could be difficult. Eneas is my son, too. I will find him."

"No. Eneas was with me. I will find him. Jehovah would not allow him to be hurt."

Maha embraced me. "He may be hurt. You do not want to see it."

I threw his arms away from me. "I will find my son. He will be alive!"

"Yaffa, will you stay with our little ones?" Maha asked.

She turned on her heel and entered our home, closing the door behind her.

I wanted to rush toward the sea. However, Maha dragged me toward the sanctuary. "We have ways we do this. If you are going, you must follow our rules."

I reluctantly followed him.

Others beside Eneas were missing in the storm. Almost every man in Cainan met in the sanctuary, where Jon assigned them areas to search. Maha and I were sent toward the sea, since that is where we last saw Eneas.

We knelt together in prayer before leaving the sanctuary, begging Jehovah to help us safely find our missing family members.

~ ~ ~

Maha and I joined a group of men who left through the east gate. We spread out, walking about two body lengths apart from the other. This close together, we hoped to see any who had fallen in the piles of debris.

Although most of the foliage had been stripped by the wild winds, tree branches piled on top of fallen trees, often covered by the leaves stripped from other trees. We picked up lengths of broken branches and prodded into the piles of debris, searching for any who may be there, living or dead.

I clenched my jaw when we found the first body— a man I did not know who had been impaled by a branch. He could not still be alive, but Maha bent and touched his throat, searching for a heartbeat. He shook his head and waved for others to help lift him from the pile. They left the body near the path where others could find him.

I swallowed my retching. I had to find Eneas. If I became ill, Maha would force me to return to our home.

We found deer, wolves, and small animals among the remnants of the raging wind, along with three other men. Each time we found a man, I hurried to gaze into his face.

Each time, I breathed a silent prayer of gratitude that the body was not my Eneas.

"Here!" Maha's brother, Zerach, shouted. "I found something!"

I raced toward him, stumbling over fallen branches that littered the ground. Maha caught up with me and grabbed my elbow. "It will do no good if you get hurt."

I gazed into his face, amazed to see his agony. He loved Eneas as much as I did.

I nodded. "Thank you."

Together we moved carefully through the mess to where Zerach stood.

"What did you find?" Maha asked.

Zerach pointed at a pile of trees and other litter. "Horse."

"No!" Maha said.

He tried to pull me away. "You do not want to see this."

"No! I must. Let me see." I pounded on the arm he held in front of me.

Maha stepped aside, allowing me to see. Eneas' black and white horse laying on his side. A tree lay across his body, crushing him. He lifted his head and made a low, pained noise.

I dropped beside him and pet his nose. "It is well, Spot. You did your best to protect Eneas. Rest. You will be with Eneas again."

The horse listened, gazing into my eyes. His pain-clouded eyes closed, and he shuddered. He did not move again. I lay my head on his neck and allowed a tear to fall.

"He carried Eneas everywhere. Eneas will be sad to hear of his death." I patted his soft neck, then pushed myself to my feet. "But where is Eneas? Is he hurt somewhere?"

It took many spans to cross the space between the walls of Cainan and where the trees had once stood outside the sandy berm that separated the trees from the sea. I found an elk away from any piles of other debris. I hoped to find Eneas where he would be safe.

As we neared the line where trees once stood, we stopped and stared. One tree still stood. All the others were scattered on the ground between the sandy berm and the wall to Cainan.

How did this one tree manage to stay standing?

Maha took my hand. "Are you certain you want to go farther?"

"I have to find our son. He will be waiting for me."

Maha slipped a part of his lower lip between his teeth, nodded, and held onto my hand. We stepped across the branches and slippery dead, stinking fish lying near the trunk of this one tree. I pushed the fish aside with my stick, hoping not to find Eneas beneath them.

Maha and another man lifted a tree that lay against this one standing tree. More fish, more broken branches, and a dead fox lay against the tree. No man. No boy. No Eneas. The stench in the heat turned my stomach.

Zerach whispered, "Oh, no. Maha."

I glanced at him as he pointed upward.

My eyes followed the direction of his fingers, into the tree.

There, in a crotch of the tree, lay Eneas.

"Eneas!" I screamed. "Eneas. I am here. We will get you down."

Maha and Zerach scrabbled across the pile of trees and debris next to the tree until they could climb into it.

Zerach pushed himself upward to the crotch where Eneas lay. He touched Eneas gently on the forehead, saying something to him.

He touched Eneas's throat, looking for a heartbeat.

I stood gazing up, willing him to open his eyes, begging his heart to beat, praying for him to speak to Zerach, to me.

Zerach spoke softly to Maha. I strained to hear the words he spoke, but I could not. My heart pounded so loud I heard little else above the roar.

Maha turned and made his way from the tree. He spoke to the other men who stood watching. Two others began to climb the tree as Maha made his way to me.

"Vida," he said, taking me by the arm. "He did not survive."

"What do you mean he did not survive?" I asked, my heartbeat suddenly stopping. I became aware of my screaming and closed my mouth.

"Eneas's heart no longer beats. He is gone." Maha wrapped his arms around me.

"How can that be? Eneas listened to Jehovah. He obeyed Him. We prayed for safety before we left the house this morning." My voice began to lift in volume. "Jehovah would not take Eneas! He lives! He has to live! Let me go to him. He is waiting for me."

"Yes, Vida. He lives with Jehovah now." He pulled me closer.

I began to beat on his chest. "No! He cannot be gone! He obeyed! Jehovah would not take him from me! No! Let me see my son!" With each word my beating increased, and my voice lifted.

Maha pulled me closer and whispered into my ear. "Wait, Vida. The men are bringing his body from the tree. You can see him then."

"I want to see him now!" I raged.

Maha used calm, quiet words as he spoke to me. "Soon, Vida. You can see him soon. They are getting him down from the tree. Wait."

He held me close and murmured words of comfort into my ear while the men worked to bring Eneas down from his place in the tree.

They set him on the ground near us. Maha kept me enfolded in his arms, close to him.

I tried to twist away. "Let me go. I need to be with him."

Zerach must have nodded, for Maha loosened his grip on me. I ducked under his arm and dropped to the ground next to Eneas.

He did not look damaged. No cuts or bruises marred his face. Nothing indicated what had taken his life.

I brushed his hair back. "Oh, Eneas. What happened?"

I bent and kissed his cold, salty face. Salt from the sea filled his clothing and his hair, covered his skin.

"Why is he salty?" I murmured.

Maha knelt next to me, touching Eneas's face, neck, and back.

"The wave … Gera said a wave took him. It must have broken his neck and left him in this tree. He does not look frightened, like the other men we found."

I looked at his face again. No fear filled it. If I had been tumbled in a huge wave I would have been frightened. His face was calm.

"Perhaps it took his life before he could be afraid," one of the men suggested.

"Or he saw Jehovah and had no fear," Maha replied.

Chapter 5

Stories

I did not cry as I helped prepare Eneas's body for burial. I did not cry after. I sat staring at a wall, remembering Eneas. I did not bathe. I did not wash my hair. I did nothing to make me appealing to my husband or others.

After we buried Eneas in the burial grounds, Yaffa took our other children to her home to care for them with her children. They needed care that I could not give them in my overwhelming grief.

More than six months later, Enos and Rebecca returned from their travels. I hardly noticed when they entered the house, until Enos set his hands on my head.

"Vida," he said. "Father and Jehovah understand the sorrow you feel at the loss of your son. They know you miss him.

Eneas listened to the words of Jehovah. He was taken to Him quickly. He felt no pain.

"Eneas wants you to stop grieving for him. Your other children need you.

"Father has commanded me to bless you. You will have other sons and daughters. One son will be honorable. He will receive power to serve Jehovah as Adam and Seth have served Him.

"Lift up your head and be of good cheer, Vida. You have much to be grateful for."

Enos said more. Tears began to flow. When he said Amen and lifted his hands from my head, the front of my dress was soaked in my tears.

I stood and Grandpapa Enos hugged me. I hugged Maha.

"Where are the children?" I asked. I had not cared enough to ask earlier.

"Yaffa has them. Are you ready for them to come home?"

"Yes." I gazed around at the dust that lay on the furniture. "We have much to do."

"It is good to have you back again," Maha said, pulling me into a close embrace.

Grandmama Rebecca and Yaffa helped me and Devora clean the dust from the furniture and floors. They brought in flowers to brighten the table.

Once more, I found pleasure in life and my family. However, the sea held no joy for me. Maha tried to entice me to walk along the shore, but I could not pass the east gate nor follow the path. It held too many dark memories.

After a year, Maha took me for a walk in the hills west of Cainan. "You are no longer happy here in Cainan."

"No. I am happy."

"Not as happy as before. I have been thinking and praying. I think we should find a new home, one without so many memories."

"Leave Eneas?"

"He is with Jehovah. He will be with you, here." He touched the side of my head. "And here." He touched the center of my chest. "You need to find joy in the other children and in our home. A group of people want to leave Cainan. We should go with them."

"Why would they want to leave Cainan?"

"It has become a dangerous place. Men from other lands have discovered us."

"Do these people still believe in Jehovah and his love?" I asked.

"Do you?" Maha countered.

"I do."

"So do they. Enos is not here to teach. They feel they do not need to stay in Cainan to worship Jehovah. We want to move inland. Find a home far away from the dangers of storms like the one … the one —"

"The one that took Eneas?" I stared at Maha.

"Yes. Most of those who plan to leave lost a son, a brother, a husband, or papa in the storm. Cainan holds sad memories for them, as it does for us."

"Do you think we will be safe without the walls and guards Jon provides?"

"We will find a new home far from the paths that men who no longer believe in Jehovah travel. They will never find us."

"Do you promise?"

"Yes."

Maha took me into his arms. I gazed into his eyes and found a surety.

"When do we leave?"

"Within the month.

In less than three weeks, Maha led a small group of people from Cainan. I rode in the first wagon part of the time. We moved back a place each day, giving everyone the opportunity to ride in the front, out of the worst of the dust.

Maha led us to the west and south. When we reached low hills, Maha knew which direction to travel and led us onward.

Each day of travel became more difficult for me. Once more, I carried a child, and the daily nausea grew worse in the dust kicked up by the horses, oxen, and our herds of cows, sheep, and goats.

I let Gera and Devora drive the wagon while I rode above the dust on the back of Beauty. I would take the younger children with me on the horse, one at a time, giving them time with me and time out of the dust.

As we traveled through the day, the sickness reduced and I could return to the wagon and my children. The little ones would crowd close to me on the wagon seat, wanting me to tell them a story.

I found telling stories let me think of something other than my stomach. I told stories I had heard Eve share with me about her life with Adam in Eden, along with other stories of our early mamas and papas.

When I told the story of Grandmama Rebecca and Grandpapa Enos living in Shem, all the children crowded close so they could hear. I had heard these stories from the time I could listen to stories in my papa's lap.

"Grandmama Rebecca and Grandpapa Enos ran from the house, looking to see who had been injured," I said. "Grandmama Rebecca told me she made certain to close the door behind her. She hurried down the street toward the noise. She found her brother, Gil, lying in the dirt, covered in blood. The bad men had attacked and beaten him. He had many injuries."

"Bad men," little Lucina cried.

"Yes. Very bad men, for Gil had been hurt badly. Grandmama could only hold his head in her lap and cry that she loved him. He told her he loved her, as well. And then, ... and then, he died."

"Oh, no! Mama, he died!" Amasa cried.

"He did. Grandmama cried for a long time before Grandpapa found her. When they returned to their house with him, they looked all over for their children."

"Were they hiding from the bad men?" Gera asked.

"Grandmama thought they might be. She looked under every bed and in every closet. They could not find them."

"What did they do, Mama?" Adiva asked.

"Grandpapa took his friends and looked all over Shulon, searching for their little son and daughter. Nat was only five and Ziva only almost three. They were too small to be out on their own."

Tamid grabbed my arm. "They found them, did they not? They were in a cupboard in the kitchen. That is where I would have been."

"Grandmama looked in all the cupboards. She moved everything from every shelf and every big space. Nat and Ziva were not in her house. Her children were not in Shulon. Grandpapa Enos went with some of the men, looking for them outside Shem."

"Was that not dangerous?" Adiva asked.

"It was, especially after the Shemites attacked. But Grandpapa wanted to find his children, as I would want to find any of you if you were missing."

"Like you hunted for Eneas?" Tamid asked.

I pulled him onto my lap. "Yes. Like I hunted for Eneas."

"Did Grandpapa find them? I do not remember an uncle Nat or an Aunt Ziva?" Adiva asked.

"No. The Shemites helped search, but Ziva and Nat were gone. They never saw them again."

"You were blessed to find Eneas," Amasa said. "It would be hard to never see him again. We know where he is. He is with Jehovah."

I hugged him close and ruffled his hair. "Yes, Amasa, we know where Eneas is. Grandmama Rebecca and Grandpapa Enos never knew for sure where Ziva and Nat went."

"Never?" the children chorused.

"Well, they heard later that they were sold in Nod as slaves. They never saw them or heard from them. They hoped it was not true." I lifted a shoulder. "I think they hope they were not taken and sold. But, no one knows where they are."

I did not expect my story telling to do more than help the children pass the time as we rode or walked the long distance seeking a new home. It helped both them and me feel better about losing Eneas. Like Amasa had said, I knew where Eneas was — safe with Jehovah.

Grandmama Rebecca and Grandpapa Enos still had not discovered any news of their children. I grieved for them and for Ziva and Nat.

~ ~ ~

As we traveled, nightmares began to plague me once more, as they had in the months since the great storm. I would see the huge wave roll toward Eneas, capturing him and his horse. In my dreams, it did not always withdraw before capturing one or all of my other children. Sometimes, I would dream of our unborn child, dragged by the whirlwind and taken in the winds. I woke screaming many nights.

Maha prayed with me. It helped. The dreams recurred less often. I would find a way to protect the children. Sometimes, Eneas would sit by my side and hold my hand, telling me he had a busy happy life with Jehovah.

That helped settle my mind and drive away the dreams.

We traveled four weeks before we reached a valley surrounded by mountains. We were safe there. The mountains were rugged enough to make it difficult for others to enter without our men knowing it. They did not need to stand guard except at the pass that led out of the valley and into the rest of the world.

The men built houses to protect our families. They prepared the soil for fields and we women helped them plant the seeds we carried with us. We named the village Ziklag.

The rains would fall soon. We worked hard to have enough food harvested to survive the cold rain time. We had no way of knowing how bad the rains would be in this valley.

The rain came as expected. It fell as snow higher in the mountains, and rain fell where we lived. By then, every family had a home where they could safely wait out the rains.

Maha told me the rain fell better than it had in Pisidia. Enough rain fell that we could easily grow food for our families. In Pisidia, the lack of rain caused children to starve and men to seek the gold rock that men of Nod and other lands desired.

Our newest daughter joined our family during the rains. I never thought of Ilka as a replacement for Eneas, although she did help to keep the nightmares away. With her birth, I no longer dreamed of wind or waves.

Ilka grew in the clean air. We all loved her. She smiled and laughed when we talked to her.

I took Ilka with me to the field, carrying the babe on my back while I worked. Many times, Adiva would take the sleeping child and lay her on a blanket on the side of the field.

Lucina, too small to help in the field, would play with her brothers, Tamid and Gera, on or near the blanket.

One day, as I stretched my back after planting the last of the seeds, Tamid shouted and stabbed at something near the other children with the stick he carried, pretending it was a sword.

Maha ran to him from the other field while I raced across the bottom of the one I worked in. I arrived as Maha stabbed at the earth one final time. He lifted a serpent on the end of his knife.

"It curled up near baby Ilka," Tamid cried. "When she moved, it stretched out. I saw its mouth open, trying to bite her. I grabbed my stick and hit it. It turned on me. Papa, it tried to bite me. I could only stab at it and hope it would race away. It did not. Oh, Papa. Thank you for killing it."

Maha's face paled as he lifted the huge serpent from the ground. Its triangular head warned us its venom would kill if it bit.

"Did it strike you?" Maha asked.

Tamid ran his hands across his arms and legs. "No. It missed me. I do not know how."

I grabbed up baby Ilka and examined her little body. The serpent had not been able to strike her, either.

"Ilka is safe. Where is Lucina?"

"Here I am, Mama." Lucina peeked from behind a nearby tree. "Gera brought me here."

"Gera? Gera, where are you?" I called.

"Here, Mama." He stepped from behind the tree. "I did not want Lucina to be injured by the serpent or Tamid's stick. I brought her here."

"Good thinking," I said.

"I wanted to grab Ilke, too," Gera said, holding onto Lucina's little hand. "I could not get to her. The serpent and Tamid were between me and the baby. I am sorry, Mama."

"You did well, Gera. You protected Lucina," Maha said.

I gathered my little children into my lap and hugged them close. How did I not know serpents lived in our valley of Ziklag?

"We will need to be more watchful," Maha said, echoing my thoughts. "We will not always be near them, and Tamid will not always have his stick to fight the serpent off."

"Will there be more?" I asked. My stomach churned at the thought.

"Where there is one, there are usually many. Yes. There will be more. I need to teach Tamid and Gera to use their knives."

I shuddered. "We all must be alert to them, until they learn this is not a safe place for them."

Maha wrapped his arms around the children and me. "We will make this place safe for everyone. Until we do, we must be extra careful."

That evening, after we were safely in our home, Maha led our family in prayer. He thanked Jehovah for protection from the serpent and begged Him to keep the serpents and other dangerous creatures far from Ziklag.

When the younger children were sleeping in their beds, he pulled his cloak on and left. "I must visit with a friend."

"Friend?" I asked.

"Yes. We need his help."

He closed the door silently behind him.

"Friend?" Adiva asked. She sat beside me, mending clothing.

"Your papa has friends we have not met. He is gone to meet with them."

"But we know all the men of Ziklag. They came here with us. Why would he not use his name?"

I smiled. "This friend is different. Perhaps your papa will tell you more about his friend when he returns."

"I never thought of Papa with a secret friend."

"Your papa has friends I have never met. Perhaps he will introduce us to this friend."

Chapter 6

Jared

"Grizzle agreed. We must be watchful until the serpents decide to leave the valley. The bears will help convince them to go. Jehovah will also help us. But we need to protect ourselves and our children until they are gone."

"Grizzle? Is this a new bear?" I asked.

Maha shook his head and laughed. "Nah. He followed us from Cainan. He has friends in this area, though, so he will have some help."

"That is good to know."

Each year the number of serpents in the valley dropped. One bit a young child. Her parents did everything they knew to overcome the venom. However, her small body could not throw off the venom in time to save her life.

After that, every mama, every papa, every older brother, and every older sister watched the grasses and the wood piles and anywhere else a serpent would hide. We all carried knives in our hands, ready to destroy every serpent we saw. We refused to allow the Destroyer's followers to hunt and hurt our children.

After five years, we saw fewer of the sneaky creatures. Maha reported to me that the bears and some of the other big birds had fought the serpents until they decided Ziklag had become too dangerous for them.

We continued to be wary, keeping our knives handy in case the horrid creatures tried to return and hurt us. No one wanted to lose a child to their venom.

Our sons grew loving Jehovah. However, they chose to do things that would not allow them to spend time teaching Jehovah's words to others. Maha would occasionally leave me at home with our children while he traveled with his papa, Cainan, or his Grandpapa Enos to share with other people in other lands.

We accepted any newcomers who found their way to our protected little valley and requested permission to stay. We warned them of our faith and belief before giving them the opportunity to live with us.

Most of the people in our small community of Ziklag loved and obeyed Jehovah's commandments. Those who chose not to, were uncomfortable with the rest of us. Within a year or two, they would move on.

We were happy to have them move on, although we missed the friendships we made with them. They could not be happy living among us.

More children were born to our family. Not often, but often enough they had a brother or sister to be their friend as they grew.

One year, we met with Papa Cainan, Grandpapas Enos, Seth and Adam and their wives in Home Valley. Eve and Ganet expressed concern that no son had been identified as one to carry on the responsibility to be a prophet and leader for Jehovah since Cainan.

None of Mahalaleel's brothers had been found worthy. Nor had Maha. I felt uncomfortable in the presence of these matriarchs, wives of prophets as my husband had not yet been identified. We were still young, then, less than a hundred years old. But both Seth and Cainan had been ordained to the Priesthood before their hundredth birth year.

It saddened me that none of our sons appeared worthy or willing. If Maha did not receive that honor, perhaps one of our sons, or one of the sons of his brothers would.

As I helped the other grandmamas prepare the meal for our men, I let it slip that I found myself with child once more.

"Another child?" Grandmama Eve exclaimed. "How exciting for you."

"I am happy to bring another child to this earth," I said.

"When should this child be born?" Mama Elia asked. "You do not seem to be sick."

"No. This child has not made me as sick. I expect him to come in another five months."

"Enough time to be safely in your own home, then?" Grandmama Ganet asked.

"Yes. We have a good healer in Ziklag. She knows me. She knows how to help my children come to this earth."

"That is comforting," Grandmama Rebecca said.

"It is." I picked up a bowl of fruit and carried it across the green to the sanctuary where we were to gather for a midday meal.

"It would be nice if this child is obedient, worthy, and willing for Jehovah to use him as a prophet," Grandmama Eve murmured as she walked beside me.

I nodded. "It would be."

We said nothing more about the child during that visit.

We returned home before the rain began to fall, preventing further safe travel. I did not mind, for my healer, Aminta, could reach me.

When Maha sent a child to get her, Aminta hurried to our home and helped to deliver another son. We named him Jared.

I had other children after Jared, both sons and daughters, but not many. I always held the hope within my heart that this child, this Jared would be willing to obey and worthy to carry on as a son of Adam.

As Jared grew, he stayed close to Jehovah and visited often with his grandparents. His connection to the other prophets gave me hope that one of our sons may follow in the tradition of his grandpapas. He traveled with them, teaching the laws of Jehovah.

Like his papa, Maha, Jared spent time with his Grandpapa Seth and Grandmama Ganet in Laish one winter. He spent time with my parents and learned to love them as he loved Maha's parents.

When Jared left Laish, he brought Helsa with him. He and Helsa went to visit Grandmama Eve and Grandpapa Adam after the marriage to receive the marriage blessing. In addition to the marriage blessing, they were asked to travel through the land for a few years to continue teaching of Jehovah. The people of the earth listened to him in a way they would not listen to the older prophets.

~ ~ ~

Our family continued to grow after that. I gave birth to three more daughters and two more sons. Our daughters married men who loved Jehovah from Ziklag or Cainan. They stayed busy providing food for themselves and their families.

Jared and Helsa had many children. However, none of their boys obeyed the commandments of Jehovah with exactness. Like our other children, they worked hard to care for their families. However, they did not choose to go with their papa or with the High Priests and Prophets, our grandpapas, to teach of Jehovah to people who had lost the truth.

During this time of our family's growth, Grandmama Eve and Grandpapa Adam decided to travel around the land to meet some of their grandchildren and to visit the homes of their sons and grandsons who were High Priests. They traveled west to visit with Jared and Helsa first, although Jared was not yet a High Priest.

At about the same time we received word that Grandmama Eve and Grandpapa Adam were traveling, we also received a message from Jared. It had been many years since their last child came. Now, after more than one hundred twenty years of marriage, Helsa was with child, once again.

It had been many years since Papa Cainan had received the Priesthood. Mahalaleel and I had decided that the line of authority, which had been promised to Adam to pass from papa to son, would miss this generation. Perhaps it would go to Jared, or one of his sons.

Maha did all he could in our village of Ziklag to ensure that the people knew and understood the commandments. He had a copy of the Book of Commandments that Adam had written. It included all the commandments and many of the stories of Jehovah's dealings with Adam. With this book, Maha could help the villagers of Ziklag and the surrounding villages remember.

We heard news of Grandpapa Adam and Grandmama Eve's visit to Laish. My parents sent word that they were finally able to meet with them and hear their stories. Grandmama Ganet sent a message telling us of Grandmama Eve's first ride in the snow. She loved it.

While Grandmama Eve and Grandpapa Adam visited with Grandmama Ganet and Grandpapa Seth, Helsa delivered a boy child. The delivery was difficult for her. We prayed for the boy they named Enoch.

Grandmama Eve and Grandpapa Adam left the north mountains in early spring, traveling toward Cainan where Enos and Rebecca lived. We waited to receive word they had arrived safely. I looked forward to hearing about Grandmama Eve's first experience with the sea. I prayed the storms and winds would be calm for them and that Jehovah would bless them with safety.

While Grandmama Eve and Grandpapa Adam visited Cainan, we received news that Enoch struggled to speak. His movements were slow in developing.

"I fear this is not the one," Jared wrote in his letter to us.

We redoubled our prayers to Jehovah.

From Cainan, our beloved Grandparents traveled alone into the mountains of Pisidia, where Mama Elia and Papa Cainan had returned, working to restore those people to an understanding of Jehovah's love. Maha spoke with his friends, the bears. He worried that his parents and Grandpapa Adam and Grandmama Eve would not be safe in Pisidia. The Destroyer had convinced them to worship the nuggets they dug from the earth more than the truths taught by Jehovah.

It did not surprise me, then, when Grandmama Eve knocked on our door much earlier than we had been led to believe they would arrive.

"We could not stay in Pisidia," Grandmama told me as we sat down with a tall glass of cool apple cider. "Those men have developed hearts of stone. They would not receive us in the community center. The few who stopped by Elia's home came only to say they had 'met the great Adam and Eve.' I have never felt such hostility among people who should have received the blessings of Jehovah."

"It is because they have given their hearts to the Destroyer," Maha told them. "My messengers tell me that it will not be safe for Mama and Papa to stay with them much longer. I sent word to them today. I hope they listen."

"Your messengers?" Grandpapa Adam asked. "Are you still friends with the wild animals?"

"I am. The bears have protected me for many years. Without them, I would probably have been dead many times over the years."

"Because you have been their friend, they protect you. You are blessed."

I smiled. I had seen bears from a distance. I knew how much they loved my husband, and Maha loved the bears. He had been blessed by the friendship many times.

While Maha showed Grandpapa around Ziklag and took him into the hills to meet his friend, Grizzle, I introduced Grandmama Eve to the women.

As we walked between our home and the home of another woman, I shared with her the news from Aenon. "Helsa gave birth, another boy child, Hadar. They fear Enoch, born to them two years ago will not be acceptable to Jehovah."

"Why would Enoch not be acceptable?" Grandmama Eve asked.

"His birth was difficult, causing him to develop slowly. He has not yet walked nor spoken."

"Enoch is still a child. We do not know what plans Jehovah has for him. We do not know who Jehovah plans to carry forward the line of authority and the High Priesthood. It may be Enoch. It could be Hadar. It could be Jared or even Maha."

I turned to stare at Grandmama Eve. "Do you think there is still a possibility Jehovah will find my Maha acceptable?"

She lifted a shoulder. "Who knows the mind of Jehovah? Anything is possible."

Later that evening we shared the news with Maha and Grandpapa Adam.

"Enoch is growing stronger each day and is a quick and intelligent boy," I read from Helsa's letter. "However, he continues to be slow to speak and struggles to get the words out. Perhaps it will be Hadar who will be chosen by Jehovah to carry the lineage of the High Priesthood."

Grandpapa Adam shook his head. "It is up to Jehovah. He will provide one to carry on the lineage. There are three besides me who have the right and responsibility to sacrifice to Jehovah and teach their brothers and sisters of His love. When Jehovah decides it is time, other men will be called to carry on the lineage. He knows more than we do."

I breathed in deeply, considering Grandpapa Adam's words. "I thought it had to be a son of a prophet."

"It has always been that way. The High Priesthood has always been patriarchal, following a line from papa to son. Jehovah will provide. He knows."

Grandpapa Adam and Grandmama Eve stayed with us nearly two months. Some of the newer residents of our village came to better understand Jehovah's plan for them to be happy. On the day they climbed into their wagons to leave, I shed many tears along with many of the other residents of Ziklag. I had enjoyed having them with us.

Chapter 6

Rites

News traveled slowly between our communities. Raiders who lost families and homes began to patrol sections of the roads and trails between communities. The roads and trails became dangerous to travel. Messages did not always arrive on time, or at all, when a messenger traveled alone along the trails.

We did hear from Jared. Enoch continued to stutter. Hadar often lorded over him. He believed he would be chosen to be the next one to receive the responsibility of High Priest. In his pride, Hadar expected others to do his chores and demanded gifts and favors.

"I have not heard of any of the grandpapas act as Hadar does," Maha complained. "How can he believe he will be chosen if he is this prideful. In his way, he is as bad as the people of Pisidia."

"Have your Mama and Papa decided to leave that wicked place yet?" I asked. "I fear they will not survive if they stay there."

"I fear for them, as well. Papa has asked Jehovah. He says these people will lose their blessings if they do not repent."

Within the year, Jehovah called Papa Cainan and Mama Elia to leave Pisidia and return to Cainan. Maha and I sighed deeply in relief. We had feared for their lives.

We continued on with our lives. I helped teach our grandchildren to read and write. I had become one of the older women in the village. Maha tried to keep me out of the fields during harvest time. The sharp scythes could be dangerous.

Instead, I cared for the grandchildren so their mamas could help harvest the fields. Sometimes, we sat by the stream and played in the clay. I helped the younger ones learn to form jars and pots. Sometimes, they made pretty little beads of the red clay.

Some days we practiced reading and writing. The little ones loved learning to read and write.

We received a message from Grandpapa Adam one day asking us to join them in Home Valley in three weeks. If we left the next day, we would arrive in time.

We did not fear traveling over the mountains alone. Although Grizzle no longer lived, his sons and grandsons still lived near Ziklag and protected Maha when he traveled.

We saddled our horses and loaded a pack horse with our travel supplies the next morning early. A few others who had family in Home Valley traveled with us.

We only knew that we were wanted in Home Valley. Adam did not tell us why. We pushed our horses to ride as fast as we dared each day. We did not want to be late.

One evening when we stopped for the night, strange men called from outside our camp, asking for permission to enter. Maha glanced at the other three men. They nodded, indicating that they were ready with their staffs and swords, although Maha still did not carry either one. Smoke from our fire disguised the smell of fear the other women and I exuded.

"Come on into the camp," Maha called, "but keep your hands well into the air where we can see them."

Two men entered the camp with their hands over their heads.

"We are cold and hungry. The smell of your food enticed us to your camp. Do you have anything extra you could share with us?" One of them said.

His eyes shifted toward our packs laying near the fire. Maha saw the glance. He did not trust this man, either.

At a nod from Maha, I dipped up a bowl of the stew for each of them. They sat with us and spoke of the ride through the mountains. It did not sound right to me. We had been out of the mountains for three days. Their descriptions did not match our experience.

I moved closer to Maha.

As we crawled into our blankets that night, Maha warned me to keep my knife handy. These men could cause us problems.

I slipped my knife from my belt and put it beneath me where I could pull it quickly from my sheathe.

I did not sleep well. I feared the men would attack.

A noise woke me. Men fought. They rolled in the dirt near the low fire. I leaped from my blanket with my knife in my hand. I glanced around. More than the two visiting men were in our camp.

I shouted.

The other women came from their blankets with knives.

Then, I saw the bears. Two big black bears lumbered into the camp.

The other women screamed.

"Do not fear," I shouted and ran to where the other women huddled away from the fire. "The bears are here to help us."

We stood together in a little group and watched as the bears roared.

Men separated and stood. Maha and our friends backed away, allowing space for the bears to come in between them and our attackers. The attacking men yelped.

The bears stood on their back legs, standing taller than any of the men who had attacked our men. The five men ran in different directions.

The bears followed two of the men. We heard them scream as the bears caught up with them. I feared we would need to bandage the men — or bury them.

Instead, they returned to our camp with their hands in the air, followed by the bears.

"We did not know you are protected by the bears," the leader said. "We will leave you alone and never attack others again." He turned back to gaze at the bear. "Will that do?"

The bear's growl was low and deep.

"We promise. We know what will happen to us if we do," the other man stuttered. Like rising from a steam bath, fear rolled from his body.

The bears nodded. They stepped closer to the strange men and nudged them in the back.

"We are gone. We will not return!"

They stepped away from the light of the fire into the darkness. The bears followed them.

"We can rest better, now," Maha said. "My friends will ensure they do not return."

Six days later we entered Home Valley. Papa Cainan and Mama Elia had arrived only a span earlier.

"Do you know why we were asked to come to Home Valley?" I asked Mama Elia.

"Have you not heard? Enoch is to be made a High Priest."

"Enoch?"

"Yes, Gr-gr-grandmama Vida," Enoch said, coming around a corner. "Jehovah spoke to me on the road. I am to preach repentance."

I closed my open mouth with a pop.

"Yes, Gr-gr-grandmama. I am y-y-young — only t-t-twenty-five years. I am y-y-younger than any of the gr-gr-grandpapas who r-r-received this honor."

"Grandpapa Adam says Jehovah knows what he is doing. He must know something about you we have not learned," Mama Elia said.

"P-p-perhaps."

In the next days as we prepared for the sacrifice and the celebration, I saw Enoch gazing toward the west trail into Home Valley. His mama and papa had not yet arrived.

"They will come," I said when I saw the longing in his eyes. "Jared and Helsa will not miss this event. It is too important."

"I know," Enoch said with a nod. "But they are l-l-late."

Two days before the planned sacrifice, Jared and Helsa rode into Home Valley. Enoch rushed to them. They hugged each other and walked to the guest house where they would stay while in Home Valley.

After the sacrifice, Grandpapa Adam announced to the village that Enoch would be given the High Priesthood. Those of Enoch's family joined together in the tabernacle while Grandpapa Adam, Seth, Cainan, and Enos gathered around Enoch to confer the High Priesthood on our young grandson. Shivers bounced up my spine as I listened. Jehovah did know.

~ ~ ~

Maha and I traveled to Home Valley often over the next years. We were called once more to join the family there when Grandpapa Adam called us to join them for a special meeting.

Once more, all the prophets and their wives, including Enoch and his young wife Zehira came for this meeting. I felt uncomfortable, left out. But Helsa and Jared had come for the meeting as well. She, too, felt uncomfortable. Our grandmamas loved us and treated us well, but I still felt unsure of my place among them.

We gathered with the others from Home Valley for a special sacrifice. Jared assisted Adam and Seth in the sacrifice. Maha gripped my hand. His frustration carried through the grip, although his smile never wavered.

After the sacrifice, Grandpapa Adam introduced Jared as the next one to carry on the patriarchal order of the priesthood. He, too, would be a prophet. Maha's grip tightened on my hand. I felt, rather than heard, his little sigh.

I do not know how Maha managed it, but he smiled and beamed the whole afternoon. Not only had our grandson been ordained, now our son had been ordained as a prophet. It could have been one of several of his cousins, but Jehovah chose our Jared.

I carried dirty dishes to the kitchen behind Maha and overheard Grandmama Eve ask him about it. "How are you doing, really?"

"Me? I am happy for my son. He is obedient and always has been. He will do well."

"And you are not concerned that you were passed over?"

"I know you are worried about me, Grandmama Eve. Jehovah knows me. He knows what is needed. If he chooses to include me in the lineage of the High Priesthood, I will be ready. Until then, I will not worry about it."

"Good for you," Grandmama Eve said. "I will stop worrying."

I could not stop.

I watched him over the years. He continued to lead the people of Ziklag, teaching them of Jehovah. We lived in a safe community. Word had spread among robbers — Ziklag had inhuman protectors, bears, and they could not be bribed.

Sometimes, Maha would travel with Jared or Enoch when they needed a partner to help them teach. The villages around Ziklag knew that Maha loved Jehovah and would always make choices based on Jehovah's laws. This, too, provided us with a sense of safety we did not find in the other places we had lived.

We were called once more to witness the blessing given to Methuselah, Enoch's son. Once more, Maha sat beside me, watching as his son and grandson participated in the priesthood blessing. His smile never left his face, but his grip tightened on my hand.

Grandpapa Adam offered Maha a blessing of comfort. He told Maha he did not know when it would happen, but he expected that one day, Maha would be receiving the same responsibility as his son and grandsons. "Jehovah does things in His own time."

"I know, Grandpapa. I am happy to see my son and grand-sons earn the blessings."

"Someday it will be you."

I watched Maha over the next hundred or more years. To-gether we taught our grandchildren of Jehovah. We enjoyed life in the protected hills of Ziklag. We were happy.

And then it happened. Mahalaleel had lived nearly five hundred years when he hiked to the mountains, as he often still did. There, the voice of Jehovah told him to bring me to Home Valley.

We expected to surprise Grandmama Eve and Grandpapa Adam, but they knew we were coming. Grandpapa Adam al-ways knew.

Later that evening, Grandpapa Adam took Mahalaleel into his study. I sat with Grandmama Eve. By this time, they had lived on this earth nearly nine hundred years since leaving Eden. Even though both had become bent and frail with white hair, Grandmama Eve had lost none of her keen intelligence nor her interest in the lives of her family. Grandpapa Adam continued to direct the family and lead those who believe in Jehovah with a strength of will.

Grandmama Eve and I were visiting, sharing stories we had heard about Enoch and his new city of Zion, when Maha opened the door to the study.

"Vida. Grandpapa would like you to join us."

I glanced at Grandmama Eve. She lifted her eyebrows and shrugged. I bent to kiss her on the cheek and walked down the hall toward Maha and Grandpapa Adam.

"Jehovah has watched you and Mahalaleel for many years. He has tested your faith. Even when you lost a child, you did not blame Him. Now, it is time to ask something new of you."

I gazed into his blue eyes. At his age, I expected them to have faded, but they were as bright and clear as they were when I first met him. "What would you like me to do?"

"Can you support your husband in the responsibilities of serving Jehovah as a High Priest and prophet?"

My gaze turned from Grandpapa Adam to Maha.

He nodded.

"Of course, I can do that! Maha is an honorable man. In all these years when others received the lineage ahead of him, he has never complained. He has continued to teach our children and those in our village."

Excitement for Maha bubbled through me. I jumped from my chair to throw my arms around my good husband.

"Who knows the ways of Jehovah. I have expected this to happen for many hundred years," Grandpapa Adam said. "I knew it would come. You have obeyed as you should. Congratulations."

All the other prophets, our son and grandsons, Maha's parents and grandparents, came to be with us when Grandpapa blessed Mahalaleel with the High Priesthood. He told me later that the weight of all their hands could not compare with the weight of responsibility to share that fell on his shoulders when they removed their hands.

After that day, we traveled among the people near Ziklag and farther to the south and west, teaching those who would listen to us of Jehovah. Every time we traveled, I saw a bear outside our camp, helping Jehovah to protect us.

Jehovah truly knows what is best. His timing is not ours. Of that, I testify.

PART THREE

Helsa

Chapter 1

Dance

L ife in this world is never easy.

I know it has never been, nor will it ever be. Sometimes, though, I would like it to be a bit easier.

I am Helsa.

Jared and I were married by Grandpapa Seth and blessed by Grandpapa Adam many years ago. We traveled together for the first few years teaching of Jehovah, as Grandpapa Adam asked.

Those were good years together. We loved the time we had alone as we traveled between the villages. After months of being alone, going into a new village became a game. Would these people accept us, or would they chase us away?

In some villages, we made good friends whom I will always love. When we met for the great family conference in

Home Valley, the good women friends I made joined us with their families to hear the last words of our first papa and mama, Grandpapa Adam, and Grandmama Eve telling us the story of her life.

In other villages, however, Jared did little more than share his name, and the men pushed us back onto our horses.

"You are not welcome here," they cried. "We have no need of you or the message you want to force on us."

We would leave, a sadness filling our souls. These men and women, and their children, needed to know of Jehovah's promises. They had refused yet again to receive His love.

~ ~ ~

I was born in the northern country of Laish to Achyan and Nitza. I loved the green meadows, the tall trees, and the deep snows. Even today, I long to return to visit my parents and ride through the deep snow in a sledge.

But it is not to be.

Jared visited his grandparents, Seth and Ganet, in my eighteenth year. He came trudging up the mountains through the deep snow to learn from his grandpapa about teaching the words of Jehovah to others. He stayed for a week before leaving for a month to go with Seth. I had not had a chance to visit Ganet in that week.

When he returned, the village celebrated the warm weather. Our fields and gardens were planted and began to show the green of life.

I loved the fragrance of newly turned earth and the warmth that came after the snow and ice melted. I danced as I carried

Mama's contribution to the celebration out to the village green. I twirled ... and almost stumbled over someone's feet.

Strong, warm arms kept me from falling.

As I regained my balance, I turned, looking up into the sun to see who had both tripped and saved me. His blond hair and light clothing glowed in the bright sunlight. His deep blue eyes shone.

"Are you well?" he asked.

I sucked in a sharp breath. "Yes. Nothing spilled and I did not get hurt. Where did you come from?"

"Ziklag."

I pulled back away from him. "You are ..."

"Jared, grandson of Seth." He laughed. "You look confused."

"You did not just come from Ziklag. That is far away from here. How did you get here to trip me?"

"Oh. That. I watched you dance across the green. I wanted to stop you before you fell into the hole here." He pointed behind him at a hole left by a mole.

My mouth rounded into an O. "I did not see that. Thank you."

Jared smiled at me. "Perhaps you should not dance across the green until you know where the holes in the grass are."

I giggled and pulled the bowl closer to my chest. "I will do that. Thank you for catching me."

My dancing ended as I walked carefully to set Mama's colorful bowl on the table with the other dishes. Jared walked beside me.

"I'm sorry I stopped your dance," he said in a soft, contrite voice. "I liked watching you, but I did not want you to fall."

I smiled up at him. "Thank you, Jared."

"You know my name," he said. "I do not know yours." His eyebrows wiggled up and down.

I giggled and spun away. "Maybe I will share it with you, but not now." I danced away. "I have to go help my mama."

When everyone came together to sit for the meal, Jared and his grandparents sat across the table from my parents and me. My older brothers and sisters sat with their families up and down the tables.

"Hello, Nitza, Achyan," Seth said as they set their food-filled plates on the table.

Mama lifted her spoon. "Good to see you came back in time for the celebration. Is this the grandson I have heard stories of?"

"I try to return in time for celebrations," Seth said with a smile as he held the chair for his wife, Ganet.

Jared set his overloaded plate on the table. "I am Jared." He smiled toward Mama and then looked at Papa with the same casual smile.

Papa nodded and set down his spoon. "I am Achyan." He waved toward Mama. "My wife is Nitza," his arm waved toward me, "and our youngest daughter, Helsa."

"I am happy to meet you, sir," Jared said, "mistress." He smiled at me. "Good to meet you, as well, Helsa." His eyes sparkled with concealed laughter.

I grimaced. "Good to meet you, Jared."

"Jared is here to learn how to teach and share the words of Jehovah. I have the joy of teaching my grandsons," Seth said as they started to eat.

"Did you not have another grandson here a few years ago?" Auntie Dita said from the other side of Papa.

Ganet drew her eyebrows together. "We have had many grandsons come stay with us over the years. Which one are you thinking of?"

"The one with a long name — Ma … Maha… something like that."

Jared laughed. "Mahalaleel?"

"Yes. That is the one. Do you know him?"

"He is my papa. That was more than seventy years ago."

"Did he not choose a wife here?"

Jared glanced down the table. "My grandmama is down there," he waved at her.

Galit waved back, then nudged her husband, Natan, who waved as well.

"I plan to spend tonight with them. Mama misses Laish. She told me she wished she could come with me to visit."

"Galit and Natan must be happy to see you here. They do not get to see their grandchildren often," Mama said in a sour voice.

I glanced toward her. She frowned at me. What did she mean?

"I am here now. My brothers and sisters have come often. We see them when we can." Jared's shoulder twitched a little.

"Do you ride?" Jared asked after we had eaten about half our meal.

I glanced toward Mama, who visited with Ganet and Auntie Dita. "When Mama lets me, she does not let me out often."

"Ah. Now I understand the dancing."

"What?" I squawked. "I was enjoying the warm sunshine. It has been a long cold time."

"I saw many hills of snow. The trail I followed had been narrowed by them as I came here. No wonder you were enjoying the sun."

I allowed a small smile to escape. "I love the snow. But it lasted longer than expected this year. Sometimes, I would like to spend some time where it is always warm."

"Even where I live in Ziklag, it gets cold when it rains. Snow does not get you as wet as the rain."

"No," I agreed. "But the snow is colder."

"Have you ever had to be out in the rain, soaking wet to the skin, and the wind trying to tear your clothing off?" Jared asked. He shivered. "It becomes mighty cold."

I shivered without thinking. "The rains that come before the snow are cold. As they get colder, we know the snow is closer. It is always a relief when the snow finally falls."

"Helsa," Mama said. "I need you to help me clear this table."

I jerked toward her. "Yes, Mama."

I turned back to Jared and lifted a shoulder. "Maybe I will see you again."

Jared smiled. "I am certain we will."

I gathered our family's plates and other dishes and followed Mama toward the house.

"Do not think that boy will want to be with you," Mama growled. "I am not going to have my grandchildren come visit me only every few years or more."

~ ~ ~

When Jared left at the end of the warm time, I rode with him. Mama was not happy about it. Jared had returned to my door often during those evenings except when he and Seth were out of town.

He and I walked where Mama could see. Jared worked to be certain Mama knew he would always be good to me. In that time, I grew to love him. I could not consider allowing him to leave without me — if he asked me to marry him.

He did, three weeks before he needed to leave to get down the mountains before the snows closed the trail.

I said yes. Papa and Mama said no.

Seth and Ganet spoke with Mama and Papa one afternoon when I was not home. I do not know what they said. All I know is that evening, Papa and Mama sat me down.

"We have learned more about Jared. We changed our minds," Papa said.

"Do you mean you will allow me to marry Jared?" I asked. Uncertainty filled me.

"Yes, Helsa. We do." Papa glanced at Mama who nodded her head. Her grim lips pressed tightly into a thin line.

I could see her reluctance. She feared I would never return.

Papa continued, "You have our permission to marry Jared, if you are certain you want to leave us behind."

I threw my arms around his neck. "Oh, thank you, Papa! Thank you, Mama." I dropped next to her chair and hugged her. "I will come often to see you."

"Do better than Vida. Come home more often," she grumped.

"You know I will," I murmured into her hair.

"And you will mean it, too, as long as you are here with me. Wait until you get into the world. You just wait." Tears filled Mama's voice.

"I love you Mama, Papa. I love it here in Laish. But ..." My voice trailed off.

"You also love that boy." Mama said it with such finality I leaned back and stared at her.

"I do. But I am not dying. I am going with my new husband, as so many other girls have done in the past. You left your home to be with Papa." I put my arms around her once more.

"I did. But I knew your papa more than one season of warm."

"Not much more," I said, glancing up at Papa.

He cringed. "Perhaps two seasons."

"See, Mama. Have you returned to your mama?"

Her long dark hair swung back and forth with her head. "I planned to return. I wanted to return. I always expected to return, ..." tears overwhelmed her voice.

I looked up to Papa once more.

"We cannot travel from here in the snows. After the snow melts, we must work hard to grow enough food for our family." He set a hand on Mama's shoulder. "We thought we would return for a visit. We have not."

Never returned to your home? Never saw your mama or papa again. Understanding overwhelmed me and tears coursed across my face.

"Mama! No wonder you do not want me to marry Jared. He promises me we will return to see you. We will be able to come visit more often. I promise."

Mama lifted her head and stared at me with red-rimmed eyes. "You say you will return now. Do not make promises you cannot keep."

"We will return, Mama."

"We shall see. I will not look for you until you knock at my door."

Seth, er, Grandpapa Seth married us the day before we left. As it was, we had waited longer than we should have. Jared wanted to be sure I spent time with my mama until then.

We stayed in the guest house that night, rising early to find Papa and Mama waiting with our saddled horses and a pack horse loaded and ready to leave.

I hugged Mama and let her cry on my shoulder until Papa gently pulled her away. Jared stood next to my horse's nose while I mounted.

Jared's grandparents, both Seth and Ganet and Galit and Natan, hugged us goodbye and stepped back while Jared swung up onto his tall horse. Tears openly dripped down the cheeks of the women. Men, too, had glistening eyes from un-shed tears.

"We must go, if we are to avoid the next snowfall," Jared said. He took the lead to the pack horse and led us down the trail toward our new life.

I sat straight in my saddle, unwilling to allow Mama to see how sad it made me to leave her and Papa. But I had wanted to leave this high valley all my life. Excitement filled me. After we started away, I would not turn back to wave. I knew I would race back to their side if I did.

Chapter 2

Attack

We left too late in the year. The journey down the mountain trail became much more difficult than it should have been. Rain fell on us on the second day, turning the trail to a slippery mess.

Cold invaded when the sun fell. Jared kept the horses close to us and built a small fire each evening. We cuddled close to each other, trying to stay warm.

On the third night, snow fell. We woke the next morning warmer than we had on the morning before.

"Why are we warmer?" Jared asked.

"The snow helps to keep us warm," I said.

"Too bad we have to move."

"We will freeze if we stay here."

Jared sighed and wiggled out of my arms. "Then we should move on. I believe we should be out of the snow to-day."

"That would be nice."

I pulled my socks on while under the blanket and quickly shoved them into my icy boots. "Brrr!" I shivered.

Jared handed me a tuber that had laid along the edge of the coals, baking during the night. "That should help you stay warm."

I held it in my hands to warm them, then moved it to my pocket while I helped gather the few possessions we had un-packed the evening before and stuffed them back into the pack. Jared put out the small fire, shoveling mud over it and smothering it. Then he lifted the heavy pack onto the pack horse. I helped tie the pack down and saddled my red mare, Pepper.

I swung up onto Pepper while Jared took the pack horse's lead and mounted his horse.

"Are you ready?"

I nodded.

He clucked his tongue. "Time to leave these cold moun-tains, Midnight."

I nudged Pepper and we moved toward the trail together, the pack horse following behind us. I pulled the tuber from my pocket and munched on it while we rode.

The snow continued to fall, making it difficult for us to see the trail. I could see Jared's frustration that we were slowed by the snow.

Jared had not lived in the cold of the mountains as I had. He had no warm gloves to keep his hands warm as I had. His hands struggled to hold onto his reins, and he began to forget where we were going.

When we stopped for a midday meal, he began to mumble. I could not understand what he said. I pulled a blanket from the pack and wrapped it around him. I needed to get him out of the cold as soon as I could.

I wrangled him back onto his horse, tied the lead of the pack horse to the back of Jared's saddle, then took his reins to lead Midnight.

"I am sorry, Midnight," I whispered to the tall black horse. "Jared is ill. We need to find our way down this mountain to-day."

I repeated the message to Pepper. She had been down this trail before with Papa and knew what to expect. I loosened my grip on her reins. "Get us out of these mountains, Pepper," I called.

Pepper moved with sure feet down the trail.

Sometime during that ride, my eyes closed. I woke when Pepper stopped. My eyes jerked open. The snow had stopped and rain fell on the leaves of the trees over our head.

In front of us lay a fence. Beyond the fence was a small cabin. I smelled smoke from the fire. Would it be safe to ask for refuge? Papa had warned me that robbers ranged along the trail, seeking to steal from unwary travelers.

"Jehovah," I prayed. "Jared is ill. It is raining and cold. We need to get out of the cold. Is it safe to stop here? Can I take Jared here seeking assistance?"

A cold chill froze my heart.

No.

"Where shall we go to be safe from the weather? Jared cannot stay in the cold much longer," I prayed.

Midnight pushed past Pepper with a soft whicker. He led us around the fence and past the house. I let him lead. I had no idea where to go differently than where the horse led.

My eyes swept across the land as far as I could see in the dim light of the setting sun. Heavy rain fell from black clouds. I saw no place to get out of the rain.

Midnight came to a halt under trees. I stared around. The rain had stopped. No. It had not stopped, the trees stopped the rain before it reached us.

I sighed. Maybe we could be safe.

Jared leaned sideways and almost fell off his horse. I jumped off Pepper and caught him before he fell.

"Wha—" Jared mumbled.

"I guess we will be safe here," I murmured.

I pulled the blanket from around his shoulders and lay it on the ground. Long pine needles softened the earth.

"Here, Jared. Lay here. I will get a fire going and we can be warm."

"No fire," Jared mumbled.

"No fire? You are freezing."

"No fire. Not safe."

"I will get us dry blankets to help us stay warm, instead. I will be right back."

I hurried to the pack horse and dragged the pack from his back. I dug into it and pulled out two dry blankets.

I hurried to cover Jared.

"Hobble horses?" Jared mumbled.

"I will take care of the horses. Do not worry. I know how to do this."

I unsaddled both the horses and hobbled them so they would not run away before I dug into the pack for food. Jared needed something to eat to get well.

I found apples and travel bars in the pack. They did not need cooking.

"Here, Jared. This is not much, but it is food. You will want to eat."

He managed to swallow the travel bar, but his teeth still chattered. I lay next to him to help warm his body. I did not dare move, fearing he would grow cold once more.

Sometime during the night, he woke up.

"How did we get here?" he mumbled.

"You fell asleep in the saddle. I gave Pepper her head, depending on her to get us down. She brought us down the mountain out of the snow. When we stopped at a fence, with a cabin and a fire on the other side, I could not cross it. Oh, Jared, I prayed."

"And?"

"And a cold deeper than any I have ever felt filled my soul. The rain soaked us through and you are sick. I did not know where to go."

"How did we get here?"

"Midnight led the way. He brought us here."

"Midnight's a good horse." The slur in Jared's voice grew deeper.

"He is. And you need to sleep more. Jehovah and Midnight will keep us safe."

I snuggled next to Jared and allowed my eyes to close. *Please, Jehovah. Please keep us safe.*

~ ~ ~

Later that night, Midnight and Pepper screamed, bringing both Jared and me up with a start.

"What was that?" Jared whispered.

"The horses."

"Stay here," he murmured into my ear.

"Me, here? You have been sick. You stay here."

"Then come with me." He pulled his staff from the saddle next to us.

I glanced at the ground. I needed a weapon. No long pieces of wood lay where I could grab them. I shook my head and silently slipped out my belt knife. I could not help from a distance, but if someone came close, he would be hurt.

The horses screamed again.

Jared ran toward the noise.

I followed at a trot.

Men were trying to drag the horses away from where I left them. Midnight and Pepper both complained with loud voices.

"What do you think you are doing?" Jared shouted.

Pepper kicked back at the man behind him. Midnight reared up on his hind legs and dropped onto the shoulders of the man in front of him. The man fell to his knees. Midnight kept his foot on his shoulder.

"Get him off me!" the man shouted as the horse shoved him from his knees to his face in the dirt.

The other man scrambled away from the horses on his knees.

Midnight set a foot on the downed man's back.

"Come help me, Si!" he called. "Si! Help!"

Jared stepped around Midnight. "Good job, Midnight."

He dropped to a knee. "What did you want from us?"

"Your horses. Ours are back there."

"Then walk back and get them, but remember, our horses do not like to be taken from us. They fight back."

"Why do your horses fight back?" the man asked from the ground, fighting to breathe.

Jared lifted his voice. "Because they are ours."

"Oh. Can you have him move his hoof? It hurts."

"I do not know. Where will you go?"

"Back to my friends. They are waiting for me."

"This is more than stealing our horses?"

"Maybe."

"If I let you go, do not come back. You cannot take our horses. They will protect us. Do you understand?"

Midnight leaned forward, letting more of his weight settle onto the man's back.

He screamed.

"I understand. Get his hoof off my back!"

Jared touched Midnight's shoulder and he lifted the hoof. Before the man could roll away, the hoof sank back on his back.

"It looks like Midnight does not believe you."

The man's eyes rolled upward toward the horse. "Let me go."

Jared lifted his eyebrows. "What are you lying about? Why will my horse not let you go?"

I heard a sound behind me and whirled around. Two men crept on their hands and knees toward us.

Pepper whirled around, kicking one in the head. The other shouted.

"Ah," Jared said. "You were waiting for your friends. Too late. Pepper is watching us, as well."

The other man rose from his knees, knife in hand. Pepper shoved into him, knocking him off balance.

"Wha—?"

"As I told your friend here," Jared called from the other side of Pepper, "our horses do not like it when people try to steal them. They are ours. We are theirs."

The man near us lunged toward me. Pepper whipped her tail into his face, then lifted a foot and tripped him. I dropped down and grabbed his knife from his loose grip.

When he stood again, he lifted his hands. "You win."

"Why are you trying to steal our horses?"

"We needed a ride. Chuza kicked us out into the rain. We wuz in the cabin first, but he kicked us out. We needed to go into town for more to drink, but it is a long walk. We saw your horses —"

"And decided they were an easy target?"

The man who stood in front of me shrugged. "Well, yes."

"Our horses chose not to join you. Go on. Get out of here."

Jared touched Midnight's shoulder once more. The horse lifted his foot long enough for the man beneath to roll away. He jumped up, his eyes twitching from Jared to his friends and back to Jared, briefly landing on me before bouncing back to his friends.

"Chuza will be angry with us," he whined.

"Harlon, shut up," the man whose knife I held growled.

"I din't say nothin', Bart." Harlon's whine grated.

"Chuza will be angry?" Jared asked. He nodded to me. I nodded back.

Jared stepped forward and grabbed Harlon. He turned the man around and held his hands behind him. Pepper and Midnight stepped closer to Bart trapping his hands next to his sides. The third man lay on the ground, still sleeping.

"Rope?" Jared growled.

I ran to the pack and pulled out a length of rope and took it to him. He tied Harlon's hands behind his back.

He pushed Midnight aside and grabbed Bart. He spun him around before he could react and tied his arms with the other end of the rope. Si, the man knocked senseless by Pepper's feet, groaned.

"What will you do with him?" I asked, nodding toward Si.

"Same as the others."

Jared pushed the horses out of the way and dragged his prisoners closer. He bent and tied the third man with the center length of the rope while I stood with my knife pointed at the men.

"You may want to help him," Jared grunted to the other men. "Pick him up and come with me."

I followed behind, wondering what Jared planned.

He poked the men with his staff, prodding them forward.

"Stop there," he commanded.

"Why here?" Harlon wheezed.

"Because I said," Jared growled. "Sit."

The men sat on the ground as demanded. Jared gathered firewood. I picked up some dry pine needles to start the fire. Jared scraped away a circle in the litter. I dropped my needles in the center and he bent over it with a fire starter. When the spark landed on the needles, he gently breathed on it until the fire grew. He added larger pieces of wood until the fire blazed.

I stepped back out of the glare. The light hurt my eyes, making it hard to see when I stood close. Jared checked the knots tying the men, then joined me.

"We must leave here," he murmured into my ear.

"Now?" I whispered.

"Yes."

I gathered the few things I had removed from our pack and stuffed them back in.

"You will need these blankets to keep you warm," I said.

"What about you?"

"My cloak was made for the cold. I will be warm."

Jared loaded the pack back onto the pack horse, while I quietly saddled Pepper, then helped Jared to saddle Midnight. We mounted the horses and moved slowly and quietly past the blazing fire. The thieves sat next to it, leaning against each other.

"What will happen to those men?" I asked in a low voice after we were well away from them.

I could barely see Jared's shrug. "I do not know. I imagine they will sit there until they untie themselves, or until their boss, Chuza, finds them. They will not freeze while they wait."

We rode a distance down the trail before light began to filter through the leaves. The rain stopped before we left the trees. Jared pulled us to a stop, at the edge of a meadow.

I gasped.

Patches of blue, yellow, and orange, pierced with spikes of red carpeted the green meadow. The fragrance of the flowers wafted toward us on a gentle breeze.

"Beautiful," I sighed.

"We will see more of these as we travel down the mountains. This part of the land does not get as cold as it does in Laish, and it stays warm longer."

"Oh," I breathed. "It is no wonder so many prefer to live lower down the mountains. I love the snow, but I understand better now."

Chapter 3

Late Birth

Wared took me to meet his grandparents, Eve and Adam in Home Valley. We were welcomed and Adam blessed our marriage. He invited Jared to serve Jehovah with me by teaching as he had been taught by Seth in Laish.

When we left, we traveled to communities that had not heard of Jehovah. Some listened to Jared. Most did not. We traveled for years, even after our first five children were born.

Then we entered a small village called Aenon. The people of this village accepted us. They had prayed for someone to find them and teach them of Jehovah. Jared and I settled in a home abandoned by its previous occupants who left to find a different life.

Aenon was a beautiful little village. Homes surrounded a green where children played, lovers strolled, and the community gathered for celebrations and discussions of village needs.

The community well stood on the edge of the green. I spent many happy hours with my friends in the early morning and late evening, gossiping and sharing. The women of Aenon assisted me with our children during the times when Jared traveled to other villages to teach of Jehovah.

Jared and I watched our sons grow. Although Jared did not know if he still lived within the possible line of priesthood authority, we hoped for a child of promise. No new High Priests had been identified in more than two hundred years. Still, we wanted a son of ours to be eligible.

Sadly, however, most of our sons were less than eligible. They obeyed the commandments, most of them, but they chose to work within the community, supporting their families and leading, some joined and led the guard protecting Aenon, rather than going with Jared to teach and share.

News came that Grandmama Eve and Grandpapa Adam decided to travel around the country to visit with their children. We would be among the first to be visited. Jared was excited to have Grandpapa Adam visit and go with him to teach.

I wanted to see them, as well, but after more than twenty years of not having little children, I found myself with child once more. I feared my sickness would make it difficult to enjoy the visit.

"Do you think this will be an obedient son?" I asked Jared after losing the contents of my stomach one more time.

"Only Jehovah knows," he said. "It would be nice to have a son who is more obedient. But at this point in our lives, I will be happy to have him born healthy and well."

"I feel the same. Perhaps Grandpapa Adam can help?"

"Perhaps."

By the time Grandmama Eve and Grandpapa Adam arrived, I felt some better. I could eat food without losing everything, by then.

I had not shared the news of the coming child with them yet. I worried about how they would accept it. Would they support me having another child at my age? Not many women continued to have children after one hundred fifty years.

I should have known there was no need to fear.

One day while we worked together preparing a meal as we waited for our men to return, I built up my courage. "Grandmama Eve. I am with child again."

"Congratulations, Helsa! How long has it been since your last child? I see no children still living here with you."

"No children live here now. My last child, a daughter, came to our home more than twenty years ago. She has a child and will have another close to the time this child is due."

I touched the growing bulge in my stomach. "We had thought I had passed the childbearing years long ago. I guess I was wrong." I bit my lip, fearing her response.

"I know of women who still give birth up to their two hundredth year, so this is not unusual. But, to be honest, most women have had their last child by the time they have lived one hundred twenty-five years." Grandmama Eve lifted a shoulder in a little shrug. "We had lived out of Eden for one hundred thirty years, when Seth was born. I do not know how many years I lived before we left Eden. Perhaps I was as old as you are."

I allowed a little sigh to escape.

"It is never fun to be miserable. It is worse when we are older. I feel for you."

"Jared prays that this child will be the child of promise, the child to whom the High Priesthood can be conferred. Even with a skip in the lineage, perhaps this child will be the one who is prepared." I sat in a chair and waved Grandmama to sit across from me.

"None of your other sons are worthy?" she asked.

"You would know." I traced the wood grain on our table. "But, no. We hoped Ruben would be the one, but he finds joy in working with horses and chooses not to leave them to preach the gospel. None of the others have been solemn and thoughtful. None have shown they are the one. Perhaps the next High Priest will come from another line, another son of Cainan."

"Only Jehovah knows which of the sons of Cainan will be the one chosen. You have no others?"

"None of the others have shown they are the one. Some have chosen to join the guards, protecting Aenon. Nathan had to kill one of the raiders when they raided from Yarmuk ten years ago."

Grandmama Eve leaned forward and took my hand. "Oh, Helsa. It has been a long hard time for you, as it has been for Elia. No man has been chosen since her Cainan. No son. No grandson. Imagine how she feels."

"She must be frantic." I gazed into Grandmama Eve's eyes and accepted the love she shared.

"She is learning to wait with patience, as you must, my dear."

Before they left, after visiting with us for nearly three months, Grandpapa Adam and my Jared set their hands on my head and prayed for a blessing for me and the unborn child. As Grandpapa spoke, I opened my eyes and sucked in my breath.

"It is given to women to suffer pain and sorrow as they bring children into this world. You cannot expect this child to come easily. He will, however, grow to be a healthy young man. As you teach him of Jehovah, he will draw close. Be faithful and strong."

This would not be an easy birth.

~ ~ ~

Grandpapa Adam spoke the truth of my struggles with the birth of this child. After they left, I struggled once more with eating. The sickness in my stomach made it difficult for me to eat, though I knew I needed to feed the coming baby. But my head pounded, causing my stomach to refuse to retain food the way it should.

I spent many days in my bed with my eyes closed, trying to stop the nausea from ejecting the food I ate. Some days it worked. Most days it did not.

I expected Jared home to be with me the following day until the birth of this child. We still had another month before we expected the birth.

However, the babe determined to be born early. I lay alone in my bed that afternoon, ordered by the healer to stay down until the baby came and too sick to move. The familiar cramps signaled the coming of the child.

"It is too early," I moaned, grabbing my stomach.

Worse. I had no one to go get the healer who had suggested I should be careful in the next few days. What would I do?

I swung my legs over the edge of the bed and sat through another cramp. The sun shone brightly outside my window. I had not been out in the sun for many days. Could I make it to Josefa's home?

I stood and made my way to the door. I clung to the door as another pain swept through my body.

"Grandmama? Grandmama? Are you here?" my young granddaughter Pia called from the kitchen door.

"Here," I cried.

"Grandmama?" Pia continued to call. "Grandmama? Where are you."

I lifted my voice louder. Still, it came out hardly more than a whisper. "Here, Pia. I am here."

I heard footsteps patter toward me.

"Grandmama!" Pia ran to me and touched my hand. "You do not look so well."

"I am not well. Thank you for coming. Be a good girl and get your mama. Tell her I need the healer."

The little girl stuck her thumb in her mouth. "You need Mama and the healer? Are you sick?"

"Yes, Pia. Very sick. I need the healer."

Pia turned away and scampered down the hall toward the kitchen. I heard her little voice floating through the open window. "Mama! Mama! Grandmama Helsa needs you and the healer. Why would she need a healer?"

I let go of the door and slid down to the floor.

Not only was the delivery early, it was not easy. In fact, none of my other birthing of babies was so difficult.

Although the little boy breathed without trouble, he did not squall as most other babies do when they see the world in which they must live out their mortal lives. This child lay with open eyes, staring at the healer and me.

Jared arrived home as the healer lay the child in my arms.

"This is too early," he cried.

"But he is here," the healer answered.

Jared kissed me and leaned close to stare at our baby son. "Are you well, Helsa?"

"Better than I expected. It hurt more than the others, but he is here. What will you name him?"

Jared lifted the babe into his arms and stared into his eyes. "Enoch. This boy child is Enoch."

Enoch grew well, though he never babbled as other children babble. He spoke little.

Not much more than two years later, another baby boy joined our family. Jared named him Hadar.

Enoch continued to be bigger than his brother, but he did not speak as Hadar did.

Soon people began to treat Enoch as less than able. They would speak to Hadar, rather than to Enoch, asking Hadar how Enoch felt or what he wanted.

I wanted to shake my child and shout, "Speak up for yourself!"

I did not. Instead, I waited for him to choose to speak.

As they grew, Enoch spoke more, but he spoke with a stutter. It further pushed the boys of the village away from him.

Hadar began to push Enoch around, insisting that he do the chores I gave to Hadar. His gang of friends bullied other children, taking their lunches and insisting they give in to his demands.

I tried to stop Hadar's bad behavior. He did not listen. He continued to push his brother around and insist that Enoch do his chores.

Hadar decided he would be the next to be a High Priest, and insisted the other young people bow to him and give him special gifts and services.

Enoch never complained.

Jared traveled often enough he could not stop Hadar's behavior. By the time he tried to take him away with him to teach, Hadar caused more problems.

We spent many nights crying together, worrying what we should do to stop his bad behavior.

On the day he and his gang surrounded Zehira, a poor young girl whose leg had twisted while yet a baby, I called him in.

"What are you doing, taunting that poor girl?" I asked.

"Who? Zehira? She likes the attention."

"No one likes to be treated like a thing, one who is of no importance."

Hadar shrugged. "She has no importance. Her parents should have thrown her on the midden heap when they discovered her deformity."

I gasped and allowed my mouth to close with a pop. "Hadar. You do not mean that!"

"I do. The world has no place for the deformed."

"I thought you hope to be a prophet for Jehovah? How can you teach of our God of Love when you treat others with such callous disrespect?"

Hadar stood staring at me with a smug grin.

"Bah. You do not understand the ways of Jehovah." I shoved an urn into his arms. "You will go to the well, alone, three times and bring me back three urns full of water." My voice began to lift. "You will not insist that your brother carries the water for you. You will not insist that others fetch or carry the water. YOU will go get it. You will bring it to me. Do you understand?"

"And if I do not?" Hadar snarled.

"You will leave this house with the clothing on your back and never return. You will no longer be my son."

Hadar's eyes widened. "You would not do that, Mama."

"Try me. This is the last time I will tell you. Go. Now." I lifted my arm and pointed toward the kitchen door.

Hadar moved toward the door.

"I am watching. I will know if you force another to carry a drop of that water."

Hadar slunk away from the door. He brought me three urns full of water, alone. None of the other boys carried any of it.

Chapter 4

News

Hadar did not change his ways.

Within two years, he left our home with his new wife, Mele. I feared for her. I did not believe he would treat her well. But I had little to say about it. She believed Hadar's lies and refused to listen to me.

He insisted on a marriage, though he was too young. The village leader joined them in marriage. They were married, and I could do nothing about it.

While Hadar bragged about his beautiful new wife, Enoch left Aenon planning to visit with Grandpapa Adam.

I worried about Enoch although he had traveled alone among robbers and thieves before. Only Jehovah could protect him. *Please, Jehovah,* I prayed, *bless my son. Keep him safe.*

More than a month later, we received a message from Home Valley. Grandpapa Adam wanted us to visit. Although the fields ripened, Jared and I took a small guard of our sons and rode away to see why Grandpapa Adam would call us to come visit.

We hurried, but robbers rode the roads between Aenon and Home Valley. We were forced off the road to stand still, waiting for large mobs to pass by us.

We did not want to battle our brothers as we traveled to respond to Grandpapa's call. I wondered if our men were unhappy to stand along the side of the road against the green trees and bushes as the multitudes of angry men passed us.

At first, our men growled. Then they listened to the enraged voices of the horde, threatening Jared, Grandpapa Cainan, Papa Mahalaleel, and anyone else who believed in Jehovah. The men of our guard stared at the ground, understanding the love of Jehovah was all that stood between them and the fury of these hateful men.

We were concerned as well, because we needed to return home as soon as we could to assist in the harvest.

When we rode down into Home Valley, Enoch stood with his grandparents. Mama Vida pointed toward us.

Enoch turned and ran to us, into our arms.

"M-m-mama! P-p-papa! Y-y-you arrived in time." Enoch said.

"What is going on? We were only told to come here by tomorrow," Jared said.

"Y-y-you w-w-will n-n-never b-b-believe what has h-h-happened to me," Enoch said.

Enoch shared the experience he had on the road. As he journeyed to Home Valley, Jehovah spoke with him. He told Enoch that he needed to go to see his Grandpapa Adam. There was something he would do for him.

"H-h-he said I had been o-o-obedient. Grandpapa is o-o-ordaining me to be a High Priest tomorrow."

Jared and I threw our arms around him.

"Congratulations!" Jared said.

I squealed and hugged him close. "I knew you would be the one. I hoped from the time I first felt you move inside my belly."

"M-m-mama," Enoch said. His face reddened.

I sat with the women, all grandmothers of our young son while Grandpapa Adam and Enoch performed the sacred sacrifice on the hill. We then sat together in the tabernacle while Adam, Seth, Enos and Cainan set their hands on his head. Adam gave our son a most sacred and beautiful blessing.

Jared held my hand, squeezing it. I glanced into his face. None of the pain I felt in his squeeze showed on his face. I glanced at Papa Maha. He, too, smiled while squeezing Mama Vida's hand.

Although we were filled with joy and excitement that our son had been chosen at a young age, we wondered why Jared and Mahalaleel had been passed over.

After they finished, Grandpapa Adam asked Enoch to speak to us.

I sucked in a breath, knowing how much he stuttered. How would he find the courage to speak to so many people?

"I-I-I am but a l-l-lad, n-n-not old enough to be tr-tr-trusted with such a h-h-high and h-h-holy calling. I am slow of sp-sp-speech, as you can h-h-hear. St-st-still," he took a deep breath, "Jehovah has c-c-called me to pr-pr-preach the g-g-gospel. I w-w-will do this. I love Jehovah. He is m-m-my Savior and Redeemer."

Tears filled my eyes. Enoch spoke more words then than he had spoken to me, or a group, ever.

I gazed around the group of loving grandpapas and grand-mamas. None had dry eyes. They accepted him, even with his stutter. If Jehovah could accept my Enoch, I could. And so could the others.

When Enoch left the following morning, he traveled alone. Grandpapa Enos asked "Where do you plan to go first?"

"I h-h-have no idea. I will f-f-follow the S-s-spirit of Jeho-vah, t-t-traveling and t-t-teaching where he s-s-sends me."

"What will be your message?" Grandpapa Seth asked.

"I h-h-have been c-c-called to p-p-preach repentance. I choose to f-f-follow Jehovah this day and always."

"May He bless your efforts," Grandpapa Adam said. "There is much too much sin and evil in our world. I pray Je-hovah will protect you and bless your work."

Enoch lifted a pack to his back and walked up the hill and out of Home Valley.

"Jehovah will provide for his needs," Grandpapa Seth said.

"We told him to stop by our homes as he passed," Papa Mahalaleel said. "Every teacher needs to know there is one place of refuge from the storm."

"He is always welcome home," I murmured.

Grandmama patted my hand. "Of course, he is."

We left for home shortly after Enoch left. We had a harvest to help with and other children who needed our help.

Jared sighed more than usual in our travels. I would glance at him, but he had his head down, staring at the dirt.

After many of these sighs, I rode close to him and asked, "Jared, what is the problem?"

"You will think I am small and petty," he mumbled.

I brought my horse closer to his and touched his arm. "I will never think of you as small and petty. You are the best man I know and love. Is it that you have been passed over?"

"I try to do everything Jehovah asks of me. I should be happy for Enoch. I am. It is just ..."

"It is a patriarchal order, and two of Enoch's papas have been skipped. It hurts that you are one?"

"Yes. It should not. But it does. I do not know how Papa does it. He should have been ordained many years ago."

"You do not know that he is not feeling as bad as you."

"He did not show any sorrow."

"Nor did you until after we left. Lift up your head. We ride through beautiful country. But it is dangerous. We need your help watching for problems."

He touched my knee. "I am sorry. You should not have to carry the weight of looking for danger while I act like a baby."

I laughed. "I do not see a baby. I see a man of God who wants to do what is right. Jehovah sees it. He will bless you for it."

"Do you think so?" Jared's voice lifted, no longer sounding dejected.

"I do."

~ ~ ~

Jared and I were kept busy with our children and grandchildren. He continued to travel to teach of Jehovah.

Enoch returned to Aenon and married Zehira. Her papa and mama fought the wedding, but they could not deny her the opportunity to be married to a prophet of Jehovah.

Enoch truly loved Zehira. Her twisted foot did not stop him from wanting her as his wife. He saw past the disability and saw the beauty of her soul.

She traveled often in those first few years of their marriage. We gave Enoch two horses to carry him and Zehira from place to place, along with a mule to carry their supplies.

Because of her limp and inability to walk without a crutch, she did not travel as often with him as I had with Jared, after children came into their family.

We brought her into our home some of the time when Enoch left. Most often, however, her parents insisted that she stay with them. They still saw her as their useless slave. I wanted to go shout at them, but Jared reminded me shouting would not help Zehira.

Mele and Hadar lived in the village for a few more years. Although Mele and Zehira had been close friends, after Mele's marriage to Hadar, they were no longer close. Perhaps they could not be close, for Hadar continued to mock Zehira and badger her and Enoch.

I understood Enoch's gentle nature, but I could not understand that he did not stand up to his brother. One day he would, and Hadar would pay for his crimes.

Life continued for us. Jared taught those in the village, his grandchildren, and worked in the fields when not teaching in other communities. I cared for grandchildren when their mothers went to the fields. I spun and wove, made clay pots, and the many other tasks of women. We were busy.

One evening, a knock on the door surprised us. When I opened the door, Grandpapa Adam stood there. We did not expect him. I looked out past him, searching for Grandmama Eve or his guards.

"I came alone, Helsa," Grandpapa Adam said. "Is Jared home?"

"He is. We were sitting down for an evening meal. Come in. Join us."

Grandpapa Adam smiled. "I would like to break my fast with you. I miss a woman's cooking."

He followed me into the kitchen.

"Jared," I said. "We have company."

"Who?" he looked up, then stood up so fast his chair almost tipped over. "Grandpapa Adam!" he said catching his chair. "I did not expect to see you here. Why?"

I set another plate, cup, and spoon on the table for Grandpapa while he and Jared embraced.

Grandpapa sat down in the chair and smiled at us. "Can a grandpapa not come visit a grandchild without question?"

Jared sat and ducked his head. "Yes. It is unusual that you would come." He lifted a shoulder in a small shrug.

"I did not leave home expecting to come visit Aenon. You have done an excellent job serving Jehovah here, teaching His word and helping others to obey. I can spend my time where I am needed in other parts of the land."

I dished food into Grandpapa's and Jared's plates. We held hands and Jared offered a prayer, asking Jehovah to bless our food.

As we ate, Grandpapa told us of his adventures in his travels toward Aenon. Men tried to capture him, but he managed to escape their trap.

"It happens often when I travel. I try not to tell Eve, for she would worry even more. I must depend on Jehovah to protect me. We both know He will."

Jared sat still, his spoon in the air. He turned to Grandpapa. "I have had similar experiences when I leave Aenon. I try not to travel alone, but sometimes I must. I always know I have been protected."

Grandpapa nodded. He looked at me and set his spoon down. "I must tell you my purpose in coming to Aenon tonight."

We nodded. I knew Grandpapa had more on his mind than a visit.

"I heard from Jehovah on my ride here. I planned to turn toward Shulon and ride farther southwest, but near the turn to Aenon I heard from Jehovah. He told me to come here to see you."

I sat still, afraid they would remember I was in the room and send me away.

"What have I done to attract the attention of Jehovah?" Jared asked.

Grandpapa leaned forward and took his hands. "You have been patient in your trials. You have been obedient as you continue to travel and teach those around Aenon of Jehovah's laws and blessings. You have been a loving husband and father. Not all men can say that."

"It is good to know Jehovah has seen this. I always try to be obedient." Jared glanced up and over toward me, lifting his eyebrows.

"Jehovah has watched you, son. You have supported your son in his new responsibilities. We will want to talk about Enoch later. But now, you need to know, I am to ordain you as a High Priest. You," he turned toward me, "and you, Helsa, are to come to Home Valley in three months. That should give you time to plant your fields before you travel. Jehovah knows you must care for your children and grandchildren."

My hand crept across the table toward Jared's. He trapped it in his big hand and squeezed.

"What I am telling you, Jared," Grandpapa continued, "is your life will change after you come to Home Valley in three months."

"High Priest," Jared breathed. "I feared I had not obeyed well enough."

"Who knows why Jehovah does things? He does His will in His time." Grandpapa picked up his spoon and brought another bite of food to his mouth. "Great food, Helsa. You are a wonderful cook."

We spent much of that evening visiting with Adam. Long after he retired to our guest room, Jared and I spoke of the changes that would now affect our lives.

Jared would travel more. I could travel with him as could others of our sons and other young men who need to learn more about Jehovah.

"Will others seek to hurt you, or … me?" I asked.

"The Destroyer has always done all he could to destroy Father's plan. He will do what he can to make our life difficult."

"I feared that. Will we need to protect our home?"

"I doubt that. We can depend on Jehovah, as we always have. He has protected us through the years."

I leaned into Jared's chest, enjoying his stroking his hands through my hair.

Chapter 5

Capture

L ife after Jared's ordination was much like Enoch's and the others we had witnessed. It changed our lives. We spent more time traveling to lands I never thought to see. We traveled far to the west and south, teaching the family of Adam about Jehovah.

Jared listened to Jehovah. Many times, as we considered taking a route or entering a village, we were warned not to follow the path. We were always protected when we listened.

Rarely, however, we were not warned. We walked into a village filled with huge men who called their land Coos. They welcomed us into their village and listened to the words taught by Jared.

"We have found a people who were prepared to hear of Jehovah," Jared said as we prepared for the night.

"That is nice. It will be good to stay in one place for a time." I lay down next to Jared in the large bed we were provided.

During the night, a hand clamped across my mouth. My eyes opened wide. I could see nothing in the darkness.

More than one pair of hands carried me from the room outside. I could see stars shining above us and felt a breeze on my face and bare feet. No sound was made and I could not shout through the hand covering my mouth.

I heard a door open. The hands set me down in a dark place. Shock ran through my body when I realized they had not hurt me, had not tied nor gagged me. They closed the door, shutting out all light.

I felt along the door, seeking a handle and a way out. I found no door.

I tried pounding on the wall and shouting. No one responded.

I shouted until my throat hurt. What now?

A lump filled my throat, making it difficult to breathe. What did these people want from me? What were they going to do to Jared?

I huddled next to the wall, hoping someone would help me escape. *Please, Jehovah, help me escape this prison. Protect Jared from these wicked men.*

The cold, dark room chilled me, but I needed to know where I was. I stood and held my arms out in front of me. Moving them around, I found the wall.

I took careful steps along the wall, touching it with one hand so I would not get lost in the darkness. I stumbled over a bag, scraping my bare foot. I bent over and felt the bag. Peas, or beans filled it.

I carefully went around the bag and bumped into something cold. I touched it. Cold, almost like a body. It swung away from me.

My scream echoed around me.

Would they keep their dead with their beans?

It made no sense. I touched the hanging body, feeling along its shape until I reached the opening where the guts and heart had been removed.

Gasping, I forced my hands to follow the body down to where the legs should be. Short and thick. In the front of the body, not along the sides like a human.

I moved my hands along the body upward until I reached what should be the arms. Short and fat, like the legs. These, too, attached to the body along the front, not on the sides as a person's arms would be.

I stood gazing in the dark toward the body in the cold storage room. This must be a deer.

Breath whooshed out of me in relief.

I knew where I was and why I was so cold. I did not yet know why my captors had taken me from Jared.

I pushed on around the room, careful to scoot my feet slowly forward along the floor to avoid tripping and scraping them. I could smell the food in the room. Perhaps I could find something to eat.

I pulled a tuber from a basket, carrying it with me. I did not want to eat a raw tuber, but it would be better than nothing. I brought it to my nose and smelled the earthy soil clinging to it.

I moved on around the room, hoping I could find the space near the door I had not found yet, again. My feet bumped into another basket. I groped in the dark until I reached into the basket. Round, knobby fruits filled it. I lifted one out and smelled it. A pear. That would quench my thirst better than the tuber. I took two.

I made my way past barrels, baskets, and bags, trying not to think of the hanging animals in the center. I plucked a plum and an apple from the baskets as I discovered them.

At last, I found the open area. I felt along the wall and found a crack that identified the door. I sighed in relief. I knew there had to be a door.

I moved to the side and leaned against the wall and munched on a pear, its sweet juiciness dripping down my arms.

I had warmed with my movement. However, as I stood still, the chill of the room seeped into me. I slid down and sat on the floor with my arms wrapped around my legs. I had on a thin night robe for sleeping. It would not protect me from this cold.

As I sat with my arms around me, struggling to get warm, I fell asleep, waiting and hoping for rescue. Certainly, Jehovah would hear my plea?

The fruit I had not yet eaten rolled unseen from my lap onto the floor while I slept.

~ ~ ~

A beam of light woke me. The door had cracked open. I gazed at a skirt, then lifted my eyes to look into the eyes of a girl.

"You must come with me," she whispered.

I tried to push upward, but my knees would not move in the cold. "I cannot stand," I whimpered.

A hand reached in for mine. "Take my hand. I will help you."

I did not know who helped me. I did not care. I would be released from the bone chilling cold of the cold storage room. I took her hand and allowed her to tug me to my feet.

"Come quickly," she urged in a low voice. "If I am caught helping you, I will be switched."

I nodded and shuffled my feet forward faster. The movement helped to warm them. Soon I could walk without shuffling.

She turned a corner, staying close to a wall, then turned at another. I followed as quickly as I could along the rough path with my bare feet.

"Where are you taking me?" I whispered.

"Out of the village. The priest wants to offer you to his god. I do not think Jehovah would like that."

I stopped. "You believe?"

"Yes. I am among the few who believe Jehovah. Most here believe Asharat can bring them wealth. I want only the peace Jehovah brings."

"And this Priest of Asharat wants to …?" I gulped.

"Sacrifice you. He thinks that will keep your Jared, and all the other prophets of Jehovah far from Coos."

"He is correct in thinking that. Or, it would bring my sons and grandsons and all their cousins in righteous indignation to avenge my death."

The girl tugged on my arm. "That would not be good for your sons. We must go quickly. I will get you out of our village."

"How will I find Jared?"

"I do not know. I only know you must be gone before the sun reaches the tops of the trees, or we will both suffer."

I followed her through the early morning light, turning first to the left and then to the right again and again until I felt certain she would lead me back to the priest.

At last, we reached the wall surrounding the village. She touched a place on the wall, and a small door opened. She stooped to pass through the door. I ducked my head but could have stood straight. This young girl stood taller than I did, and I had not been considered a tiny woman.

She pushed the door closed behind me, then hurried across the open space toward the forest beyond. I pulled up the skirts of my night robe and pumped my legs into a run to follow her. I waited for a shout from the wall, calling us back. I cringed from the expected arrows.

At last, we reached the edge of the forest. I followed her down a narrow track, trying not to stop and rub my sore feet. She stepped off the path and disappeared.

I stepped to the place on the path where she left it and saw nothing but bushes. Her hand reached out and took my arm.

"In here," she hissed and pulled me forward.

I stumbled forward, expecting to be scratched by the brambles. I found myself in a small clearing. A huge rock stood on the other side of the clearing. A stream trickled through the center.

Before I could enjoy the warmth of the sun shining on my arms, she led me forward, jumping across the stream and to the side of the rock. A small cave had been worn away, big enough for me to sit in.

"It will keep you dry if it rains," she said.

"How long do I stay here?" I glanced wildly around the small clearing.

"Until your Jared finds you."

"Can he?" Fear tore at my soul.

"Jehovah will lead him to you."

Would He? *Oh, Jehovah! Keep Jared safe. Bring him to me.*

The girl moved into the trees and disappeared. I was alone. I remembered the pears, plum, and apple I had grabbed the night before. Where had I put them?

I glanced down. I wore my night robe, not a dress. I did not have my pocket. It lay by the bed with my dress and shoes. And the food lay on the floor of the cold storage room where I had been sitting.

I sat in the grass and rubbed my feet. I picked them up and rubbed the bottoms. Small stones had embedded in them. I brushed them away, expecting to find bloody feet. They were unmarred by cuts or bruises.

I sighed. *Thank you, Jehovah. Please help get Jared free and help him find me.*

I walked to the small stream and sat next to it, letting my feet dangle in the water. The cool water soothed my sore feet. When I started to shiver, I moved back to sit beside the rock once more.

I leaned back against the rock and closed my eyes, soaking in the sun. I finally got warm and moved from the sun into the shade of a tree.

I could only wait and pray that Jehovah would bring Jared to me. I had slept little in the cold storage room the night before, and found my eyes closing in the warmth.

Men woke me as they walked past my hidden glade along the path. Their noisy steps made me think they were from Coos. "Woman? Woman?" they called. Their voices confirmed my suspicion. Men from Coos.

I ducked around the edge of the rock. I did not want them to see me through the bushes.

I did not have to worry, for they did not push through the brambles. After many breaths, they had passed by my hiding place.

I slumped to the ground and sat with my back against the rock. How would Jared find me?

When I woke again hungry and thirsty, the sun had moved more than a hand span across the sky, standing high over my head. I walked to the stream and knelt next to it, scooping water into my hands for a drink. Jared had taught me to be wary, especially when we were in danger.

No one saw me now, but that did not mean they would not return and find me.

After drinking, I wandered to the trees, hoping to find a fruit tree among them. Cherries and plums filled the lower branches. Birds had eaten the fruit on the higher branches. I did not mind, for I had no way to reach those.

I plucked some fruit from the trees and sunk my teeth into a plum. Ah. So good, especially to one as hungry as I was.

I threw away the pit and popped some cherries into my mouth. Their sweetness filled me.

After eating the juicy cherries, I went to the stream once more and washed their stickiness from my face. For now, I would not hunger or thirst, but I needed Jared. I needed coverings for my feet and a way to go home.

I set on a rock close to the trees and let the tears fall down my face. I was alone. How could I find my husband and family? How would I get home?

Tears fell for many long breaths.

~ ~ ~

The clopping feet of horses on the other side of the small clearing echoed through the brambles, bringing me to my feet.

The horses stopped moving. I glanced at my feet. I had nothing with which to defend myself, not even a stick.

I bent to pluck smooth pebbles from the stream. My aim had not been tested in many years, but there was a time I could hit a wolf in the head. Perhaps I could still hit a man.

A rustling in the bushes encouraged me to choose a stone and prepare to throw it. A man backed through the brambles. I lifted my front arm to help aim and began my throwing arc. And then he turned.

Jared.

My hands dropped the stones. The one on its way toward him flew high over his head.

"Helsa!" he cried. "They told me to ride into the forest until I saw a huge banyon tree. Take five steps forward and turn off the path to the right through the bushes. I would find you."

"And you did!" I hurried to him and fell on his neck, the tears from earlier finding new strength.

He held me close to him. "And, I did." He ran his hand through the back of my hair. "You are here, like Paco said."

"Who is Paco?"

"One of the few who believe in Jehovah. His daughter led you here. He said the priest wanted to offer you to their god, Asharat, as a sacrifice."

"That is what the girl who helped me escape the cold storage room said. She said I did not have much time."

Jared glanced down and saw my bare feet. "Your feet! Where are your foot coverings?"

"With my other clothing, in the room where we slept last night, or where we began to sleep."

"I woke early and reached out for you. You were gone. At first, I believed you had gone to help the women. Then I saw your clothing on the floor where you left it last night. I knew you would not leave your clothing to help other women."

"No. I would not leave my clothing and shoes behind," I agreed.

"Paco found me shortly after that. He told me his daughter had rescued you. I had to go with him to the sanctuary. The priest wanted me to see his sacrifice."

Jared pulled me into another embrace and kissed me. "He wanted me to watch him sacrifice ... you. He ..." Jared's tears dampened my hair.

"He did not have me. He could not sacrifice me."

"No." Jared took a step backward. "Paco and his daughter packed our things and set them on the pack mule. All had been prepared for me to leave. I had to wait while the priest ranted at the loss of his sacrifice. He sent men away to look for you." He pushed a lock of my hair back and brushed his fingers across my face.

I reached up and caught his hand in mine. "I heard horses pass by on the path. No one stopped. They must not have known about this clearing."

"No. They must not have." His warm arms encircled me, warming me in a way the sun could not.

"How did you escape the priest?"

"In his anger, the priest shouted at his men when they did not find you. Men were scurrying away from him. I stepped back. Paco wrapped a cloak around me and led me to our horses. He gave me hurried directions to your hiding place and shoved me out the back gate."

I kissed his hand. "I knew you would find me. I asked Jehovah to protect you and bring you to me. He did."

"Come with me. We must leave this land before the priest's people find us."

I lifted my feet. "Did you bring my foot coverings?"

"We will need to check the pack for your foot coverings and your clothes. You need more to protect you than that thin night robe."

I glanced down at the robe. "No. It does little to protect me from the cold."

"Wait here," Jared instructed. He disappeared through the bushes, returning not many breaths later leading the two horses and the pack mule.

He opened the pack and set it on the ground. I dug into it and found a clean dress and foot coverings. I pulled them on and sighed.

Jared tied the pack once more and lifted it onto the mule's back. He then helped me mount my red mare, Pepper's Daughter, and led the way from the small clearing through the brambles.

We rode many spans before we reached the safety of one of Jared's friends. I examined my arms and legs, expecting to find scratches from the brambles.

There were none. Once more, Jehovah blessed me.

Chapter 6

Priesthood

We returned to Aenon as often as we could, often staying there during the rain times. Sometimes, we found refuge in a village when we were caught in early rains. We were blessed to find safe refuges in those years. Most years, however, we returned to the peace of Aenon.

News of Enoch filled the land. He had defied armies of attackers who struggled to take him. Most of his attackers wanted to kill him. Whirlwinds blew them away.

We heard news of Enoch and the city he built. We heard its beauty could not be surpassed. Better still, Jehovah walked among the residents there.

Another story reached us. An army arrived at the gates of Enoch's city, Zion. He stood outside the gate and prayed. The top of a nearby mountain lifted and landed on the army, stopping the attack.

We were called to Home Valley to witness the ordaining of Enoch's son, Methuselah, to the High Priesthood. All the other high priests joined us there, as did Jared's Papa and Mama, Mahalaleel and Vida, for the quiet celebration.

I watched Papa Maha join in congratulating his grandson who received something he had not yet received himself. A sadness surrounded him. Although to see it, I had to watch him closely. As an honorable man, he rarely shows his true feelings, especially when he is sad or hurt.

Jared spoke softly to him when they were alone. I do not know what they said, but I know Jared understood his papa's concerns. It had to be hard to be passed over for a grandson, yet again.

When we left Home Valley, we traveled a short time with Enoch and Maha and their wives before we turned west toward Aenon.

Enoch told stories of the Coos giants attacking him. The people of Coos had become so large they were called giants. The girl from Coos who saved me years ago, though less than twelve, stood much taller than me. I understood them being called giants.

"What I do not understand," I said, "is why they continue to be so antagonistic toward Jehovah's prophets. All the prophets want to do is to help Adam's children to find the happiness available only through obedience."

"It makes no sense to me," Mama Vida answered. "We do not want to hurt them. We want them to be happy."

"I fear for my husband sometimes," Zehira added.

"Jehovah protects us," Jared said.

"He does," Enoch agreed. "I have been in places where I could not survive on my own. There have been too many times with too many enemies who wanted to take my life, surrounding me. I live because Jehovah protected me."

"We have had similar experiences," I said. "Although we have probably not had as many. Only because of Jehovah's love do we live today."

Mama Vida asked me about the experience. I shared my escape from the Coos giants. Even as I remembered my captivity, I shivered, although rain would not fall for another month and warmth surrounded us.

We separated as the road divided, taking us west to Aenon and the others toward Ziklag and Zion. I missed their company as we made our way home.

"Papa Maha hides his sorrow well," I said. "It must be difficult to see a son and two grandsons receive what you have longed for over the years."

"He has waited many hundred years for that blessing. I pray he will receive it from Grandpapa Adam sometime soon."

"He will have deserved it, when it finally comes. He is a good and honorable man."

Stories of Enoch's teachings and his city came to us from visitors and when we traveled to teach. Each time, the stories seemed too wild to be believed. But as we considered Enoch and his absolute trust in Jehovah, we knew they were true.

While Enoch built his city, Zehira returned to stay in Aenon. Her parents insisted that she and her children return to their home, often insisting that they provide unwilling and unappreciated assistance. Many times Zehira found her way to our home when she could no longer accept the abuses heaped on her and her children.

We tried to convince her to come to our home to stay, but she never had the strength to argue with her parents. Then Enoch came for her.

We were home when he dragged her and the younger children from her parents' home. They had heaped accusations and fear on both her and her young children.

We provided them with a cart to ride in and a pair of oxen to pull it. Her surprise filled us with joy.

We later learned that the journey to Zion had been disrupted by men who pretended to be Enoch's friends. They took him away, supposedly to help others in need, then robbed Zehira of her little cart.

We sighed in relief when we received word from Methuselah that his mother had finally arrived in Zion safely, much later than we expected. Zehira proved to be stronger than any believed, especially her parents.

Our lives continued. We loved our children and grandchildren and visited with those who accepted Jehovah's word as Jared taught, helping them to remember the covenants made.

We trusted Jehovah's protection in our travels. He always kept us safe. We did not return to Laish as often as I hoped, but we did return home as often as we could.

Mama always greeted us warmly with food and her love. She always exclaimed her pleasure that we had returned. In return, I welcomed home all my children who had left Aenon for a different life as I had left Laish so many years ago.

Finally, after much longer than anyone expected, we were called to Home Valley once more. Papa Mahalaleel waited with Grandpapa for all the prophets to arrive.

When he joined with Jared and Seth in offering the sacrifice, I glanced toward Mama Vida. She smiled through her tears. At last, Papa Maha would receive the gift and responsibility of the Holy Priesthood.

All the current prophets set their hands on his head and Grandpapa Adam spoke the words giving him the Priesthood and responsibility, then blessing him with power and love for his brothers and sisters. After Grandpapa Adam said the final amen, I opened my eyes to see Papa Maha staring into Mama Vida's eyes. The love between them evident for all to see.

I gave him my love and congratulations, knowing that the gift would change his life more than he and Mama Vida ever expected.

~ ~ ~

Men tell their stories. They will focus on the hunt, the teaching, and the other activities of men.

Women's stories are different. We care about our families, our husbands, our God.

I was there at the Great Family Conference in Home Valley when Grandpapa Adam received the blessings and love of Jehovah. He also offered blessings for each member of his huge family. In his old age, it took many days to provide these blessings to all who came for the event.

While the men carried on with men's discussions, Grandmama Eve and two others of the matriarchs shared their stories with the women.

I knew it must have been difficult to be alone in the world, but Eve's story sobered me. I had not had to bring babies into the world without another woman who knew about birthing babies. I had fire and a home and other supplies that she had to learn to build or create.

Ganet had to deal with giant serpents and men who wanted her as only a husband should. Her strength awed me. How could she find forgiveness within her for that foul man?

Rebecca's story on the third day left me sitting in tears. How could she continue with such courage and grace after losing her children to who knew who? Where were those children? I had not lost children to thieves, slavery, or some other horror. Mine had chosen to follow the Destroyer, as had many of all my grandmamas. It was our common sorrow.

After they shared their stories, they counseled those of us who were wives of prophets to write our stories for the other women of this world. Perhaps we can make a difference. Perhaps we can help postpone the wickedness. I do not know.

My story is not exciting like those of Eve, Ganet, or Rebecca. I have never encountered the serpent that follows the Destroyer. My children have not all been obedient.

I do not know if my story will help another woman. However, Grandmama Eve recommended that we write the story of our lives. I try to be obedient. This has been my attempt to do that.

Helsa, Wife of Jared

PART FOUR

Qutarah

Chapter 1

Baptism

I could not believe Methuselah wanted to spend time with me, Qutarah, a woman from tiny Shule.

While the great Enoch taught our village of Jehovah's love, a boy, not much older than me, ambled to the back where I stood and whispered to me. I tried to ignore him.

When he leaned close to whisper once more, I responded. "I do not know who you are, but I am trying to listen. This man," I nodded toward the front of the room, "came a long way to speak to us. I want to hear what he has to say."

"Yes, Enoch did come from a long way off. We left Aenon three weeks ago."

"You came with him?" I whispered without turning my head.

"I am Methuselah. He brings me with him, sometimes, when he travels to teach. He is teaching me to be like him."

"Does he teach you to visit with girls while he teaches?" I turned and stared at him.

His mouth popped shut and he turned to listen to his papa. Good. I wanted to hear.

When he finished speaking, men and women hurried forward to speak with Enoch. I joined the throng. His words filled me with warmth and my spine tingled. It felt strange to have both reactions racing through me.

The boy who said he came with Enoch pushed up close behind me.

I twirled around. "Back off. Have you never heard that women do not like to be crowded?"

He stepped back a step. "No. I thought women liked a man to come close to them."

"You thought wrong." I growled and stepped forward another step.

The boy stepped behind me. "Forgive me. I did not know."

We neared the place where Enoch stood.

"I forgive you but be quiet. I want to think about what I will say," I hissed.

When we reached Enoch, he stepped forward and put an arm around the boy. "I see you met my son, Methuselah."

"He said he came with you. He did not say he is your son," I said, glancing at him.

He lifted a shoulder in a small shrug. "I said I came with him. I thought she would see how I resemble you, Papa."

"I wanted to hear the things you said, Enoch. I did not want to hear his whisperings."

Enoch smiled. "What did you think of my words?"

"They filled me with a hope I have not had before."

"Good." Enoch's smile lifted. "And, do you have a desire to be baptized."

"I do. When can I be baptized?"

"We will see if there are others who seek baptism. If there are, we will do it soon. Maybe tomorrow."

I thanked him and returned to my home. Mama and Papa had many of the same reactions as I did. They, too, wished for baptism. We discussed the message brought by Enoch long into the night.

The next morning, I went with my parents to hear the word of Enoch once more. Those words filled me with the certainty that I needed baptism.

Others in the village agreed with our family. Enoch baptized us that afternoon in the pond near the edge of Shule.

I came out of the water feeling clean and pure. Enoch wrapped his arms around me and hugged me, as he did all those he baptized.

"Welcome to the faith," he said.

I waded out of the water into my papa's arms, who, with Mama had preceded me into the water. He twirled me around into Mama's arms who had a blanket to dry me.

"We are true Sons and Daughters of Adam," Mama said, hugging me.

Methuselah stepped close to us and poked his hand out toward me. I glanced at Mama. When she nodded, I held out mine. I did not know what to expect.

He took it and bowed over it. "Welcome to the family of Jehovah," he said.

Later, when everyone had dressed in dry clothing, we sat together in the village gathering room. There, Enoch lay his hands on our heads, one at a time, and blessed us to remember the covenant we had made. My soul felt on fire with the love of Jehovah as he lifted his hands from my head. I slowly moved to my seat next to Mama and listened as the others received their blessing.

I knew I had done the right thing, and I knew that Jehovah knew that I knew. I would never deny my faith.

Methuselah came to sit next to me. I smiled at him. How could I frown when such joy filled me?

"You know my name," he whispered. "I do not know yours."

"Qutarah," I whispered back.

He took my hand and kissed the back of it. When he let go, I stared at the spot. Boys could be so strange.

In the following days, Methuselah found me when I went out for water and carried my urn home for me. Often, when I walked outside, Methuselah waited on the path outside our front gate and walked with me.

Papa laughed at my complaints and told me to enjoy his attention. "Perhaps it will help the other young men of Shule to see you as marriageable."

I frowned at him. "I do not need that —"

"Do you have young men begging me to accept him as your husband? I see none."

"How many young men joined us in baptism? Do you really think they will allow me to serve Jehovah?" My voice dropped in volume and tone.

"Enjoy his attention, Qutarah," Papa said. "You may not receive more like it after he leaves."

I left through the kitchen door, Papa's taunts ringing in my ears. I refused to allow him to see the tears he caused.

Had he really believed the words Enoch taught? What happened to treating your wife and daughters with kindness and dignity? If Papa heard it, he forgot those words already.

I sat under a tree and quietly sobbed. What hurt most was that he was right. No unmarried young men found their way to the pond where we were baptized. And no young men were begging Papa to give me to them as a wife. What would I do?

~ ~ ~

A year later, Enoch returned to Shule. Once more, he brought with him his son, Methuselah, and two other young men.

Once again, I sat on the edge of the crowd to listen to him speak. The spark of faith he had lit the year earlier grew larger with each word until it glowed within my heart like the fire in Mama's kitchen.

Methuselah found me, once more.

"Why do you follow me around?" I asked. "I am still the ugly, too large girl no man wants."

"What are you saying?" Methuselah asked. "You are beautiful with your tawny hair and golden eyes. I have seen no other woman like you."

My hand strayed up to brush my hair off my face.

"Little things like that. You are more graceful than many more petite women. How can you not know of your beauty?"

I bowed my head. "Not even my father sees beauty in me," I murmured.

"What?" Methuselah cried. "How can this be?"

"All my friends are married. I have never had any man show interest in me. None have asked my papa to marry me."

"None?"

"Do I look like a married woman to you?" I asked.

"No. I see nothing that would mark you as married ..."

"Because no one is interested in me." My voice lifted. "Do you intend to increase my shame?"

"No, Qutarah. I ... I could not forget your face, your hair, your eyes. They filled my dreams at night and during the day. Your musical voice echoed in my memory. I begged Papa to return here. I wanted to see you once more."

"You have seen me," I whispered. "Now what?"

"I am still overwhelmed by you, Qutarah. Will you marry me?"

"You jest. I told you, no man wants me. Do not say things that will make me cry when you leave."

"I do not expect to leave this town alone again."

"You will leave with your papa and his friends. You will not be alone. You do not even know what it is like to be alone."

"No. I do not know your loneliness, but I do know what it is like to miss you." He took my hand and gazed into my eyes with his dark brown eyes. "Qutarah, will you marry me?" he repeated.

"You mock me."

"No. I am honest in my feelings for you. I want you to be my wife. Please?" His eyes softened with the plea.

"You want ... me?"

"May I speak with your papa?"

"You need to know," I sucked my lip in and chewed on it. "Papa does not live like a believer. He is an unhappy man who spends too much time drinking his wine."

"Another reason for me to take you away from here. May I ask him?"

"He will want a bride price. Will that be a problem for you?"

Methuselah touched the pocket that hung over his shoulder. "I have no land to give him. I live far away. I brought an extra horse from Aenon, one I raised to give to your papa. And," he licked his lips, "I sold a horse and brought the coins. I feared your papa would want a bride price."

"You came planning to ask me to be your wife?" My heart raced and my stomach churned. I never expected this to happen to me.

"I did. I told you I persuaded Papa to return … because I wanted to see you once more, to ask you to be my wife."

"Are there no girls to marry in Aenon?"

"None like you, Qutarah. None like you."

"What does your papa think of this?" I demanded.

"He approves. He remembers you sitting on the edge of the crowd listening intently to his words. You do believe the words he spoke?" Methuselah became suddenly serious.

"I do."

"Papa brought me with him here, knowing what I planned. He will accept you."

As expected, Papa demanded a high bride price for me, saying he would miss the labor I provided to him and Mama. He took both the horse and all the coins Methuselah brought with him.

Enoch performed the rite that married us before we left Shule, reminding us we would want to travel to Home Valley soon to have Grandpapa Adam bless our marriage.

"I cannot say the words he will use, but it will bring you great joy," he told us.

Mama bid me a tearful farewell. Papa stood outside the door with arms folded and a scowl on his face. He did not lift a hand to bid me goodbye.

I left Shule with Methuselah, Enoch, and the two young men who came with them, riding behind Methuselah on his horse.

"I do not understand your papa's lack of faith. He heard nothing of what I said about caring for his women," Papa Enoch said. "I am happy you are now a part of our family."

"I am happy she chose to be my wife," Methuselah said. "I knew I needed to come rescue her. I love her."

I squeezed Methuselah from behind. He took my hand in his and kissed it.

I felt a love I had never experienced before from my parents. I lay my head against his back and enjoyed the rocking of the horse in the warm sunshine. Life with Methuselah had to be better than life with my papa.

I still had no idea what this tall, strong man saw in me. For the time, I was grateful he took me away from Papa and his meanness.

We lived in Aenon near Enoch's parents, Grandmama Helsa and Grandpapa Jared for the first few years of our marriage, when we were not traveling together to teach. Grandmama Helsa accepted me, as she did all the other children and grandchildren who came to her door, with open arms.

From her I learned to stand up for myself.

"You must not always give in to your husband," she told me. "They like a little mystery, a little challenge from the woman they love. Methuselah told me that you told him to be quiet that first time he saw you. That drew him to you."

"My rudeness?" I struggled to believe she understood.

"Yes. He liked that you cared enough for yourself and for Enoch that you told him to be quiet. I see that your papa has treated you badly. It leaves you afraid to stand up for yourself, but you must, if you want to keep Methuselah home more than gone."

"I listen to what Methuselah wants and obey. Is that not what women are expected to do?"

"Perhaps in some villages. Those whose men listen to the words of the Destroyer. I thought many in Shule accepted Enoch's teachings."

"Many did, especially the women. But when Enoch left, they forgot. Men gathered and remembered how nice it was when women obeyed them. They began to insist we bow to their every desire."

"That must have been hard."

"It confused me. I felt Jehovah's presence that day when Enoch baptized me. I felt his love. I thought the others of my family and village did the same. Apparently, they did not." I sighed.

"How did you manage?" Helsa set her hand on mine. "It must have been difficult."

"I remembered everything I could that Enoch taught, repeating the words each night and praying to Jehovah in my heart during the day and on my knees at night. I did my best to stay close to the things I remembered."

Helsa leaned forward and touched my knee. "You must remember that Jehovah loves his daughters. He does not approve when men treat women badly."

"I can tell Methuselah I want mutton rather than beef?" I asked.

"Oh, yes, my dear. You can prepare what you like. He will be glad you make those choices for yourself."

I listened to Helsa. Her words made sense.

Methuselah never complained when I chose the meal for the evening, and often asked for my opinion. I struggled to express my opinion, but I learned.

~ ~ ~

Several years after our marriage, I had gained enough confidence to be willing to go with him to Home Valley. There, Grandpapa Adam blessed our marriage with words that could never be repeated, though they were the words he used for every marriage blessing. He told us the words were the same Father used when He married Adam to Eve. The sacred and holy words thrilled within me.

Ours was the last marriage Grandpapa Adam blessed. After us, he gave that responsibility to Grandpapa Seth.

Children came into our home. More may have come sooner, except Methuselah left often with his papa to teach others about Jehovah. Because they had come to our village, I learned of Jehovah and met Methuselah. How could I ask him to stay home with me more?

One day, Methuselah decided we should travel together. I had not traveled often, but the change from being home alone filled me with excitement.

Our three youngest children and I rode in a wagon singing together. A son drove the wagon. We traveled in an open meadow toward a small wood when Methuselah rode his horse over and hushed us.

"Someone or something is in the forest. We need to be quiet for a while." He glanced at each child. "Can you play a game with mama? See who can sit quietly and make no noise. Maybe you can take a little nap? I will have a special story for you all if you can stay quiet."

I sucked in my breath and gazed at him, wanting him to tell us more, but I knew he did not want to frighten the children. "Tell me more when you can." I said in a low voice.

"You know I will." His voice could barely be heard above the sound of the horses.

The little children dropped down into the back of the wagon. I covered them with a blanket. Little giggles floated from the back, so low only I could hear them.

The wheels of the wagon creaked, as they rolled along the hard-packed earthen trail. Horses stirred up dust as they plodded forward. I rubbed my nose, knowing a sneeze would destroy the silence of ... what?

The animals made sounds, the harness squeaked, the wheels creaked. Yet, a bead of silence surrounded us, hiding us from the danger Methuselah recognized. I sensed the human voice would burst the bubble, like a child popping soap bubbles in the bath.

In this eerie silence, we rode without haste through the forest, past a small mob of attackers hidden in a glade, and out the other side, unseen and unheard by others.

I glanced back into the back where the children lay sleeping.

I raised my eyebrows in question at Methuselah.

He shrugged.

Later that night, as we sat in our camp for the night, Methuselah told us a story.

"Your grandpapa, Enoch, faces many enemies as we did today."

"How does he fight them all?" our oldest son, Samoel asked, leaning forward and leaning his elbows on his knees.

"He does not. He depends on Jehovah to protect him, as He protected us this afternoon. You little children slept, but we rode within a silent space. The horses were quiet, but they made sounds. The wagon creaked. The harness grated. Dust stirred up from the horses' feet."

"And still, we passed by our enemies without being seen or heard. They did not know when we passed. I saw them. They did not see us." I added to Methuselah's story. "You saw that, Samoel."

The boy nodded, his mouth dropping open.

"Jehovah created this earth. He can close the eyes and ears of an enemy, allowing us to pass in safety."

Noga inhaled her surprise and put her hand over her mouth. Tamir put his hand in Noga's and crawled into her lap.

"Jehovah loves his children," Methuselah continued. "He only asks that we trust and obey Him as you trusted and obeyed today on the trail. Remember this day. Remember that we were protected against men who wanted to hurt us today. Your memory can help protect you."

"Yes, Papa," Samoel said, looking into his papa's eyes. It was as a covenant for him. His little face glowed in earnest.

"Yes, Papa, I will remember," Noga repeated. She, too, radiated confidence and love for Jehovah and her papa.

"Your mama and I will teach you many things. We want you to trust us as you did today, listen to us, as you did today, and obey Jehovah as you obeyed me this day."

With huge, round eyes, our little sons and daughter nodded, agreeing to always remember.

As the years passed, they would come to me and ask, "Mama, did we really pass by an army who wanted to hurt us that day? I slept. I do not remember seeing them."

"Because you slept, because you obeyed, we passed by them in safety," I would respond. They questioned more, trying to remember the day we were saved.

Shortly after this experience, we found a little village near low hills. The people welcomed us and asked Methuselah to teach them. They gave us a home to live in with a garden and a share of the crops from the fields.

Although the village housed few people, Pisgah became our home. Methuselah returned to Aenon and brought our unmarried children to join us in our new home.

"I did not expect to find a new home," I said when Methuselah returned with our children, "but, I have. The women welcome me and have become my friends. I am happy here."

He pulled me close in an embrace. "I did not expect to find a new home, but this place has been a blessing for both of us."

"And our children. Our little ones have new friends. They stay busy helping me, playing, and learning."

"Jehovah does bless those who love and obey him." Methuselah kissed me. Our little children snickered.

"Mama and Papa are kissing," they sang.

"Yes," I said. "We do that sometimes. I put my arm around Methuselah's neck and pulled him down to kiss once more.

Chapter 2

Pride

Methuselah left us often in the next years. His papa, Enoch, called on him to journey with him to teach. Sometimes his papa and mama needed his assistance in Zion. Other times, he traveled with a son or another young man to teach the people south of us, leaving me alone with our younger children.

I did not fear to be left home alone. We had sons and others who watched the passes into our village. More importantly, I knew Jehovah would protect us.

One day, Methuselah came home from a visit to Zion glowing with excitement.

"You will be interested to hear this, Qutarah," he said, taking my hand and leading me to our favorite seats in the sitting room.

"What did you learn?" I asked as Methuselah's hand warmed mine.

"There have been warnings and blessings given by Jehovah."

"I have heard He is unhappy with this people. Too many listen to the false priests who are supported by the Destroyer."

"He is unhappy with most of the land. However, He is pleased with Papa and the people in his city. He has plans for them."

I leaned close. "What?"

"When all who are righteous are gathered in, they will be taken up to Him."

"All? Does that mean we must move to Zion?"

Methuselah's face fell. The joy became sadness. "I am not allowed to join Papa and Mama in Zion."

"Are we not righteous enough to go with them?"

"It is not that we are not righteous enough, I have been promised that my seed, a son or a grandson, will be the one to carry our generations past a great destruction."

My face crunched together. "I do not understand."

"Jehovah grows angry with this people. When they are full of wickedness, He will wash the earth clean in a flood. It will wash away all life."

"All life? How will a son or grandson carry our generations forward if all life is gone?"

"He will be saved, with a wife, to carry our lineage and our generations into time and a cleansed earth with him."

I began to understand. "A time will come when Zion is taken, and later the earth will be washed clean?"

"It will be as a baptism of the earth," Methuselah said. The joy reappeared. "And we have been chosen to be the ones to bear the one who will survive."

"One of our sons or grandsons?"

He stood and whirled me around the room. "We will be remembered through all time. It is a great blessing."

I nodded. The rest of the story filled me with sorrow. Yes, one would be saved, but how many would be lost in this great baptism? How many of my children and grandchildren would have forgotten Jehovah and be worthy of destruction?

I hid my grief from Methuselah. His contagious joy brought me laughter and love.

Over the next years, Methuselah often shared the promised blessing of his generations with others. I warned him that pride could cause him problems, but he continued to brag that one of our sons or grandsons would be the one to take life into the future.

Within a few short years after this revelation and his bragging, no rain fell on Pisgah nor in the mountains surrounding it. No snow covered the tops of the mountains, promising water in the coming growing season.

I cut back on the food I cooked, giving Methuselah and our two young sons who still lived at home less food in each meal. I ate less than I gave them. Men and children needed more food, not women.

We carried water from the well to drizzle over the few plants that continued to grow. During the hottest of the hot times, the water we carried did not quench the thirst of the few plants in our garden. The stunted vegetables from these plants were bitter and inedible.

Over the next three years, dark, water-filled clouds rolled over our head, promising the needed rain. But none fell on Pisgah or the surrounding hills. Little Andrew and Joel lost the muscle they had developed in their early years.

Toward the end of the three years, I stopped eating every day, eating only one meal every two or three days, so there would be food for Methuselah and the boys.

"Mama, I am hungry," Andrew would whine.

"Me, too," Joel would say. "Can we have more food?"

"There is no more to give you," I said. Their little tears broke my heart, but what could I do? "Would you like a drink?" I asked, motioning toward the urn of water on the shelf.

Andrew nodded and held out his cup. Joel copied his brother.

I poured them each a small cup of water. It would not feed them, but it filled their little tummies.

Methuselah returned from the hills with a small partridge. I cleaned and cooked it and set it on the table. My mouth watered at the fragrance of cooking meat. We had so little of it in the last year.

Methuselah and the other men had killed off the animals a year earlier rather than allow them to die of hunger. The meat from these had been eaten long before. In the last year, we had no meat, only a little grain, and few vegetables.

Methuselah gave the boys each a part of the bird, then gave some to me, taking the smallest part for himself.

I traded with him. "You need more to eat than me."

"No," he said. You have not eaten for three days. If you do not eat, you will be sick. We need you."

"And we need you." I tried to hand the meat back to him.

Methuselah gave me the extra bit of meat. "Eat it. Please."

He stuffed it into my mouth. The meat tasted like ashes.

A knock at our door took me away from the table.

"Qutarah," my neighbor cried. "Is Methuselah here? My daughter lies dying in her bed. Perhaps Methuselah can convince Jehovah to allow her to live."

Methuselah had followed me from the kitchen. "I will go see what I can do."

He left with the woman. When he returned, not many spans later after the boys had gone to bed, tears dripped from his nose and chin.

"Jehovah has deserted me."

"The child?"

"Died."

I sat with my hands over my face and wept.

Other children in Pisgah began to die from lack of food. I went through our small storage of grain. If we ate this, we would have none to plant. If we did not eat it, we would not live to plant even if the rains fell.

Other women in the village had come to the same decision. Our children needed to live.

This was not enough for Andrew and Joel. Their little stomachs distended from the constant hunger. They grew too tired to complain, laying in their beds most of the day.

Methuselah sat beside them, weeping. He bowed his head in prayer. I watched for him to call on Jehovah to save their lives. He did not.

Did he cause this drought and the deaths in our village? Why would he not call on Jehovah to bless us?

Instead, Methuselah turned and left the house. He did not return for three days.

My heart ached as I watched our sons fail. In the time Methuselah was gone, the boys weakened so much they could no longer drink water. I sat between them, dripping water onto their lips. For a time, they opened their lips to accept the water. First Andrew became too weak to even lick the water off his lips. Joel soon weakened like his brother.

I cried as I sat between our sons, working to keep them alive. *Methuselah, where are you? Do not make me do this alone! Come home. Heal my sons. Why have you deserted me?*

Methuselah finally returned in time to watch Andrew gasp his last breath. Little Joel lay in his little bed struggling to breathe. Methuselah knelt between their little bodies and sobbed his sorrow.

I had cried. I thought there were no tears left in me. I was wrong. Tears of sorrow, frustration, and anger washed across my face. *What more could I have done? Why had Methuselah not been able to help our sons?*

"It is my fault... All the deaths are ... my fault." His voice cracked and broke in his grief. His tears covered the faces of our little boys, lying side by side. "I have been prideful, ... bragging that my sons would carry ... the generations past the flooding, into the new world. It ... could have been one of you, had I not been" he gulped, "so prideful. You two, ... and the other children of this village, ... paid for my sins."

He howled out his grief. "I have done this. I am so sorry. Please forgive me."

Joel lifted his hand up to touch his papa's. Methuselah grasped it, bending over the little body, until long after Joel, too, had returned to Jehovah.

"What am I to do, Qutarah?" he wailed.

I pulled him back from the little bodies and wrapped my arms around him, sobbing into his shoulder. I could never tell him of my questions. He had answered them for me. We had lost our little ones and in our shared grief, we became one again.

As we rocked together, we heard rain plopping against our roof.

"Rain?" I asked.

"It began while I prayed. Although Jehovah forgave me of my prideful sins, He did not allow me to keep Andrew and Joel. I was only allowed to be here ... for ... for their final moments on earth."

~ ~ ~

Pisgah survived three years of no rain. Too many of our children and older people died in the drought. We ate too many of our seeds. We had no way of growing more. Perhaps we would have to leave this small village we loved for another.

I stood with other women on the porch to a neighbor's home, discussing our challenge when oxen pulling wagons entered our village.

I ran with the others through the gentle rains to see who would come to visit us in our sorrow.

Grandpapa Adam stepped from within the first wagon. I saw Grandmama Eve on the seat behind where he stood.

"Grandpapa, Grandmama!" I cried. "I did not expect to see you here. You have so many wagons with you."

Grandpapa Adam gave me a warm embrace. "We have brought food for your people. We heard you were in need."

Grandpapa turned to help Grandmama Eve from the tall wagon. I hugged her, allowing my eyes to stray down the length of the row of wagons.

"We have much need. The drought has been long. We were forced to eat most of our seed grain. Methuselah is with the men in the fields, planting the little we have left." I turned and pointed toward our fields.

"That is why we brought you seed for planting and food to eat," Grandmama Eve said. "We knew you and your people would not survive without it."

Methuselah and the men must have heard the commotion, for they strode toward us from the fields.

"Look what Grandpapa and Grandmama have brought us!" I cried. "Pisgah will live."

Methuselah swallowed. Emotions overcame him as he struggled to speak.

"We must empty these wagons," Grandpapa Adam called. "Who will help us?"

Men and women, boys and girls hurried to help carry the bags and baskets of seed. None were strong enough to carry any of the bags or baskets alone. It took two or three to carry what one could have before the drought. The wagon drivers joined us in carrying the food to the storage area.

Behind the wagons trailed a small herd of goats and sheep and two milk cows.

"Your children need better food," Grandmama whispered as tears flowed from my eyes. "I insisted we bring animals for you, as well."

We led the animals to the fenced pasture and let them go. Eve dumped some feed into the troughs for them.

"We did not bring bulls with us. I suspect these cows will entice one to join your village."

"They may," I said.

Two of the women whose children still lived ran into the barn for stools and buckets. They sat beside the bawling cows and relieved them of the burden of their milk.

Children gathered around us, watching with wide eyes. I fetched a stack of cups and brought it out. We dipped the cups into the buckets and handed each child some of the white goodness to drink.

One little boy cried. He had not seen milk and did not know what to do with it. His mama stooped next to him, softly telling him it would be good, if he tried. At last, he brought the cup to his mouth and took a hesitant sip. Then he gulped it down and held the cup out.

"More?" he asked.

We laughed and the women who had milked the cows poured a little more into each raised cup.

When all the food had been placed in storage sheds, Methuselah and I invited Grandpapa and Grandmama to join us in our home. I prepared a small meal from some of the food they brought.

"We thank you for your generosity and sharing of your abundance," Methuselah said, emotion filling his voice.

"We were not allowed to come any earlier," Grandpapa said. "We knew you needed our assistance. Jehovah would not allow us to come."

"That is my fault. If I had not been so prideful, Andrew and Joel would be here to greet you. Many other little children would still live." Methuselah spoke through tears that drenched his face and robe. "Qutarah and others warned me that my pride would hurt us. I did not want to believe. I was so happy with the news, I wanted to share. I … allowed my pride to get the best of me."

I stood and set my hands on the back of his neck and massaged his tight muscles.

"I did not believe others would pay for my hard-headed stupidity. I was too proud of me, and yet it is not me. It will be a son, or a grandson. I was wrong. I was so wrong." He hung his head and held it in his hands.

"What did you do that finally allowed Jehovah to open the heavens?" Grandmama asked.

Methuselah glanced back at me, then closed his eyes. "When our Andrew and Joel lay in their little beds, too weak to move, dying from starvation, I left Qutarah alone with the boys." He turned to me. "I am sorry I left you alone with them."

I shrugged. What could I say?

He turned back to face Grandmama and Grandpapa. "I went to the wilderness and fell to my knees. I poured out my sorrow and begged Jehovah for forgiveness of my sins and weakness. I begged to be forgiven of my prideful ways, asking that no more children or others would die. If another had to be taken, let it be me."

He sucked in a deep breath. "I had to stop the grief I had caused." He wiped tears away with the palm of his hand. "I knelt in prayer for much of three days, begging for forgiveness. Too many have suffered for my pride and sins. I do not know how the parents of the lost children can forgive me."

He reached up and grasped one of the hands I set on his shoulders. "Qutarah suffered the loss of our sons. She sat beside them, watching her sons waste away. Her loss is greater than mine. At last, I heard Jehovah's voice. I was forgiven. Cool rain dripped onto my face. Rain of forgiveness joined with my tears of sorrow as I stumbled home."

My fingers dug into his shoulder. He held the other hand firmly, accepting my pain.

I leaned around and kissed Methuselah on the cheek.

"Thank you, my love." He pulled me around to sit on his lap. "When I arrived home, I found Andrew taking his last breath, and Joel nearly gone. My prayers had been too late for them. I hoped one of these boys would be the one through whom mankind would be saved." He gulped in a deep breath. "It was not to be. I pray no more children pay for my pride."

"Oh, no!" Grandmama Eve cried.

"Yes, Grandmama," Methuselah replied. "Andrew left as I returned. Joel left soon after. As I returned home, people stood silently, mouths open to receive the rain. Every family in Pisgah lost someone to the drought. We would lose more if you had not brought food for us. More would be lost to starvation brought on by my pride."

We sat together in silence, absorbing the grief.

As we sat, each lost in our own thoughts, a knock came to the door. Methuselah went to answer it. When he returned, he had brightened. "The seed you brought is now being planted in our fields. The food has been distributed to each family and some is in the storehouses for later. The people of Pisgah thank you."

I do not know what Methuselah said to the families of those who lost a family member. He went into each home, alone, and spoke with them. After, the villagers of Pisgah treated him as though nothing had happened. His sorrow and grief must have helped them to forgive him of his prideful ways.

Chapter 3

Sacrifice

Years after Methuselah's test, and after more children were born into our family, Adam met Methuselah on the road to visit his parents in Zion. When Methuselah returned, a glow filled his face.

"Jehovah spoke to me when I was with Grandpapa Adam," Methuselah said in a hushed voice.

"He ... spoke to you. What did He say?" I pulled the pot from the center of the fire to the edge so our dinner would not burn and sat across the table from him.

"I have been obedient. Adam is to confer the Holy Priesthood on me in a month. We have time to travel to Home Valley, if we leave in the morning."

I rushed around the table and threw my arms around him. "You are to be honored with the Holy Priesthood? Wonderful!" I kissed his sweet lips.

"I did not know if I would ever be the one to receive it. I have other brothers, others who live in Zion. They are obedient, as well. Probably more obedient than me."

"You are to be given the privilege. What do we need to take with us?"

"The usual travel supplies, clothing, food for ourselves and our animals —"

"Nothing special?" I asked.

"We are to take a lamb for the sacrifice. I will search through the lambs while you finish preparing dinner."

"Will you expect the lamb to walk the whole distance to Home Valley?"

"I will not choose a young lamb. He must be pure, with no blemishes. But, no. He will ride in a cage in the back of our wagon with the children."

"They will love that," I said. "They will not be so happy when Adam sacrifices him."

"No. We must teach them now that not all animals are playmates. This lamb will ride with us. They can pet him and love on him, but the children must know he will be sacrificed."

"You will teach them about sacrifice?" I asked.

He rolled his lips inward. I know his tender heart struggled with the idea of sacrificing a favored animal as much as I did.

"I will teach them tonight, and on the road to Home Valley."

I nodded. "Good, for I do not have the words."

At dinner, Methuselah shared with the children about the lamb we would be taking with us to Home Valley. "He is a beautiful white lamb — and gentle. You will want to pet him and love him and give him treats. I understand that. I did the same when we took a lamb from Aenon to Home Valley the first time."

"Is it Flower?" Tamir asked.

"I do not know the names of the animals. I do not name them, when I know some will be used to feed us later, and a very few will be used as sacrifice. This lamb will be used as our sacrifice."

"What is sacrifice, Papa?" Barak asked.

"Grandpapa Adam and other men who hold the Holy Priesthood ritually offer an animal to Jehovah as we request atonement for our sins."

"You are perfect, Papa," Atara said. "Why would you need to atone for your sins?"

"All men make mistakes. I know of no one who does not. I make more than my share. I leave your mama alone for days while I go off to visit with my parents. That is not good for your mama. I do other things that require my repentance. We all require repentance. As we travel, we should think of those things and be prepared to tell Jehovah and Father about them when our lamb is sacrificed."

"Will it hurt him?" Tamir asked.

"It may, but only for a breath. It is necessary. Be strong when the time comes. You will want to weep. Tears are acceptable. Wailing and loud cries are not."

The children nodded their acceptance. I did not believe they understood about sacrifice. Who can until you have participated in one?

We climbed into our wagon early the next morning with food and supplies for ourselves and the animals. Methuselah and our son, Tamir, rode their horses beside the wagon. Chava took the reins to the horses pulling the wagon and drove it for me so I could care for our youngest, a daughter who had come to our family less than a year earlier.

It took us most of three weeks to ride from Pisgah to Home Valley. Many days, we stopped at least once on the side of the road to wait for armies of invaders to pass. Many times, we moved forward beside a mob of men without their knowing of our presence.

We entered Home Valley from the south, with the sun setting to our right. The little village never looked better to me. I had grown tired of traveling. The children had petted and loved on the lamb, giving him treats from the flowers and weeds along the road. I knew they would not be happy on the day of the sacrifice.

Mama Eve welcomed us to her home. She led us to the guest house where we left our baskets of supplies, before taking us to her home for dinner.

"You cannot expect to prepare a meal in the time you have before your children will be hungry. I have food cooking. Adam told me to expect you today."

I wanted to weep with joy. In my exhaustion from traveling, I did not want to take the time to prepare a meal.

We women, and my younger children went with Grandmama Eve to her home. Methuselah and our two older sons went with a man from Home Valley to take the animals to a grazing area where they would be safe.

"Sit," Grandmama Eve said as we entered her comfortable home. "Sit. I know how your bones grow tired of riding after a few days."

"And we have been riding for three weeks. I am tired. You have no idea how much I appreciate your gift of a meal."

"Oh, I do. I have traveled. I know how nice it is to have someone else cook a meal." She bustled out of the room with orders to put my feet up and rest.

"Watch the baby, please," I asked Atara.

"Of course, Mama." She sat on the floor beside baby Nita and watched her play.

My eyes closed in the quiet. No horses and wagon rocked me to keep me awake. The peace felt heavenly.

"Mama?" Atara asked. "Papa wants to know if you can join him with Grandpapa Adam."

I opened my eyes. "Huh?"

"You have been asleep. Papa needs you to go down the hall to Grandpapa's study."

"Oh." I swung my feet to the floor and straightened my hair. "Will you watch the little ones?"

"I have been, Mama. I will continue," Atara said, her gentle smile and nod letting me know she did not mind.

~ ~ ~

Methuselah stood at the door to Grandpapa Adam's study waiting for me. I rubbed the remaining sleep from my eyes and smiled at him. "What is going on?"

"Grandpapa wants to speak with you," Methuselah said.

My eyebrows raised and my mouth formed a little O. "Why does he need to speak with me? It is you who will be honored."

"Yes, but you are my wife. Wives have a place and must be interviewed, or so Grandpapa tells me."

I kissed his cheek and entered the office.

"Hello, Qutarah," Grandpapa Adam said in welcome. He kissed my cheek before I took the seat Methuselah indicated. He sat next to me and took my hand in his.

I gazed at the old man who sat in front of us. Although he had lived nearly eight centuries since leaving Eden, he sat with a straight back. His hair had become a white cloud that surrounded his face. He spoke with greater vigor than many of the young men I knew. And he had lived all those years. Amazement filled me.

"Jehovah requires that I speak to the wives of those are to become His High Priests and Prophets."

I rolled my lips inward. "Oh?"

Grandpapa smiled. "Yes. I need to know if you will support Methuselah in his calling. Will you do all you can to help him?"

"Of course, I will. It is good that he has been given this opportunity."

"Have you forgiven Methuselah of the great sorrow his pride caused you?"

My eyes jerked away from Grandpapa Adam's and turned toward Methuselah. "I have not thought of those days in many years. I admit, I had anger in my heart then. Why would he leave me when Andrew and Joel were so ill? When he returned, when he begged forgiveness, when he admitted his part in it, I knew I could not be angry any longer."

Methuselah's face softened at my words. I turned to gaze into Grandpapa Adam's blue eyes once more. "I forgave him then. I have no need to forgive him again."

Grandpapa Adam's eyes lifted toward Methuselah. He nodded before his next question. "Do you know your husband will be expected to travel?"

"He travels much already. We are left home to wait." I shrugged. "I am becoming accustomed to being alone."

"It will not always be easy. There may be times you need him to be at home with you. However, if Methuselah is needed elsewhere, will you allow him to leave to do Jehovah's work?"

I glanced at Methuselah. His grip on my hand strengthened. He had been gone much during the last three years. His papa needed him to help in Zion. I had not yet visited there.

Methuselah often said we would go together. I wondered if it would ever happen. Zehira had only recently moved there from Aenon.

I turned my gaze back to Grandpapa. "I would be honored to give my husband to Jehovah's service. I know he will do those things which are needed. I have sons and daughters to help and protect me in Pisgah. I will give him the support you request."

"Very good," Grandpapa said. "I know you are a good woman." He stepped around his desk to embrace me.

When we left their home to return to our guest house, Grandmama pulled me into a hug. "Welcome. You are now one of us, a matriarch."

"Me?" I asked.

"You. We wives of the prophets have much to do to support our husbands. We work together to help the new women learn. It is not always easy to be a wife."

"Even when he is not a Prophet, it is not always easy to be Methuselah's wife."

Grandmama tipped her head back and laughed. "I can understand that."

In the next days, the other prophets and their wives and families arrived. Papa Enoch and Mama Zehira arrived two days after we did, followed by the other prophet couples: Seth and Ganet, Mahalaleel and Vida, Cainan and Elia. Enos and Rebecca arrived last, having the farthest to travel of all of us.

We gathered in the sanctuary. There we visited and shared stories of the many situations we had experienced in the time since our last meeting. Our children played quietly with Enoch and Zehira's youngest, remembering the sanctuary was sacred.

On the appointed day, the women and children gathered near the altar, waiting for Methuselah and the other men to bring our lamb for sacrifice.

"Remember," I whispered to my children, "you are allowed to weep. You are not allowed to wail and cry. This is a sacred and special event."

The children's eyes widened at the reminder and sat lower in their seats. I knew how they felt. I still remembered the sorrow of my first sacrifice. I knew Jehovah required it, and I felt a closeness to him after, but I had not been prepared as my children were. Even so, how could anyone be prepared for sacrifice?

I put my arms around the children on either side of me, pulling little Nita into my lap. Chava sat nearby, hugging Atara.

Methuselah and Grandpapa Adam arrived at the altar with the ram we brought, walking up the ramp to the top where they performed the rite.

Chava stuffed her fist into her mouth. I touched her arm. She stared forward, refusing to look at me.

When the rite ended and we walked down from the hill together, Chava touched my arm. "I did not expect Papa to kill the lamb."

"That is the sacrifice. We gave up our best lamb for Jehovah."

"I did not expect the fire," Barak added.

"There is much I did not expect the first time I observed a sacrifice. You children did well." I smiled to each of them, touching them to ensure they knew I spoke to them.

"Yeah," Barak said. "Even with the blood and the fire, I felt something here," he touched the center of his chest, "something warm. I was not frightened. Sad for the lamb, yes. But not frightened."

"I felt love," Chava admitted. "I did not expect to feel love. How is that, Mama?"

I touched her shoulder and smiled when she looked my way. "Our sacrifices bring us closer to Father and Jehovah. It helps us remember that someday, when the time is right, Jehovah, himself, will come to this earth. He will give himself as a sacrifice for our sins. Then, we will no longer need to sacrifice a lamb, for the pure son of God will have sacrificed himself for us all."

"Jehovah will come to earth?" Barak asked. "How can that be?"

"I do not know, for certain. Only that he will come as a babe, like you and every other person on earth, and He will live a perfect life."

"How can he take our sins?" Chava asked.

"I do not know."

Chapter 4

Protection

I hoped our return to Pisgah would be uneventful. We moved to the side of the road many times while other travelers passed. Methuselah tied his horse to the back of the wagon and took the reins to the bullocks who pulled it. We sat together in companionable silence as we rode along the path home.

I heard one group who traveled in the same direction grumble as they passed. Their complaints were many.

"We are sent on a fool's errand."

"Why would he want a family?"

"Why not just this Methuselah? He is the son."

"The god believes this will stop Enoch."

"Ha! The priests think it will stop Enoch. Nothing has yet. Why taking Methuselah and his family?"

I sat in the wagon with a fist in my mouth, fear coursing through me. Men searched for our family, for Methuselah! They wanted to hurt us.

"What did we do?" I asked Methuselah after the men had passed and it was safe to move forward once more.

"We obey the laws of Jehovah. That is enough for many of these men." He pulled his hat from his head and wiped his face. "It does not help that my papa is Enoch. He has been mighty in his ability to teach. Men leave their fields to listen to him. The priests do not like losing their patrons."

"I would think not!"

He shoved his broad-brimmed hat I had woven for him before we left home back on his head and sighed. "We ask no money, no service from our followers, other than serving one another in love. It hurts the priests who depend on offerings."

"And Papa Enoch has been causing them trouble with that?"

"Men are questioning the need to make offerings to the priest. I guess that is causing them problems."

"They should find other ways to feed themselves," I grumbled.

"They should, but it is so much easier for them to tax and tithe the families within their villages and live off the labors of others." He lifted his shoulder a little. "I would not know. I work in our fields and with our animals when I am home. I do not depend on others to feed me or my family."

"And I am happy that you do." I snuggled under his arm, enjoying the time we had together in the wagon.

Many times each day we moved to the side of the road to avoid travelers. Most travelers were men taking the produce from their farms to the market. One had a huge wheel of cheese. Another had a wagon full of turnips. I wanted to stop these men and ask to trade for some of the good food they carried with them.

At night, when we pulled our horses and wagon into a small glen, others found us. These were peaceful men who needed to trade for the produce from their farms. I traded them some of the grain we carried for cheese and fresh vegetables.

Three of those groups of travelers, however, were men traveling in either direction searching for us. Each time these angry men passed, we moved to the side of the road and sat in the shade of the willows.

The bands of men spoke roughly, cursing Father and Jehovah. Even if they did not say they wanted to find our little family, we knew they were a problem for us.

The children sat in the back of the wagon saying nothing. I turned once to see wide eyes surveying the cursing men who passed us.

We sat quietly, but something else protected us from the view of those men.

"What is it?" Barak asked the second evening after it happened as we sat around our campfire. "Why do they not see us?"

"I am happy they do not," Chava added, "but why can they not see us?"

"We sit quietly, not causing them to look our way, but the horses continue to snort. How do they not see or hear us?" Barak asked his papa.

"It is the protection of Jehovah. He hides whom he will. We are obedient to His commands. I have agreed to teach my brothers and sisters. He protects me and my family."

"It does not always happen that way," Barak said. "Grace told me about a confrontation Grandpapa Enoch had on the way to Home Valley."

"Oh?" I asked. "Grace is a pretty girl."

"She is, Mama, but she is also my auntie." Barak frowned at me and tossed a stick onto the fire.

"What did she tell you?" Methuselah asked, smiling at me.

"Men stopped them in the middle of the road. They wanted to take Grandpapa away with them. She said they spoke of offering Grandpapa Enoch as a sacrifice to their god." Barak shook his head. "Why would a god demand the sacrifice of a man?"

"Some of the priests fear your Grandpapa Enoch. Few of us who teach for Jehovah are as powerful with our words as your Grandpapa Enoch is. It is difficult to turn away and deny the truth when he speaks it."

I pulled a blanket up around Nita, who slept beside me.

"What did Grandpapa Enoch do about these men?" Methuselah asked, turning his attention back to Barak.

Barak stood between us and the fire. "He closed his eyes, Grace says. Then a big wind began to blow. Thick, black clouds gathered above them. Then twisting, spinning clouds dropped from the mass of black clouds."

Barak spun his hands around his head to show how the winds had blown.

"And, what happened to the men who wanted to hurt Grandpapa Enoch?"

Barak dropped his hands, then shoved them up into the air, then brought them rapidly downward. "The winds dropped on top of the angry men, spinning them until the winds lifted them into the air." He twirled around. "The men spun around inside the twisting wind until the wind blew away, across the land, taking all the men who wanted to hurt Grandpapa Enoch with it."

"It blew the men away?" I asked.

Barak nodded. "Grace says they all blew away. Those on horses were picked up and blown away like the ones who walked." Barak shrugged. "Grace showed me the horses they left behind. She told me Grandpapa Enoch could not leave them there waiting for the bad men to return for them."

Methuselah gripped my hand. "Jehovah will protect his servants. Sometimes he hides us. Other times, he blows them away."

"That would have been funny to watch," Atara said. "Can you imagine the look on their face as they are lifted off their horse and blown away."

"Can you imagine the bruises and broken bones they must have," Chava added. "Being carried in a spinning wind cannot have been safe for them."

Atara smoothed the laughter from her face. "Did some of them ... die?"

"I do not know," Barak replied, sitting down on a log near Chava. "Grace did not see them again. I suppose some could have."

"Only those who wanted to hurt Grandpapa Enoch," Methuselah said, his voice soothing the children's fears. "Jehovah is a just and loving God. He will not hurt or kill men who are obedient."

As we rode onward in the next days, the children did not shout and laugh as usual. We did not sing. We chose not to draw attention to our small group. We knew only the protection of Jehovah could keep us hidden in the open.

On our arrival home, as we had each night on the road, we gathered in our sitting room before even unpacking the wagon to kneel and thank Jehovah for His watchful care and protection.

~ ~ ~

Our children grew as children do in the days and months and years that passed by. It had been many years since Methuselah had received the honor of the priesthood. None of our sons had been invited to be the son to carry on the priesthood.

It had taken years for Grandpapa Jared to receive the Priesthood. Grandpapa Maha still waited. I knew it would come, if it was right, when Jehovah determined it was time. Until then, I enjoyed my grandchildren.

I thought I had stopped having children and hoped one of our sons would be found worthy. I had not had my moon time for more than a year when my stomach revolted at food.

Methuselah lay his hands on my head when he returned from traveling the next evening. "Qutarah, you have been called upon to pass through the sorrow of women once more. This child will be an obedient son."

I heard Methuselah say many more words, but after "Son," my ears stopped hearing. I had a son growing within my womb. I thought I had passed all that. I had grandchildren who were having grandchildren!

Lamech came to us shouting for joy. He found delight in the smallest of insects, the beauty of a sunset, and all the baby animals. We hoped the blessing would follow, that he would be a child of the promise.

One year, while Lamech was still a young man, we journeyed to Home Valley with him to observe Grandpapa Mahalaleel's ordination. Grandpapa Maha is a kind and gentle man. I do not know why Jehovah took so long to choose him to be part of the priesthood lineage. Perhaps Grandpapa Maha knows. Perhaps Grandpapa Adam does. I do not. It is not my problem.

We joined with the others in celebrating the joyful occasion. Our numbers had grown to eight couples, with Adam and Eve as the Patriarch and Matriarch of us all.

Grandmama Eve and Grandpapa Adam began to show their age. They had lived nearly nine hundred years since leaving Eden. Both were bent with age. Their hair glistened in whiteness, much as I expected Father and Jehovah would appear if I ever saw them.

However, their minds did not slow. Their memories held tiny details of their lives, and ours, many we had forgotten over the years.

Grandmama Zehira and I tried to do more cooking and cleaning up, as all the other grandmothers were growing old, as well. They did not like us to push them out of the way, insisting they could help as they always had.

As a young man, Lamech was happy to visit his ancient grandparents in Home Valley.

"Will there be girls in Home Valley?" Lamech had asked before leaving home, hoping a girl there would be friendly.

"Yes, son," Methuselah replied. "There are many women in Home Valley."

"I would like to find the right woman. My nieces are nice, but I do not want to marry them."

We laughed, and remembered his earnest face as we watched him visit with the girls in the time we were visiting Grandpapa and Grandmama in Aenon.

Grandpapa Maha received his blessing and we had shared and visited together in a way only those who feel the weight of the responsibility to teach all the world of Jehovah could.

"So many of the people we see have become wicked," Grandmama Vida said. "I struggle to understand how the women can allow themselves to be used as they are."

"How can they stop it?" Mama Helsa cried. "Their men are bigger and stronger. If the women do not give them what they want, they are punished with whips and fists."

"How can my grandsons treat their women like that?" Grandmama Eve whispered. "I taught their papas better."

"You did, but their papas did not teach their sons any better," Grandmama Vida exclaimed. "We teach our sons and they turn like dogs to the vomit of the false priests. How can Father watch them?"

"I do not know," Papa Enoch said. "I have walked among them, seen their wickedness, felt their hot spittle on my face as they berate me for trusting in Jehovah." He dropped his chin to his chest. "How can I not trust Jehovah when he has protected me through all these years."

The other women had told me stories of Enoch's stutter as a young man. I saw none of it now. He spoke with authority and power.

"The priests are filled with ugliness. Their leader, the Destroyer, wants them to be angry and hateful," Grandpapa Seth added. "Without the hatred and ugliness, no one would believe their lies."

"If they opened their eyes, they would see the chains wrapped around their souls, dragging them to the eternal pits," Grandpapa Cainan added. "They are afraid of the future."

"With reason," Papa Enoch added.

We prayed together that Jehovah would soften the hearts of our brothers and sisters, allowing them to break free of the Destroyer's chains. I prayed in faith, wondering if Jehovah would do anything to change these men. He did give them the right to choose. They had chosen the Destroyer over Him.

As we prepared to leave for home, Lamech's Grandpapa Enoch invited him to come to Zion for a time. He readily accepted the invitation and rode away with his grandparents.

Methuselah and I watched him leave with some trepidation. This last son was our last hope. We prayed daily that he would be obedient. We prayed he would be safe with his grandpapa. We had to trust Jehovah.

With all our children now out of our home, we took the long way home, traveling west to visit some of the villages where Methuselah had taught. He found pleasure in introducing me to the women of those villages.

I enjoyed visiting with them and learning about the ways they wove their blankets different than me, the way their pottery making had changed, and ways they managed their home creatively.

Some villages had smiths that created items of gold, silver, and other metals. Not many women were overly interested in those creations. They did not put food on the table or help with their chores in their homes.

In some of the villages, we saw a few women who wore shiny gold or silver around their necks, waists, and wrists. These women showed a pride, different than Methuselah had shown before the loss of our two sons.

They expected others to do their chores, carry their water, and clean their homes. Their husbands had found a way to gain much of the gold and silver, causing them to think they were better than the others in their villages.

Methuselah and I tried to counsel with these men and women, teaching them the need to be humble. They laughed at us and had their guards chase us from their homes. We were unwelcome in many of the villages where gold and silver were important after that.

Our return home was less joyful than I hoped it would be. I could not stop thinking about the men and women who had become prideful, seeking power over one another and using gold they dug from the dirt as a reason for their power.

For much of my life, men had fought each other, seeking to take the wealth of land and belongings from their neighbors. The pride of these people had changed. They wanted to control others.

Over the years, these who considered themselves wealthy would encourage battles among their neighbors, seeking to control more than their own small villages. They began to combine villages and lands into larger city states and countries.

I could see nothing good coming from it.

I understood Jehovah's sadness at the behavior of his children. How could so many listen to the Destroyer and follow his ways?

Chapter 5

Gathering

When Lamech had not returned to Pisgah by the time we arrived, I began to fear for him.

"When do you think Lamech will return?" I asked.

"I do not know. He will come when Papa has taught him the things he needs to know."

We waited for Lamech to return nearly a year.

When he did, he had changed. The laughing, teasing boy who had been looking for a woman had gone. A serious young man returned to us.

"I still need to find a wife," he said, "but I do not feel compelled to find one today, or even this year. Jehovah will help me find her when the time is right."

He stepped close and gave me a hug. I had missed his embraces in the year he was gone.

Lamech traveled often with Methuselah, teaching the commandments of Jehovah. More often, however, he traveled with his Grandpapa Enoch.

He returned one time from teaching with Enoch talking about the wind that had destroyed a village and how he helped a girl and her family.

Lamech returned to that village twice more, saying he wanted to be certain the families had survived the terrible windstorm. When he returned the second time, Lamech spoke of the blessing given to a woman, bringing her back as if from the dead.

"She had been almost dead when we found her after the storm three months ago," Lamech explained. "Her skin was gray and cold to the touch. I received a prompting to roll her on her side and smack her in the center of her back. A hunk of bread that had lodged in her throat during the storm had stopped her air. She began to breathe."

"If you helped her live then, why did she still need a blessing?" I asked.

"She lived, but she had lost her memories of life. She stared into space, unknowing and uncaring. All she could do to help the family was weave at her loom." Lamech shook his head and frowned.

"Her hands remembered what her mind could not," I murmured. I had seen that in much older women in our village.

"Grandpapa Enoch warned Angetta and her papa that De-onna may not be completely healed. They promised they would be happy if she remembered more. Grandpapa set his hands on her head and offered a mighty prayer. Papa, I have never heard one call upon Jehovah and command the person to be healed. Grandpapa did that."

Methuselah nodded his head. "I have seen your grandpapa do that. He is close to Jehovah."

"What happened to the mama?" I asked, still interested in his story.

"Almost the breath Grandpapa removed his hands from Deonna's head, her eyes opened. The fog of forgetfulness had lifted. She wanted food and wondered what was burning."

"Burning?" I asked.

"Yes. Angetta had put bread into the fire before we were called to visit with Grandpapa. We took too long, and her bread burned. Her mama helped to repair the damage, and everyone had bread with the meal."

"She is an able woman," I said.

"And beautiful," Lamech replied under his breath.

"The mama or the daughter?" Methuselah asked.

Lamech grinned, uncaring of the red that crept up his neck into his face.

Lamech returned to Tyre once more. This time, he returned with a beautiful young woman, Angetta. Her papa had married them.

They rode to visit Home Valley, hoping to receive the marriage blessing from Grandpapa Adam. He was too sick at that time. His Grandpapa Seth and Grandmama Ganet had moved to Home Valley to be near their parents. Grandpapa Adam directed Grandpapa Seth to bless the marriage.

Not many years later, Grandpapa Seth ordained Lamech to the Holy Priesthood. His grandpapa Enoch was the only one who had been ordained at a younger age.

I worked to suppress my pride and joy in this youngest son. I know better than to express my pride. It was hard. This son, or one of his sons, would carry our family into a new world.

A few years later we were called to Home Valley, along with the other prophets and others who continued to obey Jehovah.

Grandmama Eve had grown weaker in the years since I saw her last. Grandpapa Adam, too, showed his great age. No one knew how many years they had lived before Father and Jehovah placed them in Eden. No one knew how long they lived in Eden. Time there had no meaning.

Now, after nine hundred twenty-seven years, Grandpapa Adam wanted to give those of his family who were still obedient a final blessing. Many of our children joined us on the trek there and stayed in a small tent village outside of Home Valley.

While the men discussed those things men need to discuss, we women gathered with Grandmama Eve seated on a low hill. Grandmama Ganet and Ruth asked her to tell her story.

It amazed me to watch her grow in strength enough that she could speak clearly and in a loud enough voice that all who sat in front of her could hear. Although I had loved her for many years, I did not know many of the things she shared. The challenges she faced alone with Grandpapa Adam would have overwhelmed me. We were grateful to hear her words and learn of her experiences.

The next day, Grandmama Ganet shared her story. I shivered with the others when she and Seth fought the giant serpent. Between the stories of Grandmama Eve and Grandmama Ganet, I knew the reason I did not like serpents.

Grandmama Rebecca shared her story on the third day. She still mourns for her missing children, who must be grandparents now, if they still live in the wicked city of Nod. I loved her description of their escape from the Shemites before moving on to Cainan before Cainan's birth.

Before we separated for the day, those others of us who were wives of prophets were assigned to write our stories for the other women to read.

I have put off writing my story. I have done nothing special in my life. My children were born in the comfort of my home with healers and assistants, not with only the assistance of my husband who had never helped in a birth, as Eve did. I never faced serpents, nor a man who tried to take me, as Ganet did. Nor have I had to escape my home because invaders attacked. My children have not all obeyed, but none of them were stolen, like Rebecca.

I have loved my husband and stood beside him as he struggled with pride. I have trusted Jehovah to protect me in times of trouble.

I know that Jehovah loves me. I love him.

I suppose that is enough to help others. If other women find the courage to trust Jehovah, their lives will be better.

May he bless you,

Qutarah

PART FIVE

Angetta

Chapter 1

Rescue

Wind.

Howling wind.

Tearing through the valley. Stripping the vegetation. Torturing every soul.

The wind spun from green clouds, ripping and tearing homes apart, lifting anything in its path and hurling it. Limbs from trees impaled other trees. Every home in Tyre had been shattered by the winds that spun out of the clouds that day.

I had run to hide with Mama and Papa in the center of our adobe brick home. When winds like this spun from the clouds, we had found safety there before.

But these winds were stronger than any others we had ever seen in the open land where we lived. Our home, like all the other homes in our village, was left in a heap.

I stood among the remains, shoving the remnants of the roof aside, praying my parents and my youngest sisters and brother were unhurt. Praying the roof had not injured them, or ...

No. I could not think that thought. They had to be under here, alive and safe like me.

Blood trickled from a cut on my face. I brushed it away and pulled another length of wood and sod that had been the roof from where I last saw my little sister.

I heard footsteps in the litter that was once our home and glanced up. "Be careful," I called. "My family is somewhere under here."

The young man stopped where he was and backed out. He returned with a bucket. He bent over and picked up the sod and wood where he stood. When certain no one lay beneath him, he moved forward to lift more of the debris away.

I did much the same thing, lifting chunks of sod and broken wood from in front of me, frantically calling out the names of my family.

I stopped occasionally to listen. At last, I heard a small cry. I bent above where I heard the sound, and then, in a frenzy, I pulled at the torn-up roof. I clawed away the pieces of roof until I reached my littlest brother. I carefully lifted him out and searched him for any injuries.

He had cuts on him. I could not tell if they were serious. He cried and clung to my neck. He lived.

"Can someone take David for me?" I shouted.

The young man who had been dragging away the debris that was once our home, stepped forward and took him out of my arms.

David cried.

"David, honey," I crooned. "This man will help you be safe. Go with him."

"I will help you," the man said softly. "Come to me."

David released my neck and went to the man.

I stepped back and called out, "Mama, Papa, where are you?"

I saw the debris move and bent to uncover whoever had been trapped beneath it.

Papa pushed away the last of the debris and stood up. "I am here, Angetta. Who else have you found?"

"Oh, Papa. David is safe ... and I am free. I have not heard or found anyone else."

"Not your mama or your sisters?"

I shook my head and fought back the tears. "No, Papa. No one else."

Papa bent to join me in dragging away the remnants of the house. Soon, he uncovered Mama. She slept. I hoped she only slept, for she had a gash on her head that bled and would not answer when Papa and I called her name.

Papa lifted her from under the last of the mess and carried her carefully across what was left of our home and away.

I stared down at the space where Mama had lain. Beneath her were both of my little sisters. Did they still live? I could not tell. They were much too still.

I screamed their names, "Anna, Della, Anna, Della," as I reached to lift them from the space.

The young man hurried to help me. "Are these the last? If you see them, I do not have to fear stepping on them."

"They are the last of my family. Help me!"

Together we lifted a length of wood that lay across Anna's legs. I bent and lifted her out of the space. She whimpered! She lived!

The young man carefully took her from me and carried her to people waiting along the edge of the house. He returned to help me get the last of the debris off little Della's body. It had not pinned her as the wood had pinned Anna, but it made it difficult for me to lift her from the cavity in which she lay.

The young man had me step back and bent to lift a bigger section of the roof. This freed Della. As I picked her up, she began to cry.

"Oh, Della," I crooned. "You are safe now. Are you hurt somewhere?"

"No," she cried. "I miss Mama and Anna. They kept me warm. Where is Mama?"

I stepped carefully through our destroyed home with Della in my arms. The young man walked beside me, catching me once when my toe stuck on a length of wood, nearly tripping me.

"Thanks," I said.

"Sure."

We stepped off the last of the trash that was once our home onto solid earth. Even here, branches of trees and pieces of houses littered the ground.

"How is she?" my older sister, Yaffa, asked.

"Scared, mostly, I think. How are Mama and Anna?"

"Anna will be fine," she said.

"And Mama?"

"We do not know. Mama lives, I think."

I bit the inside of my lip. "Where is she?" When my sister waved in a general direction toward the center of our village, I asked, "Where do I take Della to be examined?"

"They are taking the injured to the sanctuary. It is the only place that still stands, and it was damaged," Yaffa replied.

I trudged through the mess toward the sanctuary, careful where I set my feet on the shifting broken limbs and trees.

"I am Lamech," the young man said as he walked beside me.

"Thank you for your help rescuing my sisters. I am Angetta."

"We arrived as the clouds spun toward the earth. Grandpapa and I took shelter in the sanctuary. We were blessed. We were not injured. Are you well? You were injured. There is blood on your head."

I had not thought to question where this young man, Lamech, had come from. He had been beside me and assisted me in pulling my sisters from the chaos that had once been our home.

I swiped at the blood that dripped into my eye. "Yeah, I know. But my family is more important."

"You should have the healer take care of you, as well."

We reached the sanctuary and Lamech held the door open. "If you will promise to see the healer, I will go see if someone else needs my help."

I nodded. He waited until I was in the room before he shut the door behind me.

I turned to look. Our poor healer looked overwhelmed by all the injured people. I had not agreed to see the healer. She needed help!

Papa sat next to a blanket on the floor. I danced around three friends who wanted to stop me, until I reached Papa.

On the floor, inside the blanket beside him lay my mama. Her gray face told me she did not do well.

"Papa?"

He did not hear me.

I touched his shoulder. "Papa?"

He turned toward me with a blank expression. "Angetta. Your mama is ill."

"I see. Are you hurt?"

"Me? No, I do not think so. But your mama, she will not wake up."

I found a friend to help me examine little Della. She had no bumps nor bruises on her. She must have been protected by Mama in the little cavern where I found her.

I took her out to Yaffa. "Can you take Della and find David?" I asked. "I need to help Papa with Mama."

"Is she ... is she waking yet?"

"No. I do not know that she will."

~ ~ ~

Lamech found me inside the sanctuary later with a bandage tied around my head. I stood beside Papa, touching his shoulder. Mama continued to lay still. Gray continued to color her face. I smelled papa's fear.

I bent to touch Mama's face.

Cold.

It should have some warmth. I turned my cheek to feel any breath from her mouth.

None.

"Help!" I screamed.

Lamech touched my back. "What is the problem?"

"She is not breathing. Something is wrong with her."

"I wondered. She is too gray."

Lamech stooped beside Mama and rolled her on her side. He checked her mouth and did something with it.

"Her tongue is in the way," he muttered. "Hold her so she does not fall over."

I held her by the shoulders. Lamech pounded on her back.

"What are you doing?" I yelled. "That is no way to help her."

"It is. There is something in her throat." He beat on her back once more, and a chunk of bread flew out toward me.

She had been eating when I rushed into the house warning them of the storm. A bite of the bread must have stuck in her throat, blocking the air.

Mama coughed. Her color changed from gray to bright red.

Lamech and I lay her on her back, watching to be sure she continued to breathe.

"Mama!" I cried. "Papa! Mama is alive!"

He bent over her, whispering her name.

"How did you know to do that?" I stared at Lamech.

He lifted a shoulder in a tiny shrug. "I do not know. Something whispered that I should check her tongue and then beat on her back." He lifted his eyebrows. "It worked."

"It did." I threw my arms around him and hugged him. "Thank you for saving my mama for me and my sisters and brother."

"I am happy Grandpapa and I were here to help."

"Who is your grandpapa?" I asked, stepping back. Red heat raced up my neck and into my face.

"He is over there. Enoch."

"Your grandpapa is Enoch?" My voice lifted a few tones on the end. "We have heard of him and waited for him to visit for many weeks. We received a message a week ago that he would be here soon."

"We were delayed. It is good, for we would not have been here today to help you and your family."

I sucked in a deep breath and slowly let it out. "You would not be here today?"

"No. If we had not been delayed, we would have come and gone days ago."

"And no one would have known how to help my mama," I whispered.

"Maybe?"

I looked into his deep blue eyes. A lock of his light brown hair fell across them. I wanted to brush it back for him but held my hands next to my side. "It is good that you were delayed."

Papa looked up to me. "Angetta, your mama lives. Can you get her a cup of water?"

"Yes, Papa."

Lamech and I walked to the side of the room where a big urn stood. I opened it and dipped water into a cup and carried it back to Papa.

"Would you like to meet my grandpapa?" Lamech asked.

"Meet Enoch? And speak to him?"

"He does not bite. He is a kind and gentle man."

"I have heard he can be quite fierce," I murmured.

"Oh, he can, when it is needed," Lamech said with a laugh. It was not loud or boastful, just a cheerful laugh. I liked it.

"Grandpapa," Lamech said as we reached the place where he stood helping the healer wrap bandages around a little girl's arm. "This is my new friend, Angetta. Her family was trapped in what used to be her home."

Enoch looked up and into my eyes. I felt as though he bored into my soul. "Hello, Angetta."

His gentle, deep voice surprised me. I expected a more boyish voice. He looked young, although he *was* Lamech's grandpapa.

"Hello," I said in a tiny voice. "I do not want to disturb you."

"Wait while we finish wrapping this. This poor little girl broke her arm in the storm."

I gasped and stepped back. I did not want to be the cause of any more pain for her.

Lamech stepped back beside me.

"Does he always do this?" I whispered.

"What? Help the healers? Yes. When there has been an accident or problem, Grandpapa is here to help. He often knows what to do as much as the healers."

"I thought about being a healer when I was younger," I murmured. "Until my older sister cut her arm. It bled and bled. The healer had to stitch it closed to make it stop bleeding. I decided then that I did not want to be a healer."

Lamech laughed under his breath.

I stared at him. "What?"

"I do not want to be a healer, either. I do not like to be around blood."

I laughed with him. "We are alike in that."

Enoch finished holding the little girl and handed her to her Mama. "She should heal without too many problems if you keep her in that sling."

"Thank you," the mama gushed. "She will be able to tell her friends that Enoch helped fix her arm."

Enoch smiled. I could tell he had heard this before.

"I am but a helper in a terrible tragedy. If she listens to the words of Jehovah, I will be happy."

Enoch turned to us. "Who is this lovely young lady you have with you, Lamech?"

"I want you to meet Angetta. As I said before, I helped her uncover her family from beneath the remains of her house and roof."

"And he helped Mama live. She had a hunk of bread caught in her throat. Lamech knew to pound on her back to knock it out. Mama lives. She almost did not."

Enoch's eyes flicked from mine to his grandson. "How did you know to do that?"

"I listened. It felt right."

"You listened?" I asked.

"Yes. I heard a small voice within me. I listened to it."

"Can anyone hear the small voice?"

"You can, when you obey Jehovah's commandments," Enoch answered.

I absorbed that news. Perhaps the small voice had warned me where to find my family.

Chapter 2

Healing

Our open fields grew many of the grains needed by other lands nearby. We traded these grains for milk and eggs from a neighboring village who had no space to grow grains, only space for cows and chickens. Somehow, our grains had been protected from the huge windstorm.

I watched Papa and my older brothers walk beside the oxen pulling the wagons heaped full of grains to be traded with our neighbors. I hoped the wagons would be as full when they returned. We needed the milk, eggs, and cheese these neighbors traded for the grain.

Mama sighed. "I always feel lost when your papa and brothers drive away with those wagons."

"They will not be gone long, maybe only a day or two."

"Where are they going?" Mama asked again.

"They are trading our grain for other food, cheese, milk, eggs, and other things the other villages have that we do not."

"We do not have cows and chickens here?" Mama stared around her.

Her confused face scared me, yet again. Would she ever come back to us? Would she remember? Her cloudy eyes suggested it could be many days.

We had spent much of the last two months rebuilding our home and those surrounding it. Mama still suffered from the effects of her near death. She could not remember important things, like choking on the bread and me helping to find them. No need to remind her. She did not believe me. Now, she did not remember that we traded with our neighbors for cheese and milk. I frowned.

"Angetta?" Mama asked. "Do we have things to do?"

I brightened and smiled at her. "We do. You have a new blanket to weave for your newest grandchild. I have mending to do. Shall we return to the house?"

Mama nodded and took my hand.

I led her back to the house. The little ones followed us. Della clung to David's hand. I gripped Anna's hand, determined not to lose her on the way home. Mama could not survive another loss. Being forced to rebuild our home and having few of the essential requirements for a family home had been difficult for her.

Papa had built her a new loom when we discovered she remembered how to weave. I had worked to replace the jars and urns alongside other women near the creek that ran through our valley. The mud in one section of the creek dried stronger than any we had in our home before. Older brothers had helped replace beds and chairs. Our home had almost returned to the comfortable feel we had before the storm.

We followed Mama into the room with her loom. She sat on the stool and began to weave. The little girls gathered their babies into their arms and rocked them near the fireplace. David dumped his blocks from the basket and stacked them.

I sat near Mama and dug through the mending basket. Finding one of David's tunics that needed the sleeves stitched back together, I threaded a needle, and began to jab the needle through the seam.

We always had mending to do. David and the girls were active and their clothes frequently needed repair. I found the mending basket empty only on rare days.

"Angetta," David said, "someone is outside our door. I hear them coming up the steps."

I set his tunic aside and stood by the time the knock came on our door.

"I will answer the door, Mama," I said, though I knew Mama did not hear the knock.

I strode to the door and pulled it open.

On the other side stood Lamech.

"What are you doing back in Tyre?" I asked.

"That is not the welcome I expected," he said with a chuckle.

"I am happy to see you, Lamech. What brought you to our little hamlet of Tyre?"

Lamech's mouth lifted in a grin. "That is better. I am here to see how your mama is doing. Is she well?"

"That will depend on what you mean by well." I grimaced. "Mama is alive and healthy. Something happened to her during the storm. She struggles to remember how to do little things, like cook and clean. She only remembers how to weave and dress herself. I care for the children during the day until Papa returns."

"Alive but not well, then?"

"Yes. Would you like to come in to see her?"

"May I?"

I nodded and opened the door wider.

Lamech entered and David ran to jump into his arms. "Lamech! You said you would return."

Lamech set David on the floor and ruffled his hair. "I told you I would."

"Do you want to see the tower I built with my blocks? Papa made me new blocks when we built this house again."

"Yes, David. I would."

David took him by the hand and led him to his blocks. Lamech dropped to the floor and congratulated the little boy on his marvelously constructed tower.

After a short time, he said, "I need to talk to your mama and sister. Can you build another tower like this wonderful one?"

David gazed up into his friend's eyes with a frown. "I can do that. Will you come back?"

"I will."

David smiled. "Then go talk to Mama. She needs someone to talk to her."

Lamech stood and moved to a seat near mine and Mama's. "How are you doing today, Deonna?"

Mama turned from her weaving. "Well, thank you. Do I know you?"

"Probably not. I helped find people who were hurt in the big storm here two months ago. You had some problems. Are you doing better?"

"I do not know. I remember what I am doing some days. Others, well, other days I struggle to know my name. Something happened to hurt me," Mama said, giving her head a little shake.

"You were hurt in the storm, Mama." I said, touching her elbow.

"Yes, I remember you telling me that. I do not remember the storm. Did Anna and Della survive?"

"Yes, Mama. They play near your feet. You protected them with your body."

"Oh. That was good of me."

"It was," Lamech said. He glanced toward me. "Can we get a drink for your mama?"

I stood and led Lamech to the kitchen. I dipped a drink out of the water urn and poured it into a cup for Mama and another cup for Lamech.

I handed it to him and he drank it.

"Your mama needs help," he said.

"She does, but I do not know what to do for her."

"Perhaps Grandpapa can bless her. I have seen great things when he sets his hands on a person's head and begs Jehovah to heal them."

"Would he do that for my mama?"

Lamech shrugged. "Sometimes Jehovah allows it, sometimes He does not. It will depend on Jehovah's will."

"Is your grandpapa here with you?"

Lamech's smile brightened. "He is. I convinced him he should come back this way to be certain your village will have homes to provide you the protection you will need when the storms return."

"Will you ask him for me?"

"No. Your mama must ask. He cannot bless the unwilling."

~ ~ ~

Papa and my older brothers returned home late that evening with milk and cheese filling the wagons. I hurried from the house to help bring some inside. Papa and the others stored the rest in the community cold storage room dug under the ground.

When Papa came into the house, Enoch and Lamech followed him. "Enoch has asked for a bed within our home tonight. Can you help them, Angetta?"

I scurried into the guest room to ensure the bedding had been aired and cleaned. The space had not been made large like before, but there would be room for Enoch and Lamech.

I hurried from the sleeping room to our kitchen to push the pot of stew off the hot flames, mixed bread, and pulled out bowls, cups, and spoons for all of us.

Lamech and David entered to get water for Enoch and Papa. "You can dip up cool water from this urn," David said. "Angetta and Mama do not allow me to do it yet. They think I will spill it. I would not do that."

"You are a big boy," Lamech said, grinning over his head toward me. "I am certain they know about these things."

I nodded as I stepped close to fill a pitcher with water. "David's older brother tried to do it alone and pulled the urn over on top of himself. All the water spilled. It made a big mess. Since then, Mama insists that children must be this tall," I held my hand above David's head, "to get water."

"This urn?" Lamech asked, pointing to the urn with his cup.

"It is one of the few things we found still intact when we uncovered the wreckage from our home."

"Strong urn."

"It has survived many children." I gave the stew a quick stir and pushed the bread into the fire.

"Come with us to the sitting room. Grandpapa would like you to be there."

"Will he bless my Mama?"

"You or your Papa will need to ask him, or better, your mama needs to make the request."

"David, take your cup to Papa."

"No, Angetta. My cup goes to Enoch. Lamech can take his cup to Papa."

I giggled and followed them into the sitting room.

Mama sat near her loom, staring at the low fire near Papa and Enoch. The little girls played near her feet once more.

David carefully handed Enoch the cup. "This is for you, Enoch."

Enoch took the cup from the little boy's hands. "Thank you, David."

Lamech handed his cup to Papa. "And this is for you, Maher."

Papa smiled and took the cup from Lamech.

After sipping from the cup, Papa swallowed hard, then gazed into Enoch's eyes. "I have heard that you have a gift from Jehovah."

"I have many gifts." Enoch drank from his cup.

"I have heard you can set your hands on one who is ill and restore them to health. Is that possible?"

Enoch set his cup on the table beside him. "I have been allowed to do that a few times. I am not always allowed. I have not yet been allowed to heal my own wife's twisted leg."

Papa swallowed again. "Would you ... possibly ... be able ... to heal Deonna? She has not been the same since she choked on the bread. I thought we lost her. Her skin was cold and gray. But, Lamech beat the bread from her throat and she lives. Since then, her living is not real living. She is not the same." All of Papa's words came out in a rush.

Enoch leaned back in his chair and closed his eyes. I flicked my eyes toward Lamech. He held his hand out and shook his head.

We waited.

Enoch continued to sit with his eyes closed for many more long breaths. When he opened his eyes, he smiled.

"I am allowed to give Deonna a blessing. You must, however, be prepared that she will not be healed all the way. Sometimes, Jehovah allows some of the injury to remain."

"If she can remember, if she can do more, I will be happy," Papa cried.

I nodded my head. "Please help her."

Enoch set his cup on the low table near him, stood, and moved behind the seat where Mama sat. He set his hands on her long dark hair and offered a prayer to Jehovah, calling on her body to heal in all its parts, that she could remember and take her rightful place once more in the family. At his amen, we lifted our heads and stared at them.

Mama opened her dark brown eyes. The fog had lifted from them. "Is dinner ready? I'm hungry."

"Yes, Mama," I cried. "I have dinner waiting for us."

"Something is burning in the kitchen," Mama said.

I leapt from my seat and ran to rescue the bread. I pulled it out before it had all turned black, but there would not be enough for everyone. I would not have bread with my meal.

The family followed me into the kitchen.

"What burned?" Mama asked.

I pointed to the bread, fighting back the frustration. Why did I burn the bread on the day Enoch and Lamech were here?

"We can fix that." Mama picked up the knife and started cutting. Soon she had sliced away the burn, leaving enough warm, good bread for all to enjoy.

"Mama," I looked into her eyes. "You are back."

She smiled. "I am. I do not know where I was. I only know a cloud filled my thoughts. It is gone. I am back."

I hugged her around the waist. She returned the hug, careful to keep the knife away from me.

Together we brought the food to the table. "You have had the responsibility of caring for the house and the little ones. You have done well," she murmured to me.

I felt a glow from her kind words. Mama had returned to us!

Chapter 3

Responsibility

Three months later, I left Tyre with Lamech as his wife. He returned often to visit. He said more often than he should, many times without his grandpapa.

I had loved him since we first met. I hoped he loved me. I wanted him to love me. Only when he talked to Papa about marrying me did I know for certain. Lamech loved me!

Papa married us, but we went to Home Valley, hoping for Grandpapa Adam to give us the marriage blessing. When we arrived there, he lay in his bed, sick. Grandpapa Seth had come to be with him.

Lamech carried Grandpapa Adam to the sanctuary, where we were joined by Grandmama Eve and Grandmama Ganet, and a few others from Home Valley. There, under Grandpapa

Adam's direction, Grandpapa Seth performed the marriage blessing for Lamech and me.

We had both heard of this blessing. But, until we received it ourselves, we had no idea how important it would be through the rest of our lives.

During the first few years of our marriage, we lived in Pisgah near Papa Methuselah and Mama Qutarah, who welcomed me with kindness. Mama Qutarah told me stories of her first years of marriage with Papa Methuselah. I cried with her when she told me of the drought that took so many lives. I found it difficult to believe kind Papa Methuselah had been the cause of the drought.

We had been in Pisgah only a few years when we received a message to return to Home Valley. We knew Adam's great age made life precarious for him and Eve. Although I had carried our first child only three months, we hurried to meet with those in Home Valley as soon as we could.

Grandmama Ganet welcomed us to their home. When Grandpapa Seth returned from a meeting, he, too, welcomed us.

"Where are your parents, Lamech? Did they not get the same message?" Grandpapa Seth asked.

Lamech looked toward me. "Did you talk to my parents before we left?"

"No, silly. They were gone, teaching in the south. I left them a message."

"They will join us soon, then."

"Oh?" Lamech asked. "Why are we here?"

"Come with me to my study," Grandpapa Seth said.

Lamech stared into my eyes, then turned to follow Grandpapa Seth.

"Do you know why we are here?" I asked Grandmama Ganet.

"I suspect I know, but it is not for me to say. Seth and Lamech will be out when they are finished. When they are, they will tell you. Wives are not kept in the dark."

"Wives?" I asked.

"Angetta, you are still very young. You will learn about these things. For now, take care of your little one. I have something for you to eat."

She led me into the kitchen and fed me. I wanted to jump up and help her, but she pushed me down.

"This is my kitchen. I get the pleasure of preparing a meal for you. Perhaps when you are a little older, you can prepare a meal for me," Grandmama Ganet said with a little laugh.

I giggled. "Grandmama. You are so cute."

I finished my meal and helped wash the dishes before Lamech came out of the study looking for me.

"Here you are," he said. "Grandpapa Seth needs to speak with you."

"You took a long time with him," I said.

"Well, yes. There were many things for us to discuss." He took me by the elbow. "Excuse us, Grandmama Ganet, but we are wanted."

She smiled. "Go ahead. You should not make Seth wait much longer. He will want some of this dessert."

I followed Lamech down the hall where Grandpapa Seth waited for us in a comfortable chair. He waved me to a seat and asked Lamech to take the third one after he shut the door.

"Angetta, I have some important things to discuss with you and Lamech. Are you comfortable?"

"I was," I said, shifting in my seat and glancing at Lamech. "Now I am not so certain!"

"Do not fear. This is good." Lamech took my cold hand in his warm one.

"I have asked Lamech to accept the heavy responsibility of the Holy Priesthood of Jehovah," Grandpapa Seth said.

I stared at him, then turned my stare toward Lamech. "But …"

"It is true, many men have waited many more years than Lamech. He is not the first to be asked to take on this responsibility at this age. Grandpapa Enoch was given this privilege at twenty-five."

Lamech was thirty-two.

"It is a great honor to be given the High Priesthood at any age. Few received it so young. Your own grandpapa, Mahalaleel, waited many years to be given the honor and responsibility. Your Lamech is a special young man."

I closed my open mouth with a silent pop and turned my gaze to Lamech. He lifted his eyebrows at me.

"As this will affect you and your children, Angetta, I need to be certain you understand how this will change your life. Lamech will be called on to go with his grandpapas and papa. They will travel to teach the people of the land about Jehovah.

We have an obligation to teach all the children of Adam, or at least try, before the day Jehovah grows weary and cleanses the earth of all life."

"Jehovah would do that?" I asked. My mouth dropped open once more.

"This is His earth to care for, to command, and to love. And if he determines that people have been so disobedient there is no longer hope for them to repent, He will wash the earth clean and try again."

"He will?"

"He has told me, and Adam, and all the prophets down to Enoch. I believe your papa, Methuselah, has heard the word directly from Jehovah. Your papa struggled with pride in his youth."

I nodded my head, remembering the story Mama Qutarah told me in those early days of our marriage.

"Enoch told him the one who would carry life past the flood would be his son or grandson."

I turned to Lamech. "Have you heard this?"

He sighed. "I have heard the story. Our village of Pisgah suffered a great drought for three years. Many died of starvation before Papa repented and humbled himself enough to bring the rains back. My brothers, Andrew and Joel, were among the last to lose their lives to the drought."

Grandpapa Seth nodded. "Those days were hard for all of us. We wanted to help. We were not allowed. It is an important lesson to remember. Although you are young to be given this great responsibility, you must always remain humble and remember the costs of pride."

Lamech gripped my hand and stared into my face. "I will need you to help me remember."

I grinned. "You know I will."

Grandpapa Seth barked a short laugh. "We all depend on our wives to help keep us humble. Part of your responsibility, Angetta, will be to remind Lamech to remain humble. Can you do that?"

Lamech squeezed my hand.

"I can."

"You will be called on to be alone more often than is good for a marriage. You will fear for his life, for the Destroyer will do everything he can to stop the work of Jehovah. The destroyer cannot stop it, although he believes he can. He will do all he can to disrupt the work of Jehovah's anointed prophets. Can you do this and remain loyal and faithful both to Lamech and Jehovah?"

I gulped. So much responsibility and we were so young. What had we done to catch Jehovah's eye that we should be given it?

I breathed in deeply, frantically searching my past.

"You are able to do this. Jehovah has tested and tried you. He has found you both to be worthy and able."

Even Lamech gulped audibly. "He found us worthy and able?"

"He has." Grandpapa Seth turned to me. "Can you accept this responsibility and trust? It will not end while you live."

I huffed out the extra air in my chest. "If it means babies will —"

"No. It does not. It means you will continue to struggle. You will fear. You will suffer. But you are strong. You can do this. Will you?"

I set my hand on the bump of our baby and stared at Lamech. His imperceptible nod, and the look in his eye let me know he believed I could do this.

I lifted my chin. "Yes, Grandpapa. I can do this. I do not promise I will do it perfectly. I may complain or moan amid my fears, but I can do this."

"Good." Grandpapa Seth stood. "Your grandmama has an excellent dinner and dessert waiting for us."

~ ~ ~

During the next two weeks, Grandmama Ganet and Grandmama Eve spent time with me, teaching me the things I would need to be the wife of a prophet.

Lamech went with Grandpapa Adam and Grandpapa Seth. He told me they taught him of his priesthood responsibilities. They taught him of sacrifice, and baptism, and all the other rites and ordinances. He came back to our little guest house each evening exhausted from the efforts of learning.

I could not believe all the things Grandmama Eve told me. She spent many days alone after the family began to split and go live in different parts of the land. Adam needed to leave to teach them the things their parents refused to teach them.

They taught me meals to cook for large crowds and ways to depend on Jehovah. Most importantly, I learned how much patience would be needed as I waited for my husband to return home.

"You are lucky," Grandmama Eve told me. "You can have a healer close to help your children be born. I had Adam. We had to learn together how to be parents and how to teach our children."

"What was the hardest thing for you to learn?" I asked her. I expected something like learning how to live in a new world.

Instead, she said, "The hardest thing for me to learn is the hardest for us all, I suspect. Our children have the same rights and opportunities to make their own choices and mistakes. I cannot take that away from them. I must allow them choice."

"That is hard," Grandmama Ganet added. "There are many times I wanted to force a child to obey."

"But that would mean you fell into the Destroyer's trap," Eve said. "We cannot force anyone to do anything, or we become like him, and fight on his side, rather than Jehovah's. That is the hardest thing to learn. We must give every person, man, woman, and child, the opportunity and the right to choose for themselves. We may not choose for them. We may not force them."

I struggled with that. "Mama forced me to eat carrots. I still do not like carrots."

"Small children need to be protected. They need mamas to watch over them and help them learn," Grandmama Eve said. "When they are old enough and can make decisions for themselves, we must allow it."

"All of them?"

"Yes. It hurt when my first ones left. I still miss seeing Absalom and Bilhah. They were my first children. I will always love them." A tear trickled down Grandmama Eve's cheek.

"Seth reminds me of the time you lost Abel," Grandmama Ganet said.

"Yes, and then Cain left in fear of his brothers. Those days of loss were the hardest. Now, there are so many grandchildren, I have only met a few of them. I am a myth to most of them — if they have heard of me at all."

"How can they not know you?" I asked.

"It has been many years." Grandmama pulled a square of white linen from her sleeve and wiped her tears away. "We have many hundreds of thousands of grandchildren now. Most of them refuse to hear of Jehovah. Most of them have not been taught. When they are taught about us, it is with laughter and derision. I have heard the stories."

"Stories?" I asked. "About you, Grandmama Eve?"

"Oh, yes. Many stories are told about me." Grandmama Eve sat up straighter. "They say your grandpapa's and my love together is what caused us to be sent from Eden. They say I was a harlot who enticed Adam to break the laws given to us by Father and Jehovah. How can they know what it was like? They were not there. Some even say I was Adam's second choice, that another woman refused to eat the fruit and still lives in Eden." Grandmama Eve snorted. "I would have known about another woman. There was no Lilith."

"No, Mama Eve," Grandmama Ganet said, patting her arm. "You were alone. How could you have done any different."

"It was me and Adam. We wanted to obey all of Father's commandments. But we could not. For us to multiply and replenish the earth, we had to eat the fruit. I had to be the first."

"We are happy you did," Grandmama Ganet said. "Where would we be if you had not?"

"Still waiting to come to this earth," Grandmama Eve said.

Grandmama Ganet turned to me and patted my arm. "You will want to remember how much Jehovah loves you. There will be days that only the memory of His love will help you through. You still have children to bear and a family to teach. You will have many years alone while Lamech is off teaching people who do not want to listen to him. Your responsibility will be to be there, welcoming him home to a place of refuge and peace."

"That will not be easy," I admitted.

Grandmama Eve gazed into the fire. "No. It will not be easy. But you can do it. Or Lamech and Jehovah would not have chosen you."

~ ~ ~

Within the week, all the prophets had arrived from the far-flung points of the land. Papa Methuselah and Mama Qutarah received the message and arrived a week after we did.

The others arrived by the Sabbath Day set by Grandpapa Adam and Grandpapa Seth when Grandpapa Seth met with us.

They filled the guest houses near ours, which was close to both Grandmama Eve and Grandmama Ganet.

The women welcomed me into their circle of wives, special wives, for we were wives of the prophets.

On that Sabbath day, we hiked up the hill for the sacred sacrifice. Papa Methuselah and Grandpapa Jared carried Grandmama Eve up the hill. Grandpapa refused to be carried, but Grandpapa Enoch walked slowly beside him, helping him to make it up the hill.

Grandpapa Seth and my Lamech brought the lamb up the ramp to the altar. There, they carefully performed the sacrifice.

I sat with tears flowing across my face and onto my dress. I had witnessed sacrifices before and had learned that a pure young ram would lose his life. I knew the ram represented Jehovah and his sacrifice for us. This time, I felt his love burn into my soul.

I heard a voice whisper that I would be enough for Lamech. I would be the helper he needed. My heart filled with joy and love.

Grandmama Eve and Grandmama Ganet took a hand on either side and held it. The other grandmamas rubbed my back or patted me. Each of them understood the feelings I had, for each of them had previously observed their husband's special ordaining.

After the sacrifice was completed, after the last of it had burned, leaving only a small portion for us to share, I trekked down the hill with the others to the sanctuary.

There, Grandpapa Seth lay his hands on my Lamech's head and spoke the words that gave him the right and authority to use the Holy Priesthood. Afterward, Grandpapa Seth and Lamech set their hands on my head, along with some of the other prophets. Seth voiced a special and sacred blessing for me. He supported the things I heard on the hill. I will never forget the words he spoke to me.

The other women had provided food for our meal. As we ate and visited, my little one poked me. I jumped.

Lamech turned to me. "Is all well with you?"

"It is," I said. "Feel." I set his hand over the bump of our coming child. The babe kicked a little harder.

Lamech stared at me with wide open eyes. "Is that what I think it is?"

"Our child lives."

"As if we doubted," Grandmama Zehira said from my other side.

"He moves."

The talk around the table now included the joy and hope for us and our coming little one.

"Perhaps this will be a child who is obedient?" Grandpapa Enos said.

"He may be obedient, but it is rare for a first son to be obedient enough to be a prophet," Grandpapa Adam said. "You two may wait a few years before that son is born."

We had no idea then how true Grandpapa Adam's words would be.

Chapter 4

Change

In those early days, we left Pisgah, traveling to teach others the words of Jehovah. I loved traveling with Lamech.

After four children were born, however, I did not complain when we rode into Luz to find friendly people. They accepted us, happy to receive the teaching Lamech brought for them. We settled there in that small village about three day's ride from Pisgah. We lived close enough to see Papa Methuselah and Mama Qutarah, without living in their town.

Not many years after that, we were called to a family conference planned for the warm time of the year. Everyone who could and who still followed and believed in Jehovah traveled from their home in whatever part of the land they lived to Home Valley.

So many people showed up, we camped in a tent village on the edge of Home Valley. Those of us who were families of prophets camped close to Grandpapa Adam and Grandmama Eve's home.

These ancient leaders of our family had aged, their bodies were bent and weak, their hair thin and white. Each of them required others to assist them when they moved from one place in the village to another. Young men vied for the privilege of helping their ancient grandparents. We all could see that they would not have many more years on earth with us.

During those first few days as people arrived and settled in, we shared and traded things from our part of the world. We traded skills and special foods, blankets and jars from our part of the land. In this way, we shared the ways we had changed our skills because of where we lived.

In all these differences, we found a closeness and connection because we were obedient sons and daughters of Adam and Eve. We obeyed Jehovah.

When the conference started, we all met on a hill outside the village, on the other side of the orchards. Grandpapa Adam and Grandmama Eve were helped to climb the small hill so all could see and hear what they had to say.

On that day, angels visited to honor our beloved parents, proclaiming the blessings obedience had brought them. One proclaimed Grandpapa Adam to be Michael, the prince, the archangel! Those experiences are special and sacred, never to be forgotten words.

On the next day, while the men went to another part of the village, we women gathered on the same little hill. Eve's granddaughter, Ruth, who lived with her helped her walk slowly up the hill. Rebecca walked with her on the other side. They moved slowly through the crowd, for Grandmama Eve spoke to many and cooed at all the little babies. She stopped and spoke a moment to my littlest son, Shir. We loved her for it.

When she settled into her seat, lovingly placed on the hill by Enos, Ruth and Ganet led the meeting. They shared an experience to help us better understand what had happened to Eve.

Grandmama Eve had been left alone while Adam and Absalom went on a walkabout before Bilhah's birth. The destroyer attacked her, thinking he could overcome her in her weakness.

A wolf, a bear, and two cougars protected her, driving the Destroyer away. When Adam and Absalom returned, they brought back a wolf pup, killed by a serpent.

Many years later, Eve and Ganet used a vase celebrating the event to bring women together as Ministering Sisters. Women help other women who are often left alone to care for fields and family while their husbands are gone hunting and teaching.

We met in groups with others from our villages, setting up small Ministering Sister groups of our own as Eve and Ganet had organized years earlier, organizing who would look in on whom, who would help when a new child came or someone was sick or alone.

This filled me with joy. I knew something more needed to be done to help those others in our village. And, I needed someone to be there to help me when Lamech left us.

Afterward, Ruth and Ganet asked Eve to tell us the story of her life. As she spoke, her body and voice strengthened. Many of the events of her life I had never heard. Most of us had not.

When she finished her story, Grandmama Eve settled back in her seat. Her body slumped, and her voice weakened. We saw a miracle that allowed her to be strong enough to share with us.

One of the women in the group wrote down Grandmama Eve's words. They were checked and approved by her, before sending copies out to women all over the world.

On the third day, we met on the hill again to hear the story of Ganet's life. We gasped at the gigantic serpent, the earthquakes, and other problems she faced in her early years traveling with Seth. Her words, too, were written down and shared with all the women.

On the third day, Rebecca shared her story. That beautiful mother lost her first two children to raiders who sold them to slavers in Nod. She never saw those children again. Never learned what happened to them. Still, she moved forward with her life. She is an example to us all.

Grandmama Eve spoke at the end. There would not be any more days for stories to be told, but she gazed into each of us who were married to Prophets. "You, too, must write the stories of your lives. It is in the little successes that you inspire others, not in the big things of life. It is when you triumph over your challenges and share them that other women find hope that they, too, can succeed."

As a young wife then, barely forty years old, little in my life felt successful. I supported my husband in his work. I raised and taught children who had already made the choice to leave the faith. Where would others learn to be successful from these experiences?

However, I kept Grandmama Eve's words in my heart, and remembered them.

When our turn came to enter the sanctuary to receive a blessing from Grandpapa Adam, he spoke words of comfort to us both, promising children who would obey and succeed in Jehovah's work. Lamech and I left the sanctuary in tears of gratitude. We had not had children who obeyed yet, but there would be some, and one would be the one to carry our family line through the cleansing.

After our visit to Home Valley, I felt closer to Grandmama Eve than ever before.

~ ~ ~

In only three years, the news came that Grandmama Eve had lost her valiant efforts to continue living. We were called to come as quickly as we could to participate in the memorial service.

Lamech and I took our newly born son with us strapped in a blanket to my chest, along with Shir who rode behind her papa on his big horse. We rode long through each day and late into the night, sleeping only a few spans before rising to mount our horses and ride on the next day.

We arrived in Home Valley in three days, rather than the usual weeks it often took us to travel that distance in a wagon. I would have been exhausted, but Jehovah strengthened both me and our children on the ride.

Many came from far away, although not as many as had come for the Great Family Conference. Most people lived much too far away to even consider arriving in Home Valley in time for the service.

All the Prophets, Seth, Enos, Cainan, Mahalaleel, Jared, Enoch and Methuselah arrived days before the rite. Like us, they had ridden hard and fast in an effort to arrive in time.

Grandpapa Seth stood in front of us in the sanctuary, sharing his memories of his beloved mama. Those of us who loved her shared in Seth's tears and sorrow. We, too, would miss Grandmama Eve.

Grandpapa Adam sat in the front row between Grandmama Ganet and Grandmama Rebecca, with Ruth sitting close by. I have never seen him so bent and fragile.

After the memorial service, we gathered for a meal, telling stories and sharing experiences and the love we always felt when coming to visit Grandmama and Grandpapa.

During that night, Grandpapa Adam returned home to Father, Jehovah, and Grandmama Eve. Lamech and Methuselah, his papa, helped to dig the sad pit in the earth next to the one where Eve lay.

Those of us who planned to return to our homes the next morning changed our plans. We followed the men who carried the litter with his body on it to the gash in the earth, stopping next to the sad place.

Tears dripped from our faces as young men carefully lowered Grandpapa Adam's old, wrinkled body into the hole. Each of us stepped forward to sprinkle a handful of soil over his body. Enough of us had come that the hole had been nearly filled by the time the last person stepped back. The prophets picked up the shovel and scooped more of the dirt over the sad little grave until a small heap stood over it.

Grandpapa Seth offered a prayer and we turned to leave. As we walked away, an unexpected rain fell. Even the heavens wept tears. Were they tears of sadness that we lost our original Patriarch and Matriarch? Or were they tears of joy to receive them home? I like to think they were tears of joy.

The era of Adam and Eve had ended. How would our world change in the next years?

Certainly, men and women had forgotten the covenants made between Adam and Jehovah. I saw wickedness among the children of men easier than I could discover righteous men and women.

This added to my sorrow as we sat once more, sharing in a family meal, remembering our special times with Grandpapa Adam and Grandmama Eve. As we shared, the sorrow in our hearts changed to peace and love. We had been blessed to know these two great people.

Seth and Ganet left this world a little more than a hundred years later.

~ ~ ~

Our children grew, happy to live in a home with friends as well as brothers and sisters. However, as they grew older, they began to travel to neighboring villages to find their friends. The friends in some of these villages had refused the word and commands of Jehovah, preferring instead to follow the cult god Shuja who worshiped serpents.

I could not comprehend how my children could be drawn to the bloody rites of these priests. Hearing of them turned my stomach. I would never observe them.

Our children married sons and daughters who chose to believe in these cult gods and began to follow the ways of the Destroyer, rather than clinging to the truths of Jehovah. Lamech and I spent many nights in prayer and tears, begging for help and assistance with our children.

However, I could not forget the words of Grandmama Eve as they rang in my memory more frequently as my children became less obedient. "The hardest thing for me to learn is the hardest for us all, I suspect. Our children have the same rights and opportunities to make their own choices and mistakes. I cannot take that away from them. I must allow them choice."

I sometimes struggled to take that sage advice of my dear grandmama. She knew the right thing, however. I will forever bless her.

Grandpapa had prophesied correctly about our oldest son. He left our home early to wed a daughter of the priest of Shuja. He would not be the son to save life.

I sometimes asked Lamech if perhaps he would be the one.

"No," he said. "I am not ready for that big of a task. If Jehovah plans to wash the earth clean, someone will need to build something big to save that many animals. I doubt I have the ability to build something that big."

We sat together on the front porch, watching the fireflies.

"Big?" I asked. "How big?"

"All the many different forms of animals, birds, insects, and other creatures that do not live in water will need a safe way to ride out the storm. If there are only two, and there will need to be two, a male and a female, for them to reproduce, there will be thousands of animals. There must be many more than we have ever seen." He waved his hands indicating something huge.

"Thousands? That would mean a huge something to build. What? A boat of some kind?"

Lamech shrugged. "Something. I do not believe I am the one. I am to teach and preach repentance, but not to build."

"Who then?"

"Papa was promised one of his sons or grandsons would be that one many years ago by his papa, Enoch. The right one will come and be prepared when it is time. I do not believe that is me."

I reached out and touched his hand. He smiled at me.

Not many years later, we traveled to Home Valley once more to attend the memorial service for Grandpapa Seth. His wife, Ganet had left him not a year before. We sorrowed his loss, knowing that in his death he could now spend the eternities with his wife once more.

Lamech and I spoke of it as we returned home.

"Papa Seth is happy now," I said.

"He no longer has to face the trials of this earth. His body will stand straight and he can stand in the presence of Father and Jehovah holding Ganet's hand." Lamech pulled a bit of his lip in between his teeth. "He often told me she was the love of his life."

"She loved him deeply. I never heard her complain about the days they had to be separated. She trusted Seth as he trusted her."

Lamech urged his horse closer to mine and put an arm around my waist. "I am grateful for the blessing given us by Grandpapa Seth at the beginning of our marriage. It is good to know we will continue to be together long after we leave this earth. Eternity is a long time —"

"Are you sorry we are sealed together for eternity?" I poked my lower lip out in a playful pout.

Lamech leaned toward me and kissed my lips. "No. I was wondering if eternity would be long enough. I never want to be separated from you."

"Nor do I ever want to be separated from you — except during your short journeys to teach of repentance. I have enjoyed being with you again."

"Would you like to travel with me again?"

"Could I? Our children are nearly grown …"

"And you have grandchildren who look to you. Could you leave them?"

"To be with you? Yes. I would be willing to take children on the road again, as long as we were together."

"I would love to do that, as well," Lamech said, sitting up straight on his horse again. Our horses stepped apart. "I do not know how safe it would be for you and our children."

"No. Safety is a big concern. But I would be willing to go with you."

"I will pray and ask Jehovah if it is safe. If He agrees, you can go with me on my next journey."

Jehovah agreed. I traveled a few more years with Lamech before things became too ugly and dangerous for me to go with my husband.

Besides, I had more little children to care for.

Chapter 5

Zion Has Fled

A little more than fifty years later, Lamech returned from a visit to his Grandpapa Enoch and Grandmama Zehira's home in Zion. He still shook a little as he recounted the story sitting across from me at our kitchen table.

"Grandmama Zehira gave me a package of books, her story to be shared with the good women of earth. It is so good to see her walk through the city without her crutch since Jehovah healed it. But they insisted I must leave. I kissed them both. I did not want to leave Zion."

"Why did they insist you leave?" I asked. I wanted to ask to see the books written by Grandmama Zehira, but I sensed Lamech had more to tell me.

He leaned forward on the table with both arms propping him up. "The time had come. Jehovah has tired of the ugliness of hatred and sin. He wants to protect his followers who lived there in Zion from that."

"And what happened?"

"I rode from the city a distance and turned to wave good-bye. Both Grandmama and Grandpapa stood on the ramparts, waving to me. I rode out onto the plain before I stopped and slid off my horse to pray for the people of the earth. As I prayed … Angetta, you would not believe it if you were not there."

I reached across the table and took his hands in mine. "What happened?

"As I prayed, the earth around me shook. I grabbed my horse's reins and searched for the cracks that this kind of shaking usually heralds. My eyes were drawn to Zion.

"The earth continued to shake. I felt the roots of the city tear away from the earth. I watched the city separate from the soil of the earth. Great boulders and small clods of dirt fell from the edges as the city rose, slowly at first, then more rapidly as it broke the bonds tying it down."

"Were you frightened?" My thumb traced the back of his hand.

He stared forward, as if seeing it happen once more. "No. Grandpapa told me it would happen. I did not expect to see it, however. I stared upward until Zion disappeared against the brightness of the sun. Then, it was gone. Truly gone. I stood in amazement for many spans of the rising sun before I stepped into my saddle to return here."

He took a shuddering breath. "Angetta. You would not believe if you did not see it. A huge crater fills the space where
once stood the most beautiful city in all the world. A city
blessed by Jehovah." He shook his head. "And now, it is
gone."

"I will miss them," I murmured.

"As will I. Grandpapa taught me much over these years."
He rolled his lower lip in and held it with his teeth. He spit it
out. "The earth is a sad and lonely place without Enoch and
Zion."

After that, we heard people speak in whispers of Zion.
"Zion has fled," they said.

In truth, Zion did flee. It fled the wickedness and grief of
those who refused to obey the commandments of Jehovah.

In the days and months and years since Zion fled, people
on the earth have not learned. They continue in their wicked
ways.

Men sell and use both women's and other men's bodies in
unseemly ways. Men refuse to marry or form relationships
with women, preferring to live with and join with other men.
Women join with women.

Fewer children are born, although that is good for the children who will not be born into this wicked world.

Men and women battle and kill others for their wealth,
their gold and silver, their silks and pearls, and their land. Anger is everywhere.

Men and women spend much of the day eating and drinking without thought of giving gratitude to their God, Jehovah.

Gluttony, wine, sex, perversions, among other sins, all prevail across the land.

There are still a few villages where Jehovah reigns, where people believe in Him and obey his word. But not many. For now, the Destroyer wins the battle for their souls. That will change.

I fear the day will come in my lifetime that Jehovah will determine the end of life has come and flood the earth. I would not blame Him.

~ ~ ~

Less than five years after Lamech watched Zion retreat into the heavens, when he and I had lived together as husband and wife for nearly one hundred fifty years, I found myself with child once more.

I had not given birth to children for more than twenty years before then and often wondered if any of my sons would fulfill the promise given to us from Adam or to Methuselah by his papa, Enoch. It did not look good for our posterity. Too many had joined with the non-believers. Too many did not stand for truth and light.

None of our sons agreed to follow the commandments, preferring to live as their brothers and sisters had done in the years before. They chose to leave Luz to find wives and husbands, following the cult gods of the other villages. Those few who stayed in Luz and honored Jehovah preferred not to travel with their papa to teach others of the need for repentance.

We feared this coming child would be the last chance Jehovah had to bring us a child who would fulfill the promise. I had long passed the age when women brought children into the world. I feared this delivery would be difficult.

Giving birth in my advanced years would not be easy. Lamech insisted that the best healer come from far away to assist.

The birthing was not easy. But my body knew what to do and did it as it had in the years before. In a few spans of squeezing pain, I pushed the boy child from my body.

Lamech named him Noah.

We traveled toward Cainan when Noah was about six years old. We passed by the crater that had been Zion. Lamech had returned often, remembering the day when he last saw his grandparents.

We stopped to stare at the crater.

"What happened here?" Noah asked.

"I saw it happen, years ago, son. Grandpapa Enoch warned Papa Methuselah when it was no longer safe for Grandmama Zehira to go into the world. She called me to carry her story to the other women obedient to Jehovah, as she had promised them at the Great Family Counsel."

"Did you take it to them?" the little boy asked not turning his eyes away from the crater.

"I did. Your mama waited many months for my return. She had read from the accounts of Grandmama Eve, Grandmama Ganet, and Grandmama Rebecca. She has copies of some of the books written by the other matriarchs. She received her copy of Grandmama Zehira's story when I returned. She sat and read the story for days."

I smiled at Noah and ruffled his hair. "Not too many days. I read faster than that."

"Now, she has the life story of Grandmama Zehira. It is a great gift to know the lives of our women," Lamech added.

I nodded. "The books are sacred to me. Without them, we would not know of our earlier mamas."

"What happened to Grandmama Zehira and Grandpapa Enoch?" Noah asked. "I have met some of the other older grandparents."

"They are gone, Noah," Lamech said, setting a hand on his little back. "Jehovah took them out of this wicked world. They and all in their city of Zion are gone to live with Him."

"Gone? Forever, Papa?" Noah turned his stare from the crater to his papa.

"Until a time many thousands of years in the future, when Jehovah returns in the end of time. Only then will Zion return. We will join them at the end of our lives, but they will not return to earth for a long, long time."

Noah's eyes returned to the barren crater. "Why did we not go with them, Papa?"

Lamech glanced at me over his head. I shook my head a little. Noah had not yet been chosen. He did not need that much information.

"I often wonder why we could not join them. Your mama is a good woman and I follow Jehovah. We were denied the privilege of going with them, as was your Grandpapa Methuselah and Grandmama Qutarah. Jehovah needed us and our High Priesthood to stay with these wicked people on the earth." Lamech shook his head. "We are to teach repentance to them. I doubt it will do us much good. Even so, it is our responsibility to teach the sons and daughters of Adam the light and truth taught by Jehovah, teaching them repentance and love."

We stared at the mountain near the edge of the crater, a monument to Enoch's Priesthood power. Beneath that mountain lay the bones of the army that tried to attack Zion.

Noah lifted his little arms to his papa and Lamech lifted him into his own. Their tears mixed together on Lamech's shoulder. I wrapped my arms around my men and felt their sorrow. *Would this child be the one to see the end of the wickedness? Will those he takes into a new and clean world be any better?*

We traced the edge of the crater, walking our horses along the path that had been worn by others who did the same thing, staring at the crater and the mountain sitting along the edge.

After a time, we turned from the crater to travel on to Cainan.

Chapter 6

My Little Boy

Jehovah understood the wickedness of the world better than we did, for He protected Noah. In his tenth year, he went out to retrieve the sheep one evening. When he returned, a glow surrounded him.

I had seen the glow when Lamech spoke with Jehovah and heard of it from others. Grandmama Eve spoke of it when Grandpapa Adam returned after speaking with Jehovah.

"What happened, son?" Lamech asked.

"I brought in the sheep." Noah gathered dishes to set on the table.

"And they all returned?" Lamech pressed.

"Yes."

"There is more," I said. "I can see a difference in you."

Noah turned. "Can a guy have a sacred experience without his parents asking a thousand questions?"

"A sacred experience?" Lamech asked.

Noah dropped into his chair. "Yes, Papa. I heard the voice of Jehovah."

My son was a child, far too young for such things. I opened my mouth to question him, but Lamech held his hand up to stop my words.

He knelt next to our son. "And, what does Jehovah want from you?"

"I am to ask you to take me to visit Grandpapa Methuselah." He ducked his head. "I am a child. Why would I be singled out like this?"

"You are a good boy. You obey the commands of Jehovah. He needs to protect you from the Destroyer."

Noah nodded as he gazed at his feet. "That is what He said."

Lamech glanced at me over our son's head. I nodded. Jehovah did things in His own time and in His own way.

Lamech spoke to me as much as to Noah. "We will leave for Pisgah in the morning. After you eat your dinner, you should probably try to get some rest. I know it will not be easy. Not after this, but you will need your strength to travel."

"You will take me to see Grandpapa?" Noah lifted his head to stare into his papa's eyes.

"Yes. I, too, am obedient."

The next morning, we saddled our horses and tied a pack of provisions onto a packhorse. Noah rode on the tall black stallion he had trained since its birth. He had to use a fence to climb on his back.

We arrived in Pisgah after a two-day ride. Grandpapa Methuselah opened the door.

"You are here. I was told you would arrive today."

Lamech nodded. "Noah received a message to come visit you."

I tried to swallow. The dryness in my throat prevented it. *What would they do with my little boy?*

I visited with Mama Qutarah while Noah and Lamech went with Methuselah to his study.

"What happened?" she asked. "Methuselah said you were coming, but I did not see a message."

"We did not send one. We rode here after Noah received his message."

Mama Qutarah leaned back in her comfortable seat and lifted her eyebrows. "Received his message?"

"He came home from gathering in the sheep three days ago with a glow about him ..."

"A glow?" She leaned forward. "Sometimes Methuselah returns with a glow when he has communed with Jehovah."

I nodded.

"Then Noah has ...?"

"Yes. Jehovah spoke to our little boy. He said he needed His protection." I lifted a shoulder. "He needs to be protected from the wiles of the Destroyer. How will coming here do that?"

"We must wait to find out. Methuselah has paced more today than usual."

In less than a span, the door to the study opened and our men filed into the sitting room. Noah hurried to my side and put his arms around me.

"Our son," Lamech said, "is to be given the High and Holy responsibility of the High Priesthood."

"He is but a child!" I cried.

"And he needs the special protection from the Destroyer. Only this will protect him," Papa Methuselah said. "This is the child promised to me by Papa Enoch, promised to you by Grandpapa Adam. He has a magnificent and awesome responsibility coming to him."

My arm still wrapped around my son. I inhaled a huge breath and squeezed him.

Noah turned his face to me. "It is good, Mama. I am ready for this."

"Are you, Noah? Are you really?"

"Papa and Grandpapa say I am. Jehovah says I am. Who am I to argue with Jehovah?"

Words of truth from a child. I hugged him close to me and kissed his forehead. "You will always be my little boy."

"Aw, Mama," he said, wiping at my kiss.

Our laughter broke the tension.

Papa Methuselah and Lamech set their hands on Noah's head the next day, while we celebrated the Sabbath with the small community of Pisgah. Voices murmured their concern for a child to be given such a heavy responsibility. I agreed, but I understood the need for this child to receive the special protection of Jehovah through the Holy Priesthood.

In the following years, Noah met often with his grandpapa, sometimes traveling to visit the other grandpapas so they could help teach him of his responsibilities. He joined Lamech and Papa Methuselah in their travels, often standing before villages, calling them to repentance.

Lamech told me that the villagers would either guffaw at a child calling them to repentance or kneel to beg forgiveness at his feet.

"Jehovah walks with our son," Lamech told me one evening after they returned from a journey. "Noah tells me the people will come to hate him for his vigilance. They will not want to hear of Jehovah. But it is his duty to preach repentance and baptism to all the earth, as it was Grandpapa Enoch's duty, as it is my duty and the duty of all those of his grandpapas who are prophets."

"He carries a great burden."

"He does. But he carries it well. He is being taught by the best. Only Grandpapa Adam and Grandpapa Seth are no longer here to teach him, and he speaks of Grandpapa Adam as a close friend. Perhaps Adam visits him."

I could only shake my head. We had waited for this son. And he came to us at the end of our abilities to bring children into the world.

I found myself on my knees often, praying for Jehovah to bless and protect this child prophet son of mine.

~ ~ ~

In the following years, we attended the memorial services for the older prophets. Enos, Cain, and Mahalaleel died in that next hundred years.

Each brought a sense of loss to Papa Methuselah, Lamech, and Noah. They missed the strength of the Priesthood brought by the brotherhood of the prophets. Only Jared continued to live, and he grew ever older. Where there were once eight prophets before Noah, the number dwindled to four.

Noah found a beautiful believer in one of the villages where he taught, Keshet. He brought her home and asked Lamech to marry them. Then, they traveled to Aenon to ask Grandpapa Jared to bless their marriage as so many of us had gone to Grandpapa Adam.

Noah and Keshet returned from Aenon speaking in glowing terms of the blessing Grandpapa Jared had given to them. I remembered the blessing given us by Grandpapa Seth. I understood their great joy.

Noah and Keshet had several children before leaving Luz for the small village of Mamre. She needed to find her place as wife of a prophet without me looking over her shoulder. Jehovah called Noah to live in a place where he could influence the people.

Years after Noah and Keshet moved, we received a message. Grandpapa Jared had died. We hurried to Aenon to comfort Grandmama Helsa and to remember his life. There were smaller numbers of believers who joined us in honoring the great prophet, Jared. Earth grew ever more wicked.

Now there were only three prophets left. I felt the loss of power in the world. How could our men have any effect on the children of men with so few of them to teach so many?

After we returned from Grandpapa Jared's memorial, we learned that Grandmama Helsa had also left the earth to be with him. Lamech and Noah went to Aenon to honor her. The world had become much too dangerous for me to travel in it anymore. Keshet and her children stayed with me.

Noah's children behaved much as his older brothers and sisters, refusing to remain faithful to the covenant. We sorrowed with him when he came to visit.

Then, when Noah had lived more than four hundred years, Keshet once more carried a child. We all hoped this one would be one who would obey. Keshet had lived too many years to carry another child within her. Neither the child nor the mother survived.

We sorrowed with Noah. He knew of the promises made to us and to Papa Methuselah. He would carry the priesthood lineage through the destruction of a flood. But who would continue the line now his wife had died?

Then he met Imma. Though a young woman, she agreed to marry Noah, even though he had lived many more years than her grandpapa's grandpapa. She confided in me that Jehovah had promised her that Noah could protect her when no other man could.

They had sons who listened to the words of Jehovah and married women who loved them and loved Jehovah. Lamech and I bowed our heads in gratitude to Jehovah. He had provided a way for our lineage to be carried forward.

When I learned that Noah had begun to build a huge boat he called an ark to carry life through the flood, I asked Lamech to bring me paper to write my story. There are few righteous women left in the world. I will not need many copies to share. However, I must obey the commandment given to me by Eve, our first mama in that Great Family Counsel.

I have now written my story. I am ill. I may not survive many more years. It does not matter. Noah and his family will go on the ark and survive the destruction of life on this earth. We will continue to live with Father and Jehovah in the eternities, together with our loved ones. Perhaps, we will even meet with Grandpapa Enoch and Grandmama Zehira once more.

If my story goes with Noah and his family, perhaps someone will remember me, learn from me, and find joy and success in obedience as I have.

May Jehovah bless you.

Love,

Angetta

Back Matter

Acknowledgements:

As I complete the last story in the lives of the Ancient Matriarchs, I am grateful to these women who shared their stories with me. I also thank those who have assisted me in completing this final book. Much of the writing is done in the silence of my mind. Still, others are involved in the completion.

ANWA members joined me each evening for writing sprints and have encouraged me to write better and faster. I thank them for their support.

My husband sits beside me, as always, helping me with ideas and words. His patience is never-ending.

Danica Page and Dar Albert helped make this a beautiful book, with wonderful editing and a beautiful cover. Thanks go, too, to the members of my AngelCAST team who read the book a final time for errors, problems, and typos! When you find one, however, (and there always seems to be one!) the blame is mine.

As always, my parents have helped and supported me in my efforts to write. I love and appreciate them.

Last, but never least, I thank you, the reader, who has chosen this book to spend your time and money on. I have loved working on this work of fiction. I would love to hear how you liked it.

Angelique@AngeliqueCongerAuthor.com

Dear Reader,

I will be lost not having these earliest mothers sitting beside me, whispering their stories into my ear. Without them, I would never have learned the art of writing books.

This last book of Ancient Matriarchs has been the hardest book for me to write. Each of these five stories is shorter than the other four books, yet they complete the lives and stories of the women who lived and loved in our earliest days.

I originally did not plan to write Angetta's story. She came after Methuselah, before Noah. However, she called out to me, asking that I tell her story, as well. Hers concludes the stories of the lives of the ancient Matriarchs.

I hope you enjoyed getting to know each of these women, the five who tell their stories in this book and the five others whose stories took a whole book to tell. Actually, Eve's story needed all six of these books to be complete.

May we all remember the love of our ancient mothers, for they knew we would live, and they prayed we would make the right choices. As Eve said, "We are each responsible for the choices we make. We cannot force our decisions on others, nor can we foist the responsibility for our own decisions on them."

Live in remembrance of their love.

Angelique

Did You Enjoy This Book?

If you did, will you do something for me?

I'm an independent author, publishing my books without the backing of a major publisher. That means no six-figure advances and no advertising budget. This makes it difficult to promote my novels and put them in places new readers can find them. But you can help me.

Honest reviews and genuine "word-of-mouth" advertising makes all the difference. I'm not asking for one of those awful book reports I used to try not to sleep through as a teacher. What will help me is for you to leave an honest star rating and a couple of sentences on Amazon or Goodreads. Or a short review on your blog. Or tell your friends about it on Facebook or Twitter.

Let people know what you liked about this book and why they might like it, too. And, if there was something you didn't like, you can say that, as well. Constructive criticism helps me write a better book next time.

But, please. No spoilers!

Thanks for reading.

Books by Angelique Conger

Ancient Matriarchs:

Eve, First Matriarch
Into the Storms: Ganet: Wife of Seth
Finding Peace: Rebecca, Wife of Enos
Moving into Light: Zehira, Wife of Enoch
Out of Darkness: Imma, Wife of Noah

Lost Children of the Prophet

Lost Children of the Prophet
Captured Freedom
Abandoned Hope
Brotherly Havoc
Betrayed Trust
Convicted Deliverance
Trouble Escaped
Contrary Devotion
Impassioned Grief
Love Defied
Hidden Purpose
Concealed Innocence

Would You Like More?

If you enjoyed this story, you may enjoy a **Free Micro Story**, written about Eve in her travels with Adam, later in their lives. Eve must find a way to rescue Adam after he was taken by servants of the Destroyer. No one else is near and it is up to her.

Avenging Angel is **free** and only available when you subscribe to my **Ancient Historical Fiction Reader.**

Go to: http://www.AngeliqueCongerAuthor.com to get your **free copy.**

If you have something to share with me after reading, you are welcome to email me:

Angelique@AngeliqueCongerAuthor.com

ABOUT THE AUTHOR

Angelique Conger writes historical fiction about the earliest days of our earth between Eden and the flood. Many consider her books Christian focused, and they are because they focus on events in the Bible. She writes of a people's beliefs in Jehovah. However, though she's read in much of the Bible and searched for more about these stories, there isn't much there. Her imagination fills in the missing information, which is most of it.

Angelique followed her Navy husband around the world and later worked as a teacher in the years her children were growing. Writing about the earliest days of our earth, those days between the Garden of Eden and Noah's flood, helps in her efforts to change the world.

Angelique lives in Southern Nevada with her husband, turtles, and cat. Her favorite times are visiting children and grandchildren.